Best Wishes

Lexa

LOVE IN
ANOTHER TIME
A Sardinian Saga

GW00568309

LOVE IN ANOTHER TIME
A Sardinian Saga

Lexa Dudley

Matador
Unit E2 Airfield Business Park,
Harrison Road, Market Harborough,
Leicestershire. LE16 7UL
Tel: 0116 279 2299
Email: books@troubador.co.uk
Web: www.troubador.co.uk/matador
Twitter: @matadorbooks

ISBN 978 1800465 343

British Library Cataloguing in Publication Data.
A catalogue record for this book is available from the British Library.

Printed and bound in the UK by TJ Books, Padstow, Cornwall
Typeset in 11pt Aldine401 BT by Troubador Publishing Ltd, Leicester, UK

Matador is an imprint of Troubador Publishing Ltd

For Kit

Without whose patience and kindness, I would never have become a writer.

To the elusive and magical Spirit of Sardinia

In other times and in other places, people have lived and loved. Where lives are touched, leaving a profound effect the one upon the other.
Where memories linger forever, and love is never forgotten.

CASTEDDU

Ageless stronghold with medieval walls,
beneath which Villanova idly sprawls.
Here where past and present merge as one
under a radiant halo of golden sun,
nut-brown children spend carefree hours
in narrow streets, mid ancient Pisan towers.

Cool dark streets, illuminated by shafts of light
open on warm chequered squares of black and white.
From windows, cast in shade, peering eyes are met
as half-glimpsed figures form their silhouette.
Here through darkling doorways, almost concealed,
flower-filled courtyards are fleetingly revealed.

The noiseless step of time passes by unheard
leaving only a breath of wind, gently stirred
amidst washing, billowing like painted sails.
whilst overall an enchanted peace prevails.
Out on azure water, a dancing light gleams,
luring fishermen to gentle noonday dreams.

This city's magic catches the eager wandering eye,
from lofty cathedral, outlined against cloudless sky,
on over the reeling drop of San Remy, to Marina below,
past silent *stagni*, reflecting the sun's fiery glow,
to the devil's saddle towering over Golfo degli Angeli
faithfully watched by the Sette Fratelli.

Spread before me from Buoncammino can be seen
the Campidano patchwork fields of gold and green.
Nearby Tuvixeddu, veiled in her hushed mystery,
shares the splendour of this ancient history.
This city is no fading dream or passing shadow,
but alive with a vibrant race I'm proud to know.

(Poems from my Island)

INTRODUCTION

As a passing note, I set the first part of this story in 1961. Times were very different then; the age of adulthood, and parental control, was 21 and not lowered to 18 until 1970. It was not until 1968 that media censorship was abolished, and bedroom scenes did not have to be played with one foot on the floor! Being gay was only partially legalised that year, and divorcees could enter the Royal Enclosure at Ascot. Discipline and respect were paramount.

When Ellie goes to boarding school, she has a tuck box. In 1947 the country was still on rationing, which wasn't finally lifted until 1954. The tuck box was probably your most treasured possession. It was where you kept your sweets, only four allowed in the evening, under the strict eye of Matron; although it was possible to put some in the pocket of your long grey knickers if you were quick. Biscuits, homemade cake, Marmite, Bovril, jam or honey, were only allowed with your bread at teatime. Tuck parcels from home were always eagerly awaited to keep the supplies topped up.

No mobile phones in fact, in the early 60s, homes that had a phone, often had to share a party line. If you wanted to make a call and the other party was on the line, you had to hang up and wait until they had finished. Calls abroad were difficult. It was necessary to book a call to the country and then wait hours or days for it to go through, unlike today, with the wonderful way you can talk to someone in Australia on your iPhone instantly.

Sardinia is not Italy. It is an island that has changed little over the centuries, from the invading Phoenicians to the coming of the Piedmontese under the Duchy of Savoy in 1720, when Italian became the dominant language, until the present day. The fiercely independent islanders have retained their languages, yes languages, not dialects, through all the millennia together with their folk traditions and local costumes. Although UNESCO has now classed them as 'endangered languages'.

I have been told that there is a lot of reference to food. All I can say is that's the way it is in Sardinia. Food for friends, food for strangers, any excuse to sit at a table and share stories. Their hospitality is second to none.

The Sardes have a profound pride in their country, which is both refreshing and endearing.

With my books, I try to impart a little of the beauty of Sardinia, hoping others will come to love her too.

Finally, if you have read my previous books, *The Whispering Wind* or *Children of the Mists,* you will know that I am a passionate lover of Sardinia and it is a character in its own right, in my books.

Lexa Dudley 2021

ACKNOWLEGDEMENTS

I want to thank everyone who has helped me with this book.

My numerous friends in Sardinia who patiently answer all my questions about their island, and include us in their family celebrations.

And those who sent me pictures of Cagliari in the 60s with stories about that era.

To Ignazio Carboni for his original photo of the Antico Caffe.

To Alberto Piso for his help with the photo for the back cover.

With many thanks to Giovanni D'Angelo for his inspired design for the cover.

My great doctor NR who kindly gives me his time to tell me about symptoms etc.

Finally, my wonderful husband who takes me down to the island every year to renew friendships and do research.

PROLOGUE

England, January 1947

Ellie stood in the doorway of the large late-Victorian mansion watching her mother's chauffeur climb the broad steps to her new school. He puffed as he dropped her shiny new trunk on the marble floor. After pausing for a moment to catch his breath, he returned to the car and collected her tuck box, which he put beside her bright-red trunk. Ellie had chosen the trunk with her father, in preference to the brown or black ones. Her tuck box was of new white wood with black metal bands, and her name, ELEANOR di MONTFORD, stamped on both in big black letters. Her mother, Isabel, always insisted on the 'di', but Ellie left it out, thinking it pretentious.

Ellie turned to see her mother standing on the step below her.

'I can't stay, we have a dinner party tonight. You make sure you behave yourself. I don't want any trouble from you. Do you understand, Eleanor?'

'Yes, Mother.'

Her mother, dressed in a long black mink coat and black crocodile shoes with a matching handbag; her hair pulled up in a French twist, gave her a hard appearance. Ellie noticed her mother was in a hurry to leave and appeared ill at ease, she looked overdressed in her expensive clothes, as most of the women were farmers' wives or country people in their tweed suits and sheepskin coats.

Isabel dropped a perfunctory kiss on her daughter's cheek and went down the steps to get into the waiting car. The chauffeur closed the door and climbed into the driver's seat.

Ellie waved to her mother, but Isabel did not return the gesture. She did not look back, and Ellie knew her mother was already thinking about the dinner party that evening – whom she could impress, or who would be in a high enough position to help her husband's career.

Ellie watched as the large black Rolls Royce made its way down the long drive.

Her father had said his goodbye to her at breakfast and had pressed a ten bob note into her hand, whispered. 'Don't tell your mother,' and given her a quick peck on the cheek, then checked to make sure no one was watching.

Ellie turned to look at the large, red-brick building. It had all the hallmarks of an institution: bare wooden floors, curtainless windows, and the distinctive smell of carbolic soap reaching out into the morning air.

She walked inside and watched the other girls being enfolded in their mothers' arms or hugged by their fathers and wondered what it was like to be loved by such adoring parents.

A clattering noise caught Ellie's attention, house shoes banging on the wooden stairs, and then someone called her name.

'Ellie, oh, Ellie.'

A young girl came rushing toward her with outstretched arms and a broad grin across her face.

'Polly,' cried Ellie, as the two girls embraced, both wearing the school uniform of grey gym tunic, white shirt, and a house tie, grey lisle socks and black house shoes.

'Gosh, Polly,' said Ellie, pulling away and looking at her friend. 'It's been over a year and you have grown so tall.'

'And you are still as skinny as a beanpole. What have you been doing? What was London like? You look so pale. Come on, we are sharing a dorm. I have so much to ask you and so much to tell you. I've missed you so much, we all have.'

'I've missed you, too. Is everyone okay?'

'Yes, come on, follow me.'

'What about our trunks?' asked Ellie.

'Manning will bring them up. Come on. Tuck boxes go in the dining room. You must remember, the front stairs are out of bounds during term time, back stairs only,' said Polly, without pausing for breath.

Ellie smiled and followed her friend up the impressive oak staircase and down a long corridor to a compact room at the end. Two beds occupied most of the room, with two chests of drawers, a washbasin, and a rather motheaten-looking mat beside each bed.

Polly went to her chest, opened a drawer, and rummaged around until finding what she was searching for. With a great flurry, Polly handed a bag to Ellie.

'Heavens, sweets!' said Ellie peering into the bag 'Where did you get them? We couldn't get any in London, even with our ration books.'

'Simon knows a boy at school whose father makes them, so we always have the ones that are misshapen or wonky.'

'But they still taste great. What a treat – thanks,' said Ellie, relishing the sugary flavour.

'Now, tell me what has happened to you,' said Polly. 'I'm dying to know.'

'First, tell me, how are your parents and Simon and Laurence?' asked Ellie.

'Parents are well, and my brothers are back at boarding school. Simon still hates it, and Laurence loves it. Funny how two brothers can be so different. Papa says one takes after him and the other after Mother, but I can't remember which one is which. Enough about my brothers, tell me what happened to you. Your father rang mine to see if he could arrange for you to come here. Are they going abroad again? Can't you go with them? It was all such short notice.'

Ellie sat on her bed and looked at her dear friend with her green eyes and auburn hair, which she wore in two thick plaits but when loose became a halo of curls.

They had spent the first five of their seven years in each other's company playing together and at the local Playgroup. Polly's father, Adam Smythe, was a farmer and had been exempt from military service during the war to produce food. He lived on the farm next to Ellie's grandparents' home, and they were lifelong friends; the women had always kept in touch with each other.

When Ellie and Polly and the boys were babies, they were all put out in prams together, then playpens, and finally they could play in the fields, always accompanied by the two Labradors from the farm. It was during the war, and they all played in the one remaining unploughed meadow, built camps, and fished and swam in the river; idyllic days without a care in the world, returning at teatime dirty, hungry and tired. Only the occasional dog fight between the Luftwaffe and the RAF disturbed their carefree childhood.

'Come on, tell me,' said Polly.

'I don't know,' began Ellie, 'but I know I angered my mother, which is never a brilliant move.'

'That's true,' laughed Polly.

Ellie pushed the sweet into her cheek. 'Well, as you know, my mother was desperate to move back to London as soon as the war was over, although Father wanted to stay here. I can't tell you how much I hated it. No friends, only a nanny for company. I hardly saw my parents, as they were always out attending dinners, luncheons, or some puffed-up function or other.

'Anyway, about two weeks ago, Father was at an Embassy lunch, Mother was at home and told the nanny, she was expecting an important visitor and did not wish to be disturbed under any circumstances. Nanny decided we should play hide-and-seek in the garden. It was cold, and Nanny wanted to get some hot chocolate. So, I went to hide in the summerhouse. When I got there, I could hear strange moans coming from inside, so I looked in through the window.'

'What did you see?' asked Polly, her eyes wide with expectation.

'My mother was lying on a couch, her skirts up around her waist, her blouse open, and her naked legs wound round a dark shadow, which was moving slowly over her. At that moment Nanny returned and pulled me away. When I asked her what my mother was doing, Nanny put her finger to her lips and whispered, 'Your mother is securing a job for your father.'

Polly stared at her friend. 'Did your mother find out you had seen her?'

'Well, they had a formal dinner party that night for all the usual top people. I had to perform my party piece, which I hate. Anyway, one woman asked me.

'And what have you been doing today?' pulling me towards her.

'I went to play hide-and-seek with my Nanny.'

'How lovely. And how old are you? And where did you hide?'

'I am nearly seven, and I wanted to hide in the summerhouse, but I couldn't because my mother was in there securing my father his new job.'

Polly sniggered.

'There was a terrible hush in the room. My mother turned as white as a sheet and demanded that Nanny take me to my room. She was laughing in a most curious way, and said, 'Children have too much imagination when left on their own'.'

Polly took Ellie's hand and laughed. 'No wonder your mother sent you away. I bet she was furious.'

'I knew I was in trouble as soon as my mother looked at me. She insisted on sending me to school in London, but Father put his foot down and said he would only agree to send me away if I came here to be with you in the country. The row between them could be heard down the street.'

Ellie sucked her sweet. 'So, they bought my school clothes and Nanny sewed on name tags, and when they were all done, Mother gave her notice.'

Polly rose and put her arm around her friend. 'You will be happy here, I can assure you, and we are like sisters.'

'Will you teach me to do my plaits? I still can't do them on my own,' said Ellie.

'Of course, it just takes practice.'

The term started well until the weather took a sudden turn for the worst. The girls took to sleeping in the same narrow bed, with all the blankets over them for extra warmth. Later in the month, snow started falling and the forecast was bleak. After two weeks of snow, ice, and arctic winds, the old boiler finally gave up the ghost and the school had to close. They contacted the parents and the girls started packing their trunks.

Polly rushed into their dorm fling the door against the bed.

'You're coming home with me. The head has just told me your parents are abroad and your grandparents are not well and have gone to their London apartment. Papa is coming today. Do say you're pleased.'

Ellie looked at Polly and burst into tears.

'Oh. It won't be that bad. Simon and Laurence will be there too.'

'No. I'm so happy.'

Polly's father arrived in the early afternoon to collect the girls. He hugged them both and then loaded their trunks and tuck boxes into the back of the ex-army Austin 'Tilly', which was covered by a tarpaulin. The girls clambered into the remaining space in the back, where they snuggled down on the blankets laid over straw for warmth. There was a large flask of hot chocolate and some slices of fruitcake in a tin. Ellie sat back and thanked her lucky stars for such caring friends.

A slight break in the weather came in the afternoon, but the clouds were heavy, and the sky promised more snow.

When they arrived at the farm, Simon and Laurence greeted them; both boys had returned the day before. They helped their father unload the 'Tilly', while Mrs Smythe hugged and kissed both Polly and Ellie.

'Put the girls' trunks up on the landing by their room, please, boys. Nanny will want to sort everything out,' called Mrs Smythe. 'And then come down, wash your hands and get ready for tea.'

They finally sat together at the kitchen table, waiting for Mr Smythe to say grace. He thanked the Lord for the food, and they all tucked in.

Mrs Smythe turned to Ellie. 'I have put you with Polly in her room. I thought you two might like to be together. If you are not happy with that, we can move you into a room on your own.'

'Thank you, Mrs Smythe, I would love to share with Polly, but doesn't she want her own room?'

'Of course, she won't mind,' Laurence cut in. 'She can chatter to you all night long.'

Polly kicked her brother under the table, and he feigned being hurt. The friendly rivalry was something that Ellie always enjoyed; she loved this family life, which was lacking in her own home.

Slices of ham were piled on a large oval dish. A huge pile of toast rose from a basket. There was homemade butter, and pots of jam, together with a chocolate sponge and a fruit cake. Ellie felt her stomach rumble; she was suddenly ravenous.

'Tuck in, Ellie, there's a good girl. You know you don't have to wait to be asked in this house, otherwise, you will find it has all gone before you can get your hands on it,' said Mrs Smythe, slapping Laurence's hand as he reached for three pieces of toast in one go. 'And, Ellie, I think you are old enough to stop calling us Mr and Mrs Smythe. My name is Beatrice, so you can call me Bea, and you can call my husband A-J as all his friends do. Agreed?' she said, a warm smile spreading across her face; then turning to Nanny said, 'Nanny would you be kind enough to pour the tea for us all.'

'Agreed,' said Ellie, 'and thank you.'

Wonderful, carefree days flew by. The boys were up early to bring in the coal and the wood for the fires in the house and the Aga in the kitchen. The girls helped make bread every day and baked cakes on alternate days. It was their job to collect the eggs, wash them, and grade them, so A-J could take them down to the shop to help with supplies for the village.

They took turns milking the house cow, and Ellie had Polly in stitches as she tried to learn to get the milk in the pail. They took the milk and poured it into large enamel pans in the dairy. The following day they would skim off the cream; some they kept for the house, while the rest was hand-churned into butter by Bea. They put the whey to one side to be fed to the pigs.

At eleven o'clock they all went into the dining room, where the fire had been lit, and their Nanny would make sure they carried out the work they had been sent home with from school, and where Simon always made sure he sat next to Ellie. At night they snuggled down into their beds with feather filled mattresses and pillowcases topped with linen sheets, woollen blankets and large feather eiderdowns, making it difficult to rise on the cold mornings.

Some days it was so cold with a bitter wind from the north that they hurried through their jobs, eager to get back into the warmth of the farmhouse. On those days, it was necessary to break the ice on the animals' water troughs, which they did every morning and late evening, making the house even more inviting. Simon rubbed the chilblains on Ellie's hands and feet every night with witch hazel or calamine lotion to stop the itching and rubbed lanolin into them in the morning. He became her constant companion, and they did most things together.

On the farm, their water came from a well, and they would come down every morning to the kitchen to collect their pail of water from a hand pump over the sink, add some boiling water to it and wash in the bathroom next to the kitchen. The tin bath was dragged out twice a week, and they took it in turns to have a bath in front of the Aga with hot water straight from the tap on the range.

They had fresh eggs, butter, and cream. Over the next month, Ellie gained a little weight and a rosy complexion, rather than the pallid look when she arrived; but more than that, Ellie felt alive among these wonderful, loving people.

At last, the snow stopped, and the temperature rose, after one of the worst winters on record. England had come to a standstill and the economy had been hit. But with the thaw came flooding; acres of farmland lay underwater, and the crops they had planted in the autumn had either frozen in the ground or drowned by the floodwater. It wasn't until April that everything on the farm got back to any semblance of normality.

During this time, Ellie got to know the family and family life. Polly played chess with her father, or Laurence, and swore he always cheated. Ellie and Simon always sat reading books together and looked up the secrets of natural history.

'Will you come back here every hols now?' asked Simon, peering at her over the top of his book.

'I don't know. I shouldn't think so. I may have to go to my grandparents' if they come back to the country; or see my parents wherever they are. But it wouldn't be fair for your parents to look after me all the time.'

Simon lowered his book, looked at her, and smiled. 'You know what, Ellie? You will become a permanent member of this family because one day I will marry you.'

Ellie looked at him and laughed. 'Don't be so soppy, Simon.'

PART ONE

CHAPTER ONE

Sardinia, Late May 1961

Ellie watched from the deck as the old ferry pulled into the port of Cagliari. Great cranes stood like sentinels by the dock, swinging from side to side, as they loaded or unloaded the various cargoes, while swarthy men pulled and heaved at ropes and chains. Young, olive-skinned boys stood chattering beside the quay, waiting to run errands or carry luggage.

The main road in front of the port ran on either side of an extensive garden in which were planted young palms. Further down the road, there were large trees, by which stood the trams waiting for an assortment of passengers. All along the buildings on the far side was a grand arcade, where people walked or sat at tables, drinking coffee, smoking, or just watching the world go by.

The early morning sunlight shone on the golden city that rose from the harbour to the Castello at the top. It had all the promise of a beautiful day, with a clear blue sky. A gentle breeze rippled across the sea and stirred Ellie's long blonde hair as she watched the men below secure the ferry with ropes.

Ellie thought of the book she had bought by D. H. Lawrence: *'And suddenly there is Cagliari: a naked town rising steep, steep, golden looking, piled naked to the sky from the plain at the head of a formless hollow bay.'* But it was not naked: there were trees planted in the streets, there was colour, and the bay was wide and welcoming. Cagliari had moved on.

The crossing from Livorno had been long and she had slept briefly in her cabin, waking to the rocking of the ship. It had been almost twenty-four hours and Ellie was glad to see the port.

She looked over the rail at the milling crowds below and watched as a large car was making its way through the throng of people. It stopped at the bottom of the iron stairway, which had been manoeuvred across the harbour, and now rested against the ship, waiting for the passengers to disembark. Ellie smiled to herself, knowing she would enjoy this magical-looking city.

Ellie watched as her mother stepped from the car and spoke to her chauffeur. Isabel was impeccably dressed, as always. Not a hair out of place, not a crease in her dress. Her mother dismissed the chauffeur with a quick gesture of impatience. He gave a slight bow and walked over to speak to a man dressed in a neat white uniform and handed him something, which Ellie guessed was a tip. The man looked around furtively as he took the money and waved the chauffeur up the stairs. Ellie moved inside and stood beside her luggage near the doorway at the top of the iron stairway. She knew someone would collect her, as her mother always arranged everything.

It did not matter where they were in the world, Isabel di Montford organised people with a charm that was reserved for others, rather than her family, and people always fell over themselves to help her. It was said it was her steely nerves and charm that got her husband all the best jobs in the Foreign Office, but Ellie knew that her mother used more than her feminine charm to get what she wanted. At home, Isabel ruled the household with a rod of iron, and Ian, Ellie's father, always gave in to her – anything for a quiet life. The only time he had stood up to her and won, was when he demanded Ellie went to join Polly at her school, rather than a school in London, but he had paid for it with Isabel's demands to move abroad again.

Ellie looked up to see the chauffeur collecting her luggage and stepped forward to introduce herself.

'Good morning. I am Ellie Montford.'

'*Signorina.*'

A brief handshake and he was off down the huge metal stairway, a suitcase in each hand.

Ellie followed him down the stairs, carrying her vanity case. At the bottom, there was a young boy, no older than twelve, with large brown eyes and a mischievous smile. He was wearing a cotton shirt and shorts but was barefoot with a small green ribbon tied around his big toe.

'Can I take that for you, *signorina*?' he said, gesturing to her vanity case.

'Thank you,' she said, handing over her case and following him to the car where he handed it to the chauffeur.

'Go away, go away, little vagabond,' said Isabel, shooing the boy away.

Ellie felt in her pocket, found a five-lira note, and handed it to the boy. His face lit up as he smiled at Ellie. His smile was wide, his face angelic, but there was a wicked twinkle in his eye.

'*Grazie, signorina.*'

'Ellie,' cried her mother, 'I would be grateful if you did not encourage the little ragamuffins. They are a real nuisance.'

Ellie smiled at the boy and gave him a broad wink behind her mother's back.

Isabel turned to greet her daughter with the usual peck on the cheek and her obligatory criticism.

'Your hair is too long, you've gained weight, and you have been eating too much pasta. You must take yourself in hand while you are down here.'

Ellie sighed, wondering how she would cope with her mother over the coming months.

They settled themselves in the car and Isabel continued.

'I have a letter for you from Simon. I wish you wouldn't encourage him to write to you.'

Ellie sat in silence as her mother moaned on. She turned to look out of the rear window of the car and watched the young boy as he went to find someone else to help.

'There will be no need for you to write to him, Eleanor, do you hear me? I do not want you to encourage him. It is not as if he has anything to offer. He comes from farming stock, and the family is hardly out of the top drawer. Besides, Laurence will inherit the farm. Simon will have a minor job in the Foreign Office,' said her mother.

Her last words brought Ellie back from her thoughts. 'Like Father,' said Ellie, looking at her mother. Then added, 'Yes, I mean no, Mother.'

'You know, Eleanor, your father has worked hard for his position; you should respect that. And know that Simon is not a suitable match for you, even if it is time you thought of settling down. Your father should get his knighthood for his work in the Foreign Office. I want nothing to jeopardise that, do you understand?'

Ellie sighed again. 'All you are interested in is being Lady di Montfort. I like Simon; I have known him since childhood. With you and Father always away, we grew up together – shared our secrets, climbed trees together, grazed our knees together. He is kind and caring, and he is almost family.'

'Not very ladylike, and you always defend that family against me, and Simon is always standing up for you.'

'That is because I spent more time with them than I did with you and Father.'

Her mother turned away and sighed with the all too familiar look when she wasn't getting her way.

Ellie was fond of Simon but had always said she would not consider marrying until she reached twenty-four, and that was three years away. They had always said they would marry each other if they had found no one by that time. There was little doubt that it had come around quickly.

The car halted outside a large, imposing building. The chauffeur jumped out and rushed round to open the doors for the two women. A manservant came forward to take the cases, as Ellie followed her mother into the grand cool hall.

Black-and-white marble tiles were on the floor, covered with expensive-looking Persian rugs. Fresh flowers filled the hallway with their fragrant scent. The ceilings were high, leaving room for numerous pictures and portraits on the walls, giving the entire place an air of grandeur.

Whatever Ellie thought of her mother, Isabel knew how to organise things, even if they were over the top at times.

'Your father is in a meeting with the Consular from Rome this morning, but he should be back for lunch.'

The young woman who came forward to greet them was short and slender with raven-black hair clipped up in a French twist and dark, almond-shaped eyes that watched everything. She smiled, making her face light up.

'Ah, Giovanna, this is Signorina Eleanor. Take her upstairs to her room and help her to unpack, then show her around,' said Isabel in a dismissive tone.

Ellie raised her eyebrows in surprise at her mother's manner and followed Giovanna up the wide marble staircase.

'Did you have a pleasant journey from Livorno, signorina?' asked Giovanna. 'It can sometimes be choppy.'

'Yes, it was calm, fortunately,' replied Ellie. 'Thank you.'

They reached the first floor and walked down a wide corridor. Giovanna pointed to the doors as they passed.

'Those doors lead into the private sitting room and dining room. We hold all the big functions downstairs in the grand room,' said the girl.

They reached the door at the end of the passage, and Giovanna opened it to reveal a spacious, airy room with windows on two sides and a large pair of French windows on the far side that overlooked the port.

Ellie walked over to one window and looked out. There was a wonderful view of the port. Below was a colourful array of terracotta-tiled roofs as the buildings stepped down toward the port. She went over to the French doors, opened them, and stepped onto the balcony. Warm, salty air came to meet her, followed by the sounds of the city which came on a gentle breeze. Ellie smiled as she surveyed the scene.

She turned back to look at the room. It was painted a pale blue and had a blue carpet. The curtains were the palest of blue with a floral design of pastel shades. Her bed, facing the French doors, was large and its cover was the same material as the curtains. A cool room. A dressing table was on one side of the room, and a big double wardrobe on the other.

'Signorina, can I help you?' asked Giovanna, who was standing by the luggage, which had magically arrived in the room.

'Thank you, Giovanna.'

They unpacked Ellie's cases and found places for everything, all the time chatting together.

'Tell me, Giovanna, what is Cagliari like? Do you live here in the city? Do you get any time off?' asked Ellie in her broken Italian.

Giovanna laughed. 'So many questions, signorina.'

'Sorry, but I like to know everything.'

'Yes, I live here; Cagliari is my city. I love it. I live up in Casteddu, which is the old part of the city. And yes, I get time off when we are not too busy here.'

'Would you take me around Cagliari, show me the places that only the locals know, plus all the sights everyone should see? And would you introduce me to your friends, please?'

Giovanna looked round to make sure no one was listening.

'It's most irregular.'

'So am I,' Ellie replied.

They looked at each other and laughed.

'What is Milan like? I have never been there,' said Giovanna, putting Ellie's shoes in the wardrobe.

'It was wonderful; 'Polly, my lifelong friend, begged me to go to Italy with her to help organise everything for her wedding. It turned out to be an amazing experience. We did a lot of shopping in the big shops and small boutiques; they have beautiful clothes and shoes. I had always dressed plainly, not wanting to draw attention to myself, as my mother insisted, I should not be showy, but Polly changed all that when she made me buy the suit you are holding and coloured scarves to brighten up my plain dresses. I always feel more confident in that suit. They had beautiful things.' Said Ellie, laughing.

'So, I see,' said Giovanna, holding up the pink Chanel-style suit trimmed in navy. 'You also speak good Italian for an English person, and it will improve down here. Please, go on with your story.'

'Polly and I went to university together. That is where she met Mario. He was in London improving his English, while Polly was at college learning Italian. They met at an Italian evening arranged for the students at the university. From then on, they were inseparable. Eventually, she took him home to meet her parents and told them they wanted to get married. Mario explained to her father they wanted to get married in Italy but would like his permission.'

'How lovely,' said Giovanna, hanging another dress in the wardrobe.

'Anyway, Mario – whom the family, and Polly, thought was a young, impoverished student – turned out to be the second son of the owner of a large wine estate near Rome.

'Simon, Polly's brother, arrived to be with us for the wedding. Laurence, Polly's elder brother, sent his love but could not get back from Africa, as his mother-in-law was ill with malaria.

'Polly and Mario had the civil ceremony in England in a registry office before returning home. Then her parents came down to Italy for the marriage ceremony, which was held in a private chapel on the estate. Everyone was so welcoming. The meal afterwards was long and noisy, like all Italian weddings. It was a perfect day.

'When Mario's father stood to give his speech, he thanked Polly's parents for allowing him to have the wedding in Italy. He wished the young couple all the best and then, with a slight tear in his eye, he announced that they would spend their honeymoon in Australia! And that they would stay down there for a few months; I was so surprised by the announcement, as it had been a secret.

'The following day we all said our goodbyes and the newlyweds left for Australia. Polly told me they were going to visit various vineyards down there to get ideas for more modern wines.'

'Australia,' said Giovanna, closing the suitcases, 'I should like to go there one day.'

'Thank you for all your help, Giovanna.'

'Signorina, if you need them, your parents have the big suite upstairs. Your bathroom is the first door on the left as you leave your room.'

Left on her own, Ellie thought back to the wedding day. She had gone to find Polly to say her goodbyes. Her dear friend had brought out the best in her, giving her confidence by always being there to help her.

'I will miss you so much, Polly. I hope you have a wonderful time in Australia. Don't come back with too much of a twang.'

Polly pulled Ellie down to sit next to her on a nearby bench. 'I will miss you too. But, Ellie, there is something I have wanted to say to you for a long time, my last piece of advice. You need to find yourself a lover. You need someone to show you how lovely you are, not the plain Jane your mother insists on calling you. But not my brother – Simon is great, but you need a stranger.'

'Don't be silly,' laughed Ellie, somewhat taken aback.

Polly took Ellie's hand and held it tight. 'I'm serious, Ellie. Love frees a woman, gives her wings. I know what it has done for me.'

'But you are beautiful; everyone falls in love with you, Polly.'

'Ellie, listen to me, please. You are beautiful, with your golden hair and green eyes, and you have a wonderful nature. You may not realise it, but you are an extremely attractive woman.'

'Polly, you always make me feel so good.'

'Don't forget that then,' said Polly, kissing Ellie on the cheek. 'I must change. And you look amazing in that pink suit, I am so glad I made you buy it. Love you.'

And with that Polly had gone, leaving Ellie to think over what her friend had said. Then, laughing at the thought, went in search of Simon.

'Ellie, dearest Ellie, what am I going to do without Polly? Laurence has gone, and now you are going away too. I will miss you all so much,' said Simon, putting his arm around her.

'I promise to write, as long as you write to me too,' she said, kissing him on his cheek.

'I will, I promise. There should be a letter waiting for you. I will be interested to know the reaction it receives.'

Ellie laughed.

Simon said a fond farewell to Ellie before they took him to the airport.

Later, Mario's father drove Ellie to Livorno, to catch the ferry down to Cagliari.

It had all happened so quickly – Ellie smiled at the thought of Polly and Mario – it had been a wonderful experience.

★

Ian returned from his meeting with the consulate in time for lunch. It was the usual formal affair, Isabel in charge, and Ian eager to tell them everything that had happened that morning together with any fresh gossip.

He had welcomed Ellie with a perfunctory kiss on each cheek.

'I'm glad you've come. I have arranged for you to go to the university to have Italian lessons with Professor Serra. He is about to retire from the university, but he still does the odd bit of tuition. It will be good for you to do something with your time when you are not helping your mother with the entertaining. You will start after the weekend, so you have two days to sort yourself out.'

Ellie sighed. Nothing changed. The Foreign Office moved her parents every three years in the service, and wherever they went, if Ellie joined them on her holidays, her father would send her to school, college, or whatever educational place was on offer to learn the local language and to mix with the local people. As a result, she could speak French, Portuguese, Swahili, and a little Urdu. Her father, a brilliant linguist, expected his daughter to follow him. Ellie was lucky to have inherited her father's love of learning a language, which pleased him. The thought of learning Italian was pleasing as it was such a pretty language.

After lunch, while her parents took their usual nap, Ellie walked through Cagliari to get her bearings. Turning right outside the house and walking down the narrow, steep street towards the port below, where a gentle breeze greeted her with its salty smell of the sea.

At the port, the boats were so close together that it was possible to walk from one to the next all along the port. Fishermen with dark, weathered skin were resting on their boats, some lulled into their afternoon sleep after the night's fishing, others mending their green and ochre-coloured nets spread out on the Quayside to dry. A few waved idly to her or called a soft greeting.

Ellie sighed, feeling at peace here.

She turned to walk across to the Via Roma, where little cafes had seating under the grand arcade, away from the now intense Sun and sat at a table to watch the world go by. It was the quiet time when the Sards took to their beds after a good meal before the evening rush started.

She ordered a lemonade and sat sipping it... There was something about Sardinia that was so very different from Italy.

The following morning, Ellie took her place at the breakfast table. Her father was reading an out-of-date copy of *The Times*, while her mother was busy going through her mail.

'Coffee, signorina?'

'Yes, please, Giovanna,' said Ellie, helping herself to a brioche and some jam.

'Simon has said that he hasn't heard from you.'

'You said that yesterday, Mother. Besides, I saw him in Milan.'

Isabel passed the letter to Ellie. It had already been opened and read by her mother, who deemed it her duty to read all her daughter's mail before handing it over to her.

Ellie took the letter, read it, and smiled. It was a few weeks old, written before they had seen each other at Polly's wedding. Simon had said he would be interested to know what her mother's reaction would be, as he had written a vivid account of the birth of some piglets; how he had to assist and had become covered in the sow's blood.

Ellie looked up to see her mother looking at her with disdain. Simon knew that Isabel read all of Ellie's letters, so he always put some lurid details in to upset her. He would have been well pleased with today's result.

'We have a drinks party this evening for some local charities. I expect you to attend, Ellie, and I expect you to smarten yourself up,' said Isabel.

After breakfast, Ellie went to find Giovanna, who was sitting in the kitchen enjoying a quick coffee.

'Signorina, can I help you?' said Giovanna, jumping up from her chair.

'Please, Giovanna, sit down and enjoy your coffee. Then perhaps you would be kind enough to tell me where I can go to get my hair done. I would like to have it put up for this evening.'

Giovanna put her hand in her apron pocket and pulled out a piece of paper and a pencil and wrote a name and address and handed it to Ellie.

'Tell them I sent you and ask for Giorgio; he is a wizard with long hair.'

'Thank you,' said Ellie, taking the piece of paper.

'Excuse me, signorina, but does your mother always read your mail?'

'Yes, but all my friends know that she does, so they think up some wonderful stories. Today my friend, Simon, gave a rather vivid description of the birth of some piglets, much to my mother's disdain.'

The two young women looked at each other and giggled.

Ellie found the hairdressers in a street off the Piazza Yennes and was introduced to Giorgio. An hour later, Ellie left with her hair put up in a beautiful French twist with flowers for decoration.

Back at the house, everyone was busy getting ready for the evening's drinks party. Ellie had a quick bath, then slipped into a little black dress she had bought with Polly in Milan. She put on her pearl earrings with a matching pearl necklace and stood in front of the long mirror. Giovanna knocked and entered.

13

'Signorina, you look very elegant.'

'Thank you, Giovanna – your hairdresser is wonderful. Don't you think you could call me Ellie, rather than 'Signorina' all the time?'

'I don't think your mother would approve,' said Giovanna with a smile.

'Please, Giovanna, call me Ellie.'

'I will, but only when we are alone together, agreed?' Ellie smiled and nodded in agreement.

Downstairs, the guests were arriving for their free drinks and canapes. A babble of gossip and greetings filled the room. When Ellie entered, it was already filled with smoke, as men puffed on their cigars and women on Gauloises or Sobranie cocktail cigarettes. She took a glass of champagne from the tray of a passing waiter and stood to sip it.

Ellie watched the surrounding people. Most of them were from the Diplomatic Corps, while others represented various charities. There were dignitaries, councillors, and foreign diplomats. She wandered among them, listening to snippets of conversation in a variety of languages.

Giovanna came past with a tray of Vol-au-vents. Ellie took one and popped it in her mouth, then took another.

'If you are hungry, go downstairs. They are preparing all the goodies there; you can help yourself.'

Ellie smiled and followed Giovanna down to the kitchen. She selected several delicacies and sat at the end of the table to eat them while sipping her champagne watching the activity in the kitchen.

When she had finished, Ellie picked up a tray of goodies from the table and returned upstairs to hand it around to the guests, giving her a chance to chat with them as she passed from guest to guest.

'Eleanor, what do you think you are doing?' asked her mother, looking shocked at her daughter taking the role of a servant.

'Mingling, Mother, mingling,' Ellie said, moving on to a couple who looked lost.

'Would you like some of these?' she asked the girl who blushed and looked awkward. She was short and lean-looking with dark eyes. Her hair was straight and as black as a raven's wing.

Ellie pushed the tray forward. 'They are delicious, please have some. Don't be shy, help yourselves.'

She was rewarded with a winning smile.

'Are you from a charity?'

'Yes,' she replied. 'I am Antonia, and this is my brother Franco. We run a small shack to help the young boys who live in the port and try to find work for them in the docks or around the town of Cagliari.'

Ellie turned to the youthful man; he too was short and lean-looking. It was easy to see that they were related, with their similar features and colouring.

'Yes, I saw some at the port when I arrived. Tell me about it,' said Ellie.

'There's not a lot to tell,' continued Antonia, 'we rent an old fishing shack on the beach near Giorgino. We sleep about twenty boys at a push and feed them as best we can. That is why we came today, to see if we could get someone to sponsor us or help us, but nobody is interested.'

'How do you feed them?' asked Ellie.

'The people in the markets are extremely kind, and they always give us what they can't sell. At night, we collect whatever they have left behind. Plus, the bread shops and the pasta shops always give us what they would have thrown away.'

'Why do you do this for the boys?'

'Because there is no one else to help them, and we were orphans ourselves, so we know the problems the young boys have.'

'What about the young girls?'

'They are luckier, as they get taken into domestic service.'

'May I come to see you one afternoon?'

'Yes, please, that would be wonderful, thank you,' said Franco. He pulled a rough piece of paper out of his pocket with instructions on how to reach the shack.

'Leave it with me; I will see what I can do. Perhaps I could come and see you next week. Would Monday be all right?'

Another winning smile from both of them and Ellie tucked the address into her pocket.

It was around nine-thirty when the last guest left. Ellie went into the sitting room to join her parents and plonked herself down on the sofa.

Giovanna came in to ask if they wanted anything to eat.

'Scrambled eggs and toast with a little salad,' said Ian, dismissing Giovanna, he turned to Ellie. 'Who were the young couple you were talking to?'

'They look after the waifs and strays, the young boys who work at the docks doing odd jobs –'

'I would be grateful if you didn't get involved, Eleanor,' Isabel cut in. 'They are not waifs and strays, but vagabonds, ragamuffins, thieves or ne'er-do-wells. You give them money and they just become a pest. I do not know how they got an invitation to come here. People are not interested in that kind of charity. I know I didn't invite them.'

Ellie was about to argue with her mother but caught her father's look, which said, *not now,* and she smiled at him.

Supper arrived, and after coffee, Ellie said goodnight to her parents and went along the corridor to her bedroom. The young couple's card was in her pocket, and she would see them on Monday.

Sunday was always church in the morning, followed by a large lunch, after which her parents would retire to the sitting room and fall asleep. In her bedroom, Ellie went through her vanity case and taking out her wallet, counted out the lira she had leftover from her holiday in Milan. She smiled as there were about a hundred pounds, enough to help Antonia out for the time being.

When Monday morning arrived, Ellie happily walked up to the university with her note of introduction to the old professor.

He proved to be a man in his late sixties, and ready to retire.

16

He had thin, sallow skin and narrow lips. His eyes were a watery brown with dark circles that made them retreat into their sockets. His head was covered with wiry grey hair which, like his eyebrows, grew in every direction. His grubby suit looked as if he had slept in it for the past week.

The professor stared at her over his half-rimmed glasses and, with no preamble, began his lesson. He was an exacting teacher with little patience. He also had a pronounced lisp, which made him hard to understand. Ellie found the lesson boring and difficult to follow but knew her father would never hear of her quitting.

The afternoon was much more interesting, as she visited Franco and Antonia. Ellie wandered the length of the port toward the shack, following the instructions on the piece of paper Franco had given her. Men sat on the Quayside, smoking, or talking about the night's fishing and what tomorrow might bring.

The brown-boarded shack looked to be in a state of collapse. It desperately needed repair and a coat of paint. Outside, lines of washing hung at odd angles under the weight of the dripping garments. Ellie knocked at the door.

A young boy answered her knock. Ellie recognised him at once as the brown-eyed, mischievous-looking angel who had taken her vanity case the day she arrived at Cagliari, and Isabel had shooed him away.

'Hello, I'm Ellie, and what is your name?'

'I'm Tommaso. I remember you.'

Antonia came to the door. 'Don't leave the signorina standing outside, Tommaso, have you no manners? How many times do I have to tell you it's rude to leave someone on the doorstep?' Turning to Ellie, she added, 'I am so sorry. Please, come in and sit down,' she said, opening the door wide and inviting Ellie in.

One of the other boys stood up from the table where he was sitting and offered Ellie his chair.

'Thank you,' said Ellie. She sat down and was immediately surrounded by a crowd of nut-brown children with black hair and eyes to match. They all looked so young and thin, but not malnourished.

'Now, boys, away, please; allow the signorina to have some breathing space.'

They all moved but still stood staring at Ellie.

Tommaso came forward and touched Ellie's hair.

'Tommaso please,' said Antonia, 'leave the signorina alone.'

'I'm sorry about that,' said Antonia, 'but we all find blonde hair fascinating. Now can I get you a drink – water, coffee?' asked Antonia.

'No, but thank you.'

Ellie turned to Tommaso.

'May I ask why you wear a green ribbon on your foot?'

'To show I'm not so poor that I can't have something on my feet.'

Ellie smiled and ruffled the young boy's hair.

She turned to Antonia.

'I came to give you this,' she said, pulling an envelope out of her bag. 'There is not a lot, but enough to help with the rent or whatever.'

Antonia took the envelope, holding it as if it were about to explode in her hands.

'Open it. It should help until we can get someone to fund you.'

Antonia dropped the envelope onto the table. 'Where did it come from?' she asked, looking nervous.

'It's all right, I promise you. It is from my bank account – nothing illegal, promise. It is some money I had leftover from when I was staying in Milan.'

Antonia opened the envelope and looked at the money. Tears came into her eyes.

'You have no idea what this means. It is the answer to all our prayers. We are about to be evicted, as I can't find the rent. I've been at my wits' end. Thank you, Ellie, thank you,' cried Antonia, and put her arms around Ellie and wept. Then pulling away, asked, 'But what do you want from us?'

'Nothing, silly. I just wanted to help.'

'Thank you. But people usually want something from us,' sighed Antonia.

'Well, I don't. Now let me help you with the laundry.'

They chattered together as they did the washing. When they had finished and hung out the clothes to dry Antonia pulled at Ellie's arm.

'Come and see inside and I'll show you where the boys sleep.'

Ellie followed her into a sizeable dormitory room at the back of the shack. Chairs stood beside the beds with odd bits of clothing. The room was dark and dingy but smelled clean and fresh.

'We top and tail the younger boys, so the older boys can have a bed to themselves.' Said Antonia.

'What is the age range?' asked Ellie.

'We have one boy who is only five years old, but he has an older brother who helps to look after him. The ages range up to eighteen, by which time we hope they have found permanent work and shelter, but they know they can come back here if they are desperate.'

'Tell me, why do they come here?'

'Because they have either lost their parents or their parents can't afford to feed all their children, so the older ones get turned out. Whatever the reason, they are welcome here.'

'Can I come back again?' asked Ellie.

'Whenever you want; we are always here. Remember, Ellie, if you ever want anything done, you only have to ask. The boys will always be glad to help you.'

The two girls embraced.

'Thank you, Ellie, thank you.'

It was early evening, and the light was fading as the large red sun sank into the sea.

'Tommaso, come here, please,' said Antonia, 'I want you to see Signorina Ellie back to her house.'

'Yes, Mama,' said Tommaso. He took Ellie's hand. 'Come with me. I know all the shortcuts.'

He chattered to her all the way back to her house, then stood at the bottom of the steps.

'Good night, Signorina Ellie, and thank you.'

Ellie fumbled in her bag for a note, but when she looked up, he had disappeared into the twilight.

CHAPTER TWO

It was two weeks later when Ellie arrived at the classroom, dreading another depressing lesson with the professor. She had been busy helping her mother over the weekend and had not done her homework, which would mean a double amount today. Ellie knocked on the door and entered, but there was no sign of the old professor. At that moment, a man entered the room.

'Sorry I'm late. I understand you are Professor Serra's pupil?'

Ellie stared at the man. He was tall and dark-eyed, and his curly brown hair covered part of his face. He put his hand up to push it back from his eyes, which were dark brown. He was wearing a beige linen suit and an open-necked white linen shirt. Finally, he looked at her and smiled. It was a smile that lit up the whole of his face.

'*Buongiorno, signorina,*' he said, coming towards her to shake her hand. 'I'm Professor Giovanni Puddu, but everyone calls me Gino, which is so much easier. The professor is ill, so I am standing in for him. You are…?'

'I am Eleanor Montfort, but everyone calls me Ellie,' she said, feeling her heart jump.

'Good, well, Ellie it is. Now, I do not know what Professor Serra does for his lessons, but I like mine out of the college. So, grab your things and follow me down to the local café for starters.'

Ellie smiled; it was as if a breath of fresh air had blown through the dusty room.

Gino opened the door wide for her, and she, grabbing her bag, followed him out of the university, down the road to the Piazza Constituzione and across to the Caffé Genovese.

He took Ellie's hand and led her through the crowded room, which was hazy from cigarette smoke, but smelt deliciously of coffee, to a table with a reserved card on it. He pulled out a chair for her, then settled himself next to her.

'Now, what would you like to drink?' he asked in Italian.

'Café, please.'

'Right, you ask for it.'

'And you?'

'They know what I want, but you can tell them I will have my usual.'

Ellie thought for a moment. The waiter arrived and Gino nodded to her.

'Cafe for me,' she said in Italian in a shaky voice, 'and the usual for the professor, please.'

The waiter took the order and smiled at her.

'Bene,' said Gino, a wide grin spreading across his face.

The coffee soon arrived, hot and with a wonderful aroma that filled her senses. Gino passed her the sugar, and taking a packet, she held one end with her thumb and forefinger, tapping it on the table to make sure all the sugar was at the bottom. Then, opening the packet, poured the contents into her double coffee. Ellie sensed him watching her intently as he sipped his coffee.

'Is it true, what they say here, that you can trust a man who takes his coffee straight – no sugar?' she asked.

He laughed and gently pinched her elbow. 'It is, but where did you hear that?'

'The young girl who helps at the house told me.'

They sat and talked about the people in the Café; Gino correcting her Italian and Ellie asking him for unfamiliar words.

'This place is famous,' he said. 'It has been frequented by many well-known writers, like D. H. Lawrence when he wrote *Sea and Sardinia*.'

'He got it wrong about Cagliari being naked,' said Ellie.

'Why is that?

'Because from the sea now it looks green and colourful.'

'It was a while ago,' he said.

'Who else, what other writers?'

'Grazia Deledda lived here. Have you heard of her?'

'No, who is she?'

'A Sardinian writer from Nuoro, who came to live in Cagliari before going to Rome with her husband. We are proud of her, as she won the Nobel Prize for literature in 1926. You will read her work when you have learnt a little more Italian.'

Ellie took in the surroundings: fans slowly turning on the domed ceiling with its raised plasterwork; long glass cupboards with a large mahogany counter in front; the column in the middle of the room with half-panelling, which matched the walls; large windows were on the front of the café; waiters in their thin white cotton shirts, black waistcoats, long white aprons, and black trousers; girls in white tops with black skirts and little white aprons, all looking so smart.

The hour spent with Professor Serra always dragged, but the time with Gino flew by and he seemed in no hurry to leave.

'Should you be teaching someone else?'

'No, not until this afternoon. Do you have somewhere to go? Why don't you stay and have lunch with me?'

Ellie hesitated. 'My parents are expecting me home; they will wonder where I am and what has happened to me. If they discover I am having lessons with a young professor instead of Professor Serra, it will be difficult. I think I ought to get back, but thank you.'

'I understand, another time perhaps. Lesson same time tomorrow, but here, okay?' he said, rising from his seat.

Smiling, Ellie collected her bag and said, 'Thank you. I'll look forward to it.'

Ellie walked back to the house. Lessons would be better now and decided not to tell her parents about her new teacher.

The daily lessons became more interesting as the days flew by. One morning Ellie avoided her mother, who had been murmuring about going shopping in the city and wanted Ellie to go with her, but Ellie stressed she had an important lesson and slipped out of the house.

At the Café, Gino was sitting in his usual place on the terrace. He was reading one of the house papers that hung on pegs with wooden spines for the clients, like those in an English gentlemen's club. Ellie sighed.

He looked up and smiled at her, then rose and pulled out a chair for her to sit next to him.

'What would you like to drink?'

'Cafe and water, please.'

Her Italian had improved over the past weeks, and Ellie was becoming more confident and comfortable in Gino's company. He delighted in her interest in the language and his city. They met every morning in the Caffé Genovese, and he told her where they were going or what he had planned for her.

Ellie knew he was looking straight into her eyes. His intense stare made the colour rise on her cheeks.

Gino smiled at her again, a wicked grin that spread across his face and was irresistible. He put his hand on her arm and gave it that gentle squeeze she had come to love.

He waved to the waiter who nodded in return and came to take their order.

Ellie looked at Gino. His eyes were deep and appealing; they were brown with long lashes, and they stared out from under a mass of dark curly hair.

Their coffee came and they sipped it.

'Ignazio, a fellow professor, and a great friend is taking his class to Nora today. I thought we could join them. It would make a change from Cagliari.'

'How lovely! What is Nora, and when?'

'The coach leaves in twenty minutes,' he said, looking at his watch. 'I'll explain about Nora on the coach.'

They finished their coffee, and he took her hand as they hurried up to the Via Universita. The coach was waiting, and a crowd of students was climbing in to find a place to sit.

'I'm just going to see Carlo and see where Ignazio is. Find a seat in the front. I won't be a minute.'

Ellie watched as Gino hesitated and then walked across to a man in his thirties with black hair and eyes to match. He was of a stocky build, and holding a clipboard, and looked to be in charge.

'Come on, *signorina*,' said a junior student, 'come and sit with us.'

Before she could say anything, the young group had manhandled her into the back of the coach.

'We haven't seen you before, have we?' asked one.

'No, I am only a part-time student.'

'Are you new here?' asked another.

'Yes. I have only been here just over a month.'

'What nationality are you?' asked the student who had first approached her.

'I'm English,' replied Ellie, looking around to see if Gino was anywhere.

'I am Riccardo and I'm studying art and literature. The English all love Italian art and literature. What are you studying?'

'Italian…'

'You speak it well. What is your name?'

'Thank you. My name is Ellie.'

They all started chattering, asking her questions, and again, Ellie looked to see if Gino was on the coach.

He was standing in the doorway, looking down the rows of seats, searching for her. Ellie caught his eye, and he came down towards her.

'Sorry, boys, I know she's pretty, but the signorina belongs up in the front with me.'

A chorus of 'Spoilsport' and 'She's with us' came from the group.

Ellie blushed as Gino put his hand out to her and pulled her towards him.

'I got hijacked,' she said, as they sat together in the two front seats, Ellie by the window.

'I know, I'm sorry for leaving you. Are you all right now? Or would you rather sit with the group?'

25

'No, thank you, I'm happy here.'

'Ignazio isn't here today, but Carlo is taking the tour.'

He took her hand and gently squeezed it, then held it by his side. Carlo came and sat on the other side of the aisle.

'Ellie this is Carlo, as I said, Ignazio couldn't make it this morning, so Carlo has taken over.'

'Pleased to meet you, Carlo.' Said Ellie.

Carlo and Gino talked together while Ellie looked out of the window at the scenery passing by. She felt Gino holding her hand and squeezing it gently every so often.

They drove out of Cagliari, over the old rusty bridge, past the port where Franco and Antonia had the shack, past the little round tower nearby. Ellie saw the ribs of an old boat lying on its side, bleached by the constant sunlight. The salt flats, where the flocks of flamingos, with their heads down, were sifting the waters.

The students were all chattering and calling to one another.

Ellie was so absorbed by the scenery that she did not realise Gino was talking to her until he squeezed her hand hard.

'Are you all right?' he asked.

'Sorry, I was miles away. What did you say?'

'We are going to see Nora.'

'Yes, you said you would tell me about it.'

'Well, the story is that it was the first city in Sardinia, inhabited by the ancient Nuragic people. An Iberian Phoenician called Norax invaded it and gave it his name. The Phoenicians were known for their ports, of which Nora has three, guaranteeing safe anchorages whatever the weather. Then came the Carthaginians, followed by the Romans, who built over everything. It became the most important city in Sardinia until the Imperial Age when it was overtaken by Cagliari. After which the Vandals arrived, and then the sea level rose, putting two-thirds of the city underwater. They had a great storm here in 1889 and it unearthed the Phoenician temple. But we only really started excavating in 1952.'

At that moment, the coach turned off the main road, drove through the village of Pula and over the river, and then turned down towards the sea. Finally, it stopped, and they all got out, the students milling around and asking for guidance on where to go.

'Ignazio arranged a guide, so will you all please follow me,' said Carlo, as he strode off toward the ruins, the students following in his wake.

Before them was a wide bay, with a little church on the beach. The land ran on out into the sea and there was a tower at the end of a promontory. The sun was warm, but a gentle breeze came off the sea, giving a salty tang to the air. Ellie breathed it in.

'Lovely,' she said, more to herself than anyone else.

'Come with me, Ellie,' said Gino, and he pulled her toward the little church. It was cool inside. 'I have always loved this church; it is so simple, but there is something wonderful about it. In the crypt are relics of our patron saint, Sant'Efisio. The Romans beheaded him here and he became our martyred saint.'

'Is that what Cagliari celebrates every May?'

'Yes, the Sagra di Sant'Efisio and they make a feast of it. For four days they parade the saint from his church in Cagliari down to Pula, then to Nora, then back to Cagliari with a candlelight procession on the fourth evening. People come from all over the island dressed in the costumes of their towns or regions. It is a wonderful sight. Next year, if you are still here, we will go together; you will love it.'

'It sounds wonderful.'

He put his hand out to take hers. 'Let's see Nora.'

'You Seem disappointed, are you all right?'

'It's nothing, just that I was looking forward to seeing Ignazio. Let us go and find the others.'

They spent the rest of the morning walking around the ruins: the temples; the mosaics, which were covered with a corrugated tin roof to keep off the sun; the old streets with brick-built Roman sewers. They stood looking at the old theatre.

'It's the only ancient theatre in the whole of Sardinia. They came here to watch plays, not the gladiators. Perhaps they were more civilised here, at least I like to think so.'

Ellie looked at him. 'Sardinia and its history are important to you, aren't they?'

'Yes, and I hope you will come to love it too.'

They walked back to where the group had gathered and where Carlo was issuing instructions.

'Everyone into the coach, please,' called Carlo, trying to rally the students. 'Where are we going now, Carlo?' asked Gino.

'We have a table booked at a restaurant in Pula, so we can relax and discuss the morning.'

With everyone accounted for, the coach drove to a small restaurant just outside Pula.

'Ignazio knows the owner well,' Carlo said. 'He always puts on a good spread for the tour – it helps them, and the students like it.'

They were all welcomed by a short, thickset man and his equally stocky wife. After visits to the washroom or a quick smoke outside, they were shown to their seats. A table was laid out for them, so large it took up almost the entire room.

Antipasto, pasta, a main course, and dessert, followed by coffee were all demolished, leaving the table as if a horde of locusts had descended on it.

With thanks and numerous *ciao*s, everyone was, once again, back on the coach. There was a contented silence as they made their return journey to Cagliari; some dozed, while others watched the passing scenery.

At the university, the students poured out of the coach.

'I want a detailed account of Nora together with a brief history of the area for tomorrow please.'

There was a loud moan from the students as they said thanks to their professor and made their way home.

'Coffee?' asked Carlo. 'It's been an excellent day.'

They walked down to the Caffé Genovese and found a place to sit out on the little terrace.

'What would you like, Ellie?' asked Gino.

'A glass of water with lemon, please.'

'Carlo?'

'Coffee, please.'

Gino went to order their drinks.

'Did you enjoy the trip?' asked Carlo.

'Yes, very much, thank you. Do you do it often?'

'About once a term; it depends on the students. This year they are a good bunch, so it is great. Tell me have you known Gino long?'

'A couple of months, why?'

'You do know that students fraternising with the professors is frowned on by the faculty.'

'Whatever gave you that idea, he is my tutor, and I am simply a part-time student. Nothing more.' Said Ellie somewhat nettled.

Gino returned and sat beside Ellie.

'Are you all right Ellie?'

'So, what are you doing this evening?' cut in Carlo, looking at Ellie.

'I have to get back. My parents are old-fashioned; they always want to know where I am and what I have been doing.'

'What about you, Gino? Tell me, how is Angelo?'

'He's well. But I have a class, in fact,' said Gino, looking at his watch. 'I will be late if I don't get a move on.'

They drank their coffee and said their goodbyes.

Gino took Ellie's arm as he walked her down to her house.

'I didn't realise you had a lesson this evening.'

'I don't, it's just that Carlo can be overbearing sometimes. Besides, I want to be with you. A walk down to the port and back?'

Ellie looked at him, smiled, and said. 'You are funny,'

'Why funny?'

'Preferring to spend time with me.'

'But of course, silly, much better than an old grumpy professor. Did Carlo say something to upset you, there was a cold atmosphere when I returned?'

'He just remarked that the faculty doesn't look kindly on professors having close relations with students.'

'And what did you say?'

'I told him I was your student and that's all.'

Gino put his arm around her as they walked down to the port together.

'Student and professor relationships are indeed frowned on, but I don't class you as a student, but from the consulate.'

'I wouldn't want you to get into trouble over me.'

'It would be worth it.' He said smiling at her.

Ellie felt her heart miss a beat and returned his smile.

They walked on down the via Roma where Gino stopped at an ice cream parlour where Ellie had a hard time choosing which flavours she wanted. Finally, she chose pistachio and panna, while Gino had coffee with chocolate. They took their ice creams and sat on the steps of the harbour to watch the fishing boats head out to sea for the evening catch.

'Do you like it here in Sardinia, Ellie?'

'I do, I love it, it is so different from anywhere else I have been, so different from Italy and I love the people too.'

'That's good,' he said, looking at her, and they both laughed.

CHAPTER THREE

'I thought we could take a walk up to the museum this morning,' said Gino, taking Ellie's hand, and looking into her eyes. 'It's not huge, but I think it's interesting. And you will see some things from Nora where we went yesterday.'

They finished their coffee and made their way up to Casteddu. He took her hand as they crossed the road to walk up the Via Mazzini, past the lion gate, and on up the road to the university. They carried on up, under the arch, into the coolness of Via Lamarmora, which was half cast in the shade of the tall buildings rising on either side. Flowers in pots clambered over rickety-looking balconies. Washing hung from lines strung across the road and dripped onto the street below. Finches hopped and fluttered in cages outside French windows; the air filled with their chattering. Above all, this could be heard the women gossiping with their neighbours across the narrow ravine.

'They watch everything,' said Gino.

Ellie sighed.

'My, that was heartfelt,' said Gino, putting his arm around her.

'Yes, there is something rather enchanting about Casteddu that I love. I can't put my finger on it. I have been to many cities, but this has a magic all its own. Time seems to stand still.'

'I know what you mean,' he said as he pulled her closer to him.

They reached the Piazza Indipendenza, which opened on to a large, cobbled, sunlit square. It was a perfect July day, the summer heat starting to take hold of the city.

The museum was a pink-washed building with steps that led up to massive doors and dominated by the large Pisan tower. A man in uniform came forward to greet them and Gino paid for two tickets.

Inside, tall glass cases in each room held objects from all over Sardinia dating back to the ancient Nuragic people. The *bronzetti* fascinated Ellie; they were votives, or items of worship, that had been found on various digs by holy wells or places of worship. There was gold Phoenician jewellery, so intricate and beautiful; and Ellie thought that they could be worn now and still look modern. There were Roman remains and a *stele* from Nora with strange writing on it.

'That stone was found back in 1773 and is supposed to date to the late 9th Century and considered the oldest Phoenician inscription found in Sardinia.'

Ellie stared at the stone with its odd-shaped letters.

'They are planning a new museum,' Gino explained, 'but with all the war damage, it will be some time before they can raise the money.'

They were so engrossed in the various objects that they lost track of time. It wasn't until the little man in uniform returned, cleared his throat, and pointed at his watch that they realised it was one o'clock – time for Cagliari to sleep for the afternoon siesta.

They thanked the man, and as they left, he immediately shut and locked the great doors behind them. Out in the square they looked at each other and laughed.

Gino walked Ellie down to the Piazza Yennes, where they found a table under the shade of some trees. He ordered pasta and a bottle of wine.

'What did you tell your parents today?' he said, taking her hand in his and looking into her eyes.

'I didn't tell them anything. My mother wanted to go shopping. My father is busy today with a committee meeting, so I am alone,' she said, feeling her heart thump from his intense stare.

He reached across the table, took her other hand, and squeezed it gently.

'Tell me about your family, Ellie. Do you have any brothers or sisters? Where did you go to school? What do you want from life?'

Ellie laughed. 'Do you expect me to tell you all of that in Italian?'

'We have the time, and your Italian is more than up to it now.'

They ate their lunch, Ellie chattering away while he watched her.

'No, I don't have any brothers or sisters. I think I was a shock to my mother. Having a child at all was a surprise, but a daughter was not high on her wish list. My mother wanted a boy and has made that clear ever since I can remember.

'I spent my early years in the country because of the war. Something happened, so they sent me to boarding school. I was just seven, but I didn't miss my parents.

'My father was in the Foreign Office and my mother dutifully followed him everywhere. During the holidays, I went to my grandparents. They were kind but strict, and I found it lonely. But I also stayed with wonderful friends who lived on the neighbouring farm. There was Simon, who works in the Foreign Office now; Laurence, who is married to Fiona and living in Kenya; and Polly. I was staying with her in Italy before I came down here. Polly met and married an Italian, and we all went to her wedding. It was wonderful.'

Ellie sighed. She had told her story – with a few interruptions as she searched for a word or Gino corrected her Italian.

'Is Simon your boyfriend?' he asked, searching her face.

'No. I like him a lot, and he is an exceptional friend and a gentle person. We have always said that if we haven't found someone to marry by the time I am twenty-four, then we will marry each other for the company if nothing else.'

'How old are you?'

'Twenty-one this year.'

'Will you marry him?'

Ellie looked at Gino, shaking her head and feeling her heart thump again. 'I don't know.'

'Ellie, you must marry for love, not for the company. You need a man to love and to cherish you.'

She turned away, aware of her rising blush from his intense stare.

Gino hailed a waiter, ordered two coffees, and turned to her.

'Mirto?'

'Yes, please.'

The drinks came, and they sipped their coffees and liqueurs. The afternoon heat relaxed Ellie, making her feel drowsy after the meal.

'Did you always spend your holidays away? Didn't you see your parents?' asked Gino.

'Yes, but like now, my father always insisted on me learning languages or doing some suitable works.'

'Now you are adding Italian to your collection. That time in Milan before coming here gave you a good grounding.'

'Yes, now Italian.' Ellie smiled, loving his effortless way of talking to her, so unlike the formality of her own family. His amiable manner fascinated her.

'Your parents must be ready to retire soon?' he said.

Ellie continued chatting, aware of him watching her.

'Yes, this is Father's last post. They asked him to come here as he has so much experience in the so-called developing countries. My mother says she can't wait to return to England. All she wants is a rose garden to tend and a good cup of English tea. I can't see it lasting long though; she will soon miss London life. My mother has always been the driving force behind my father. Isabel is persuasive and controlling and has a tremendous amount of charm but has no compunction about using it whenever she wants something. Many say it is her charm that got Father so many outstanding posts in his career.'

'Where is home in England?'

'My grandparents have a house in Suffolk. It is next to Simon's parents' estate. We will go back there, and Father will, I suppose, hunt and shoot in his retirement.'

'And you?'

'I expect I will become a diplomat's wife, as Simon also works in the Foreign Office. His elder brother, Laurence, will take over their father's farm if he comes back from Kenya. He married a woman out there and loves it.'

'It is complicated, the English way of life.'

Ellie smiled, nodding in agreement.

They finished their drinks, and Gino caught the waiter's eye and made a scribbled sign for the bill.

They walked down the wide tree-lined Largo Carlo Felice. A little breeze came up from the port, catching Ellie's summer dress and folding it around her slender figure.

Gino took her arm, squeezing it again.

'I love that dress; that colour blue looks so lovely on you.'

Ellie looked at him and smiled again.

At the Via Roma, they walked down to the harbour to see the fishermen sitting cross-legged and mending their nets. Their suntanned faces were weather-beaten, and their smiling button brown eyes seemed to take in everything.

Gino said something to them in Sardu. The men replied, crossing themselves.

'I asked them if they've had an excellent catch today,' said Gino to Ellie. 'They said they have, thanks to the good Lord.'

One man looked at Gino with a mischievous twinkle in his eye and said something to him. Gino smiled and took Ellie's hand, replying in Sardu. He waved goodbye and drew Ellie toward him as they walked along the port.

'What did he say?'

'He said you are pretty, and I agreed.'

Ellie could feel the blush once more rising on her cheeks.

'You are indeed lovely, and you are special, Ellie.'

Ellie felt the blush rise further up her cheeks and turned away, wishing she did not always blush.

'I'm sorry, I've embarrassed you,' he said.

Ellie looked at her watch. Where had the day gone? Every time they were together the hours flew by.

'I ought to get back. They will expect me back for supper,'

'Must you?'

Ellie looked at him, feeling her resolve weaken.

'You don't know my mother. If she finds out about you… well, Isabel can be extremely vindictive.'

'I'll walk you back.'

They climbed up the narrow streets once more, the breeze cool on their backs, and finally neared the house.

There was a large archway next to a building nearby and Gino led her into it, holding her in his arms. Ellie was taken aback as he drew her toward him and placed his hands on either side of her face, gently stroking her cheeks with his thumbs, and kissing her. It was a gentle kiss that hid the passion from whence it came. She fell into him, putting her arms around him. This time he kissed her with a passion that left Ellie feeling breathless and slightly faint.

'You are wonderful, Ellie, and I think I'm falling in love with you.'

Ellie pulled away.

'Please, Gino, please don't, don't make fun of me,' she said with a sob.

He stood back, looking at her.

'Why do you think I would do that? I would never do that to you, Ellie. I am far too fond of you for that. Come and see me tomorrow, come early so we can spend more time together, *cara* Ellie.'

Then kissing her again, he released her, 'See you tomorrow, at the café.'

Ellie climbed the steps to the house and felt she was floating on air.

Her parents were already waiting for her in the sitting room, with their before-dinner drinks in their hands.

'Where the hell have you been?' demanded Isabel. 'You knew I wanted to go shopping today and I wanted you to be with me.'

'Sorry, the lessons ran late, then we all went out and had lunch together.'

'Really, Eleanor, you have no consideration for anyone except yourself,' said Isabel with a heavy sigh.

They sat at the table. Ellie, lost in a world of her own, toyed with her food. Gino's kiss came back to her; she could still feel the imprint on her lips, feel his thumbs as they stroked her cheeks, and tried to hide the flush on her face at the thought of him so close to her.

'Did you hear what I said, Eleanor?' Her father's voice broke into her thoughts.

'Sorry, Father, what did you say?'

'I said, tomorrow there is an important meeting here with several high powered people coming for lunch. I expect you to be here to help your mother. Do you understand?'

'Yes, but after my lesson.'

'No, Eleanor, you will be here to help organise the tables and flowers. It will do you good to see what your mother does, and I know Isabel could do with some support. Besides, there are some people I want you to meet.'

Ellie was about to protest but knew it would be pointless to go against her father and wondered if it would be possible to get a message to Gino but thought better of it. If anyone found out he was her professor, there would be trouble.

She spent the rest of the evening making lists with her mother and the housekeeper. Tomorrow would be a boring day.

CHAPTER FOUR

The room was full of people. Ellie watched them as they talked among themselves. It was the same the world over: those who did a wonderful job, were modest about it and were unrewarded for their work; and those who did nothing but thought themselves indispensable, above everyone else, as if they owned the world, and always stole the glory.

Ellie sighed and wandered around the room to chat with the various officials, but her thoughts were elsewhere. In her mind's eye, she saw Gino sitting in the café waiting for her. Was he wondering where she was? Did he think she had taken offence at his kiss? She hoped not.

'*Signorina,*' said a short man with a large red sash across his chest.

Ellie looked at him for a moment, trying to collect her thoughts.

He was thin and pale with a trimmed moustache. His eyes were brown under heavy brows, which were clipped and shaped. His hair, greying at the temples, was swept back and neat. He carried an air of arrogance about him.

'You seem far away,' he said in perfect English with an Etonian accent. He leaned in closer to her. 'These meetings must be very dull for an attractive young lady like yourself. I understand you are the hosts' daughter.'

'Yes, I came to join them for the summer.'

'What is your name? How long have you been here? Are you enjoying our city?'

'My name is Eleanor. I have been here for two months and the time has just flown by. And yes, I love Cagliari very much. It is beautiful.'

'Well, Eleanor, have you seen any other parts of Sardinia?

Perhaps I could persuade you to let me show you around the island sometime?'

'I have been to Nora, which I found fascinating.'

'I could take you to other places you will find even more interesting.'

'Thank you, I am busy most days. But I have to say your English is perfect.'

'I went to school in England; my parents love anything English. Please say you will come. I am sure you would love our island, and I am sure your parents would not object to me showing you around. Please allow me to introduce myself: I am Count De Melas, at your service, *signorina*.' He bowed, clicking his heels, and Ellie, having caught Giovanna's eye from behind the Count, found it difficult not to laugh.

'Thank you, Count, but as I said, I am busy most days.'

A waiter came with a tray of drinks, momentarily distracting the Count, and Ellie slipped away to find her father.

Her mother came toward her and drew her to one side.

'I saw you talking to the Count. Such an agreeable man, very influential, and very wealthy, I hear, and it seems he likes you.'

'For heaven's sake, Mother, please stop trying to palm me off on every eligible man who comes my way.'

'I don't know what you are talking about, child, but someone in his position would be a significant help to your father. You never know when we might need a contact like that.'

Rolling her eyes, Ellie walked off to find another drink.

They announced lunch. Ellie went to look for her seat, only to find her mother had placed her next to the Count. Was there no end to her mother's conniving?

Everyone stood for grace, which was given by a short, bald priest. His cassock pulled so tight across his protruding stomach that the buttons looked as if they were in danger of firing off at any moment.

Chairs scraped across the marble floor as the guests sat at the long table. A hubbub of conversation soon filled the room.

The Count tried to engage Ellie in conversation, but she turned to the man on her left. He was small with a large moustache. He had a birdlike quality, but work-worn hands, and pecked at his food.

'I am Eleanor,' she said to the man.

'I can see that.' he said, pointing to her name card with his knife. 'As you can see, I am Professor Cabeddu. I am a professor of archaeology here in Cagliari.'

'How very interesting. I would imagine there are many wonderful objects on the island.'

'So much,' he muttered, 'so many, but so little money. Unfortunately, archaeology is low on the list of priorities, what with the bomb damage, and poor land. But it would bring in visitors and much-needed money for the island, if only we could excavate. So many treasures to be found, so many, but they won't listen to me.'

The Count tapped Ellie on her shoulder to attract her attention, but she focused on the professor.

'Tell me about some of the items you have found. Did you find any of the *bronzetti*? I saw them in the museum the other day; they are so beautiful.'

The professor, not used to anyone being interested in his cause, laid down his knife and fork and spent the rest of the meal detailing all the items he had found and their significance, and the problem of artefacts being stolen and sold abroad for vast sums.

The Count, unable to attract Ellie's attention, turned to the woman on his right. Ellie noticed how annoyed he was by his facial expression as the woman gave him her views on the incapability of the Sards to organise themselves. Coming from a long and noble Sardinian family, the Count, taking offence, rebuked the woman in a loud voice, momentarily silencing the table.

At last, it was all over, and the guests left. Ellie sank into the sofa in the day room and kicked off her shoes. Her mother came in a coffee in one hand, and a brandy in the other. She was a little worse for wear after all the wine she had consumed at lunch.

Isabel lurched toward Ellie and said in a slurred voice, 'The Count has asked me if he can take you to see some of the sights on the island tomorrow.'

'Well, I have my lesson tomorrow. I don't want to miss it.'

'It won't hurt you to miss one. He will speak Italian to you, so you will not miss anything. I told him it would be all right, as he may be some help to your father.' said Isabel, slumping down in a nearby chair.

Ellie said nothing. With luck, her mother would not remember in the morning. Ellie would leave early, saying nothing. To hell with the Count.

*

When Ellie woke, it was already hot and humid, and the morning air was oppressive, making her puff as she walked up to the Via Manno, across the Piazza Constituzione and into the Caffé Genovese. The café was busy with all the early morning office workers having a quick coffee before starting their day.

She had not slept well; it had been a sweltering night and she had tossed and turned, unable to sleep. Gino invaded her thoughts, his kiss, how he had said he thought he was falling in love with her. That would be beyond her wildest dreams. But wondered why he had been so eager to end their time with Carlo. Did he feel he could not let his friends know about her? At last, she had dropped off to sleep, only to dream Gino was being pulled away from her by her mother and his friends. Ellie had woken to find herself wound in her sheets and sweating profusely. She showered, and then made her way up to the Caffé, to find something to eat.

Ellie was early, so ordered a coffee and *amaretti* and sat waiting for Gino to arrive. When he walked in, he came across to her and dropped a quick kiss on her cheek, making her blush to the roots of her hair.

'I'm sorry I'm late – bad night. It was so hot; I couldn't get to sleep.'

'Me neither.'

He looked at her and smiled, then waved to the waiter for his usual coffee.

'I thought we could have lunch at a restaurant up in Casteddu today if you agree? We can have a casual stroll up there and look at some local workshops on the way up. I want to show you the cathedral. It will be cool in there.'

'Sounds ideal,' she said, blushing again.'

'Where were you yesterday? I waited, but you never came.'

'I had to help my mother with one of her charity lunches. I couldn't get a message to you. I'm sorry if I wasted your time.'

'I was just worried. I thought you might have been offended by my kissing you.'

'You would have known it there and then if I had been, I can assure you.'

'So, you are not cross with me?'

'No, not at all, simply happy.'

They sat talking about yesterday, she telling him about the Count as they drank their coffee.

Later, they walked up the street leading to Via Universita, then up the Via Lamarmora.

'We will have a storm today: it's so hot and humid, the wind has turned, and the clouds are coming in,' Gino said, wiping his forehead with his handkerchief.

As if on cue, there was a distant rumble of thunder and large blobs of rain began to fall. Taking her hand, he started to run as a deafening clap of thunder boomed above them and the drops of rain turned into a torrent. In moments, the streets were running with water and the rain was falling so hard that it bounced off the street and up their legs.

'Come on,' he said, dragging her beside him. 'Be careful, these stones become treacherous in the rain.'

He went towards a large door, and opening it, he pushed her inside, then shut the door behind them. They laughed as they shook themselves and looked at one another in the dim hallway.

Both soaking wet, hair tight against their heads, water dripping from everywhere. They laughed again.

'Come with me,' he said.

'Where are we?

'My house.'

'You didn't say you lived here the other day when we passed it on our way to the museum.'

He made no answer but took her hand as they climbed up the white marble stairs to the second floor. The rain beat down on the lantern roof, which gave a sombre light to the stairwell. He opened the door to an apartment and let her in.

It was large and airy, with a high, wooden-beamed ceiling on which fans turned slowly, moving the air. The French windows, framed by big blue-and-white-checked curtains, were closed against the weather, the rain making strange patterns as it beat against the glass.

Bookshelves, filled with books, lined the white walls on two sides. There was a dining area on the left, and more books and magazines lay on the table. Two white leather sofas sat opposite each other, big, red cushions bringing a splash of colour to the room. A coffee table between them was also piled high with colourful magazines. A collection of antique prints of Sardinian costumes hung on a wall. The whole place had a comfortable feel about it.

The kitchen led off from a narrow hallway, and a large archway led through to what Ellie presumed were the bedrooms and bathroom.

Gino shook off his jacket and shirt, then turned to Ellie.

'Take off those wet clothes or you will catch your death.'

He looked in a cupboard to find a couple of towels and a newly laundered shirt which he handed to her.

'Go into my bedroom, take everything off, and put this on. It's the first door on the left,' he said pointing to the door.

Ellie did as he said. His bedroom was also large with French windows. A fan turned here too. A pair of single antique beds

43

were pushed together to make one double bed, over which hung an ornate crucifix.

Ellie rubbed her hair until it was reasonably dry, then, having dried herself, put on his shirt. She hunted in her bag for a comb and dragged it through her bedraggled hair.

'Are you decent?' he asked, tapping on the door.

Ellie turned to look at him. He was wearing just a towel around his waist and watching her intently. Gino moved forward, took her in his arms, kissing her, tenderly at first, but with growing passion.

He pulled away and looked at her. 'You look wonderful.'

'And you look very wet.'

He picked her up and carried her across the room and laid her on his double bed, kissing and caressing her, while slowly undoing the shirt he had given her.

'It's like undoing a beautiful present,' he sighed, nibbling her neck.

'Be gentle with me; it's my first time,' she whispered.

'My darling, I will, I promise. But are you sure you want to do this?'

'Very sure,' said Ellie, not caring if he loved her, but wanting him close to her; wanting him to make love to her.

Tenderly kissing her, Gino ran his hands over her body, sending waves of pleasure sweeping over her. He was a patient and generous lover, waiting for her to savour the pleasure of his lovemaking. When she could not hold back anymore, he took her in a long, passionate embrace, finally bringing her to a quivering climax.

Ellie lay in his arms, unable to move and sighed a long, contented sigh, while he held her and kissed her cheek.

'Happy?' he asked.

'Yes, darling, so happy.'

'My life has a new meaning now, Ellie.'

'Why?'

'Because you have become part of my life, part of me, part of my soul.'

Ellie drew away from him and looked into his eyes.

'Mine too.'

Gathering her back into his arms, he began caressing her again. She felt the weight of him on her as he rested on his elbows. A shiver came from deep down inside her and she let out a long, low moan as he once more made love to her.

Feeling him naked beside her made her glow inside, and it also reflected on her cheeks as a blush spread across her face.

'Don't be shy, my darling, you have the most beautiful body and I love every part of it.'

Ellie turned away, feeling tears sting the back of her eyes; and fought against them falling down her cheeks.

Turning her face toward him, he wiped the tears from her cheeks with his thumbs and kissed her.

She smiled at him. He was lovely, with his dark curling hair, his deep brown eyes, his seductive voice, the fine sprinkling of hair over his body. She wondered what a man like him saw in her. His lovemaking had taken away her girlhood and made her feel like a woman as she lay in his arms. Ellie closed her eyes. So, this is love, and turning to her lover, kissed him.

'Love in the afternoon, what could be more romantic?'

'Even better, the sun has come out,' he said.

He turned to kiss her again, pulling her into his arms once more.

It was late afternoon. The sunlight had travelled across the floor, marking the passing time.

He made spaghetti Genovese, the aroma filling the room. He smiled at her as he opened a bottle of white wine and put the plates on the table.

They had showered together and now sat at the table opposite one another, he in a dry set of clothes, she still wrapped in his bathrobe.

'Not the meal I had in mind this morning, but much better.' He took her hand in his and kissed it. 'You are beautiful,' he said, his eyes fixed on her. 'Come now, Ellie, eat something; you need to build up your strength.'

'I must get home. They will want to know where I've been all day.'

'What will you tell them?'

'That I spent the day loving you and being loved by you, and that it was the most wonderful thing in the world.'

'Really.'

'Yes, really, it was wonderful. But no, I will not say that I have been with you. I will say I met some friends from the university, and we got caught in the rain and went back to someone's house to dry out. I was supposed to go out with the Count I told you about, who had lunch with us yesterday. Hopefully, they have forgotten all about that.'

'Will you tell them I love you?' he asked, a smile on his face.

'Do you?'

'You know I do.'

'One day, if you still love me, then yes.'

'Tell me, Ellie, why did you never make love to Simon or anyone else?'

'Simon is a dear, dear friend, but not my lover. He has always been there for me. As for anyone else, I find boys of my age immature.'

He kissed her on her nose. 'Your clothes are still not very dry. If you are wearing them, go straight home and change or you will catch your death.'

He walked her home, and when they neared the house, he pulled her into the same deep doorway where he had first kissed her and kissed her again.

'I love you, Ellie, never forget that. Whatever happens, whatever is said, know that I love you. Do you understand? I love you with all my heart and soul. We say here that the soul passes from one to another in a kiss.'

Leaning into him she gave him a gentle kiss on the lips.

'I love you too, Gino,' she sighed. 'But I must go.' She said slipping from his grasp and leaving him breathless.

Letting herself into the house, without looking back, Ellie felt alive and fulfilled. She was loved; it was an electrifying and liberating feeling. Polly was right: love gave you wings.

CHAPTER FIVE

Isabel was standing in the hall when Ellie entered the house. Her stance left Ellie in no doubt that there would be trouble.

'Where the hell have you been?' demanded Isabel. 'I told you the Count wanted to take you out today. He has been clicking his heels in the house since early this morning. I tried to contact your professor, but it appears he is away today, so where have you been?'

'Another professor took our lesson, and several of us had lunch together. Then we walked down to the café for coffee, and we got caught in the storm, so we went back to someone's house to get dry.'

'Eleanor, I have told you before, you have no consideration for anyone other than yourself,' Isabel cut in. 'I told you last night the Count was coming. Now you go in there and apologise to him.' she said, pointing to the sitting room.

'I told you I didn't want to go,' said Ellie. 'I will not apologise. If he is daft enough to spend the entire day waiting for me, he is stupid. He should realise he cannot have everything he wants when he wants it. He's only a spoilt Count, not a king.'

Her mother opened her mouth to speak, then shut it again. Isabel was not used to such open defiance from anyone, and certainly not her daughter.

'Whatever has come over you? You will go in there; you will say you are sorry, and you will arrange to see him another day. Do you understand?'

Ellie pulled herself up to her full height and looked her mother in the eye.

'I will not.'

Ellie did not see the quickness of her mother's hand but felt the sting of it on her cheek. Indignation and anger rose in her.

'That's the last time you ever do that to me, Mother,' said Ellie, striding off up the stairs to her room.

'What shall I tell the Count? This is not good for your father. Will you see him another day?' called Isabel.

'No, Mother, no.'

In her room, Ellie sat on her bed and thought about the day. The passion and gentleness of Gino's lovemaking came back to her and she smiled to herself.

Later, there was a tap on the door and Giovanna let herself in.

'Are you all right, Ellie?' asked Giovanna, coming forward and touching Ellie's still-burning cheek.

'I'm fine. It will soon go down; it usually does.'

'My mother has never struck me,' said Giovanna.

'Perhaps you have never deserved it.'

'Nobody deserves that, Ellie.'

Silence fell between the two girls, then Giovanna continued.

'Your mother apologised to the Count, but he was having none of it. So, when your mother realised she was out of her depth when the Count refused to leave without seeing you. They sent for your father, and he has sent him packing. I don't think he will be back in a hurry.'

The two girls looked at one another and laughed.

'Did you have a pleasurable day? It's good for you to get away from here with young company.'

'I had a wonderful day, thank you. I had lunch with a very good-looking professor from the university–'

'That will be Professor Puddu,' Giovanna cut in, smiling.

'How do you know?' Ellie gasped.

'Because he's the only good-looking professor at the university.'

Ellie smiled but felt a slight flush on her cheeks as Giovanna continued.

'He's an extremely popular man; all the girls at the college or who know him are in love with him. My brother knows him, and people chat. Mind he doesn't break your heart, Ellie.'

'So, the whole of Cagliari knows?'

'No, not the whole – your parents don't know yet. But it will not take long. If you do not want them to know, be careful.'

'Giovanna, he is so different, so special. When I see him it is wonderful – being with him, talking to him, sharing time together. But when we are apart, I find I have a heavy heart. I miss his touch, his voice; sometimes it's almost unbearable.'

'I know how it feels to have a heavy heart, believe me, Ellie, I know. But you must tell your parents before they find out.'

Ellie sighed.

'Who is here for dinner tonight?'

'No one. Your parents are going out to some function given by the City Council of Commerce. I don't think they will be back until late. Would you like me to have your supper sent up here on a tray?'

'No, I think I might go out for a pizza and coffee. Thank you for everything, Giovanna. I can manage now.'

Ellie undressed and stood under the shower, letting the water wash over her, loving the feeling as it splashed on her skin. Ellie hugged herself. To be loved by someone was the most wonderful feeling. She would go to see Gino; it would be a surprise for him. Besides, she wanted to see him so much.

Stepping out of the shower, Ellie grabbed a towel and went back into her bedroom to dry her hair. She put it up in a French twist, placing a diamanté comb in the side. She applied her makeup, then dressed, choosing her dress with care, and put on a pair of flat shoes. After a quick look in the mirror and a small spray of perfume, and then collecting her handbag, let herself out of the house once more.

The area was buzzing with young people. The café was full, and people spilt out onto the pavement, laughing, and talking among themselves. Late-evening coffee drinkers sat at tables or just stood around smoking together. The young girls, with their beehive hairdos, wearing cardigans and wide skirts with full petticoats or pencil skirts and twin sets. The boys, with drainpipe trousers, string ties, slicked-back hair, and dark glasses, stood with a cigarette in their mouths, James Dean style, or leant on their Vespas, trying to look cool.

Ellie, walking up toward Casteddu, noticed where there were still ugly scars from the Anglo-American bombings, enormous holes with piles of rubble where houses or shops had once stood, beside the other houses untouched by the raids. After such an assault, Ellie wondered why the Sards ever welcomed the English.

Ellie stood under the portico with the Madonna della Grazie above, before crossing to walk up the Via Lamarmora, and smiled; Gino was in the street talking to a group of people. Ellie was about to call out, but something stopped her. Gino was standing with his arm around a young woman who was looking adoringly at him. Ellie stood transfixed as he kissed the woman on her cheek, she drew back into the shadows and watched as Gino picked up a young boy and, carrying him on his shoulders, went into his house.

Ellie felt light-headed and faint. Turning on her heel and, without a backward glance, walked back down the way she had come. It was obvious that there were other women in Gino's life.

Once at home, Ellie raced up to her room, undressed, and threw herself into bed. She felt betrayed, used, and angry with herself for her feelings, and stupid for believing that a man as wonderful as Gino could be hers alone.

The members of the household rose late the next morning. Isabel and Ian had been out until the early hours of the morning, and Ellie had had a restless night and was about to get out of bed when her mother came into her room.

'Eleanor, I need your help.'

Her mother looked decidedly the worse for wear.

'You had too much to drink last night; it shows on your face and in your bloodshot eyes.' said Ellie. 'I'm glad I don't feel how you look, Mother. What do you want this morning?'

'There are two important luncheons today. I am going to one with the Mayor of Cagliari. Your father needs to go to the other, some business luncheon, and I want you to go with him. He needs someone at his side when he is at these meetings.'

'Yes, of course,' said Ellie. She would not have to face Gino at the university today and that would make life easier.

'Thank you. I thought you would object. You haven't been very sociable over the past weeks.'

'What time is the luncheon? How formal is it?' Ellie replied, ignoring her mother's sarcasm.

'Twelve-thirty on the dot. So, you must both be there by twelve. And the dress code is smart. Do you understand?'

Ellie nodded and ushered her mother out of the room. She showered, did her hair up in a French twist, and put on a dressing gown to go down to breakfast. Her father was already at the table with his usual out-of-date copy of *The Times* newspaper propped up against the toast rack. His copy of *L'Unione Sarda* was on the floor beside him.

'I understand you are coming with me. That will be good, thank you,' he said, looking at her over the top of his newspaper, with his glasses on the tip of his nose. 'You look different, Eleanor. Are you all right?'

'Yes, thank you, Father. In what way am I different?'

'More self-assured. Overnight you have gone from being a young, awkward girl to a beautiful, radiant woman.'

Ellie dropped her napkin on the floor to give her time to compose herself.

'Tell me, how are the Italian lessons going? Is the old professor a frightful bore?'

Ellie looked at her father, but his head was once more buried in his paper. Ellie helped herself to toast and marmalade as Giovanna entered, bringing fresh coffee, the aroma filling the room.

'Coffee for you, *Signorina* Ellie?'

Ellie looked at her, smiled, and nodded. 'Thank you.'

At noon Ellie, dressed in her smart pink Chanel-style suit trimmed in navy, with navy patent-leather shoes and handbag to match, stood beside her father, who was dressed in a dark suit with a very sober-looking tie, as they waited to be greeted by their hosts. They were then handed drinks and introduced to some important people until they announced lunch.

Ellie sat next to an Italian businessman from Milan, who had just invested an obscene amount of money in the oil business. He had joined forces with a Sardinian so they could work together on the project at Sarroch. Ellie soon became bored with the talk of oil and money and turned to her left. If she thought it would be any better, she was in for a surprise. Evan Jones came from Wales. He was a hill farmer looking to see how the Sards worked their sheep and how they managed their milk and cheese production.

Ellie thought of Gino and wondered what he was doing. Was he with the young woman? Had she lost him already? The thought frightened her, making her heart thump against her chest. She was so deep in her thoughts that she was still sitting when everyone had risen to toast the honoured guest and rose hurriedly.

They all sat down again. The businessman turned to her and, in a pompous tone, said, 'I like to think I am helping the Sards out of their poverty with my investment.'

Ellie bristled but turned to him.

'With your vast investment, perhaps you could help the less fortunate, like the poor children who live near the docks and work for next to nothing to keep body and soul together. Most of them are orphans. I know that any help would be greatly received. After all, they are the future of Cagliari.'

Silence fell over the table. Ellie, staring at the man, did not give an inch.

'I think, young lady, that you do not understand. The poor are the poor and always will be. They do not help themselves, so there is nothing I can do for them.'

Ellie glanced at her father. He had his very disapproving look on his face and she knew there would be trouble, but having started, she was not backing down.

'I think, *signore*, you are the one who does not understand that money always goes to money, so the poor children don't have a chance – no schooling, no social help. So how can they possibly help themselves without some sponsorship? Surely if you are investing in the island, you could help its people and its children, rather than just yourself and a few elite shareholders?'

As Ellie spoke, the prominent people listened to her argument. Ian coughed to attract his daughter's attention, but she held firm, not willing to give up so easily.

The woman sitting opposite Ellie rose. 'I think the signorina is right. We should consider the children. This is my card, my dear. Come and see me tomorrow morning and we can talk.'

Ellie took the card and read the name embossed on it: *Contessa DeLogu*. She was the wife of the Sardinian partner in the oil deal, to whom her father had introduced Ellie to before the luncheon.

The conversation resumed at the table and Ellie smiled at the smart, elegant-looking woman.

At last, the speeches, the massaging of egos, and the commemorative awards were done, and Ellie and her father thanked their hosts and made their way home.

In the car, Ian turned to Ellie. 'You should be careful you don't make enemies here, Eleanor. Remember, we are guests here, so it is not for us to interfere.'

'But, Father, surely that is what you all do here every day.'

Her father sighed.

Back at the house, Ellie went upstairs to change out of her clothes and slip into something more comfortable and was surprised to find Giovanna waiting for her.

'I have a note for you from Professor Puddu. He said it was urgent.'

Ellie took the note and opened it.

Please could you come to my place tomorrow, instead of the café? I need to talk to you.

It is important. Gino.

'He wants to see me at his place tomorrow. I don't know why when he has someone else to keep him company. Besides, I have to see Contessa DeLogu tomorrow morning.'

'What are you talking about? There is nobody else.'

'I saw him last night. I thought I would surprise him, but it was I who got the surprise. He was with a bunch of people. He had his arm around one of the young women and he kissed her –'

'Long, black hair down to her waist, black eyes, slender, with her skirt, or hot-pants, just covering her bum?' Giovanna cut in.

'Yes.'

'That's his cousin. She adores him, but Gino has no feelings for her, I can assure you. You go and see him. I am sure it is important if he has asked you to go to his place.'

'I didn't know you knew him. You said nothing.'

'He is a friend of my brother's. Ellie, as I said before, mind, he doesn't break your heart. All the women in Cagliari are in love with him.'

Ellie felt the colour rise in her cheeks and turned away.

'If you see him, tell him I'll see him in the afternoon.'

At that moment, Ellie's mother came into the room.

'Can you do my zip up, Ellie?' said her mother, turning her back for her daughter to zip her into the neat black cocktail dress. 'Your father is busy, and I will be late.'

Giovanna let herself out of the room, leaving Ellie to mull over the words she had said.

CHAPTER SIX

The following morning, Ellie arrived at the address on the Countess's card and rang the bell in the wall. The gate buzzed into action and Ellie let herself in, closing it behind her. It was a grand house that stood in a sizeable garden surrounded by fruit trees and flowering shrubs. A flight of marble steps led up to the front door, which was opened by a maid dressed in a black uniform with a white apron and cap.

'Good morning, *signorina*. Madam is waiting in the morning room. Please come in and follow me.'

Ellie stepped inside the cool, grand hall. Sardinian rugs covered the marble floor and grand family portraits hung on the walls and up the stairs. Beautiful antique Sardinian artefacts were everywhere.

Ellie followed the maid into a big, airy room. The Contessa was sitting in a wing chair, a tray set before her on a low table with two glasses of water and coffee cups.

'Coffee now, please, Maria,' said the Contessa, then turning to Ellie. 'Come in, my dear, and sit down opposite me so I can see you. You can call me Dee; all my friends call me that – although some call me other things,' she added with a smile.

Ellie sat down in the chair and looked at the woman. Dee seemed to be in her early thirties, tall and elegant. Her black, shiny hair was tied back in a bun. Her soft brown eyes had a twinkle of rebellion in them. Ellie smiled, recognising a kindred spirit.

'I am Eleanor, but Ellie to my friends.'

'By the look in your eye, they no doubt call you other things too?' said Dee, laughing. 'Now tell me about yourself.'

'There's not a lot to tell. School, college, holidays either in

England or with my parents, wherever they were. I have just come back from Milan after staying with a friend who married an Italian. Then here, which I love.'

Dee moved forward to touch Ellie's hand.

'I understand you have been to see the boys down by the port. And you have lessons with Professor Gino Puddu. Such a lovely, but tragic young man.'

Ellie drew in a sharp intake of breath at the mention of Gino's name and blushed.

'Don't worry, my dear, your secret is safe with me. But I make it my business to know the people I want to help or become involved with. Cagliari is a small city for information.'

Ellie tried to compose herself and took a quick sip from a glass of water. She wanted to ask why Dee had described Gino as tragic, but the moment passed as Dee continued.

'Now, I have been thinking about what you said to my husband's partner at the luncheon. I have decided to see it for myself. You will take me to this shelter for the orphans and introduce me to the people who work there to help them. I have already done my research on the couple. I think they are doing a wonderful job; they just need some extra help. I have started the ball rolling; it just needs my say-so.'

Maria returned with the coffee and poured two cups. They drank it straight, the hot liquid strong enough to fell a horse.

'We have no children of our own, which has been a great sadness to both of us. My husband is often away on business, so the thought of being able to help some children would be a great comfort to me.'

Ellie listened, sipping her coffee, believing the Contessa was testing her.

'I am from one of the old Sardinian families. I see change coming to my island, some good, but mostly bad. The so-called intelligentsia and councillors in Cagliari are influenced by the Continentals, and not always for the best. If they don't want something on the Continent, they send it to Sardinia, as they treat us like a colony. Our people suffered in the war, which they felt was nothing to do with them. The occupation was difficult for many. Mussolini banned the Sardinian language and speaking it could be punishable by death, but we still spoke it in our houses among ourselves as children. It was our way of defying them, of defending our dignity.'

'I can understand that,' said Ellie.

Dee sipped her coffee.

'Yes, I believe you can.'

'I love Sardinia and its people. I have only been here for a few months, but I love it. It is unique in so many ways.'

Dee smiled.

'I am not surprised that you want to help young people. You haven't had a lot of love in your own life, so it seems natural you want to help others.'

Ellie was taken aback.

'I know all about you and your family,' Dee said. 'Your mother is hell-bent on getting some recognition for your father and will do it by any means. Your father is a brilliant man, but he is dominated by your mother, and you have paid the price. But you have turned out to be a loving young lady, and I am pleased to know you.'

Ellie stared at Dee. 'How do you know so much about me?'

'Cagliari is extremely small, and the Diplomatic Corps is even smaller. A few well-chosen questions and I had all the information I wanted, and more. So, you see I know you, and I hope I can count myself as one of your friends.'

Ellie smiled. 'I would like that very much, thank you.'

'Now, I want you to give Franco and Antonia this,' said Dee, taking an envelope from her pocket and handing it to Ellie. 'They will need some cash for beds and things. It would be better if you gave it to them after I have gone. Less embarrassing for them. Well, now let us go to see your friends.'

Ellie took the envelope and placed it in her bag. Dee rang a bell on the mantel shelf and Maria came in and stood beside her.

'Aldo is outside, *Signora.*'

'Good. Come, Ellie my dear,'

Ellie followed Dee out of the dayroom into the hall and down the steps to the waiting Continental Bentley. It was so highly polished it looked as if it had just been delivered from the showroom. Aldo fussed around his charge, making sure Dee was comfortable in the back seat; then, standing back, he gently clicked his heels and closed the car door. He opened Ellie's door for her, and she stepped in next to Dee.

'You know where to go, Aldo?' asked Dee. 'Not too close, please. I don't want to frighten everyone.'

Aldo nodded, and they set off.

'He knows Cagliari like the back of his hand. His father was chauffeur to my father. He had an extensive family. We had to send him away during the war, to the mountains to fight with the Resistance, rather than sending him to the Continent, the family came with us to the country. Their family has always looked after us, and I hope we have looked after them in return.'

They drove in silence along the Via Roma towards the old port, out by the rusting iron bridge that crossed the broad expanse of water to Giorgino.

'I'd better stay here, *Signora,*' said Aldo, pulling into a side road off the dirt track. 'I will be here if you need me,' he added as he jumped out to open the door for Dee.

Ellie and Dee got out of the car and walked beside the rough port. Fishermen sat mending nets of green and ochre, laying them out to dry in the sun. A strong smell of the sea hung in the morning air without the usual breeze.

The fishing boats moored by the quay were so close to one another it was possible to walk the full length of the port without getting off the boats, just as in the port of Cagliari. The air full of men singing, whistling, or calling to one another in their ancient language.

'The Sards happy at their work,' said Dee to Ellie.

They walked to the old shack where they found Antonia and

Franco hanging out the washing on long lines strung from the shack to posts, which stood at all angles under the weight of the clothes.

'They certainly do look as if they need some help; the place is about to fall down,' whispered Dee.

Antonia looked flustered as she pinned the last of the garments on the line, then came towards them.

'Antonia, this is Contessa DeLogu,' said Ellie.

'I am honoured to meet you, Contessa. I am so sorry, *Signora*. Ellie didn't say she would bring anyone. It is all a bit of a mess. We had some extra boys in last night; they were turned out of their hideout, so they needed somewhere to sleep. Please come in.'

Antonia showed Dee into the shack.

'May I sit down?' asked Dee with a smile, moving toward a rather rickety– looking chair.

'Not that one, please,' said Franco, and he offered her a large, sturdy wooden one.

Dee sat down, and Franco and Antonia found chairs for Ellie and themselves.

'Dee this is Franco, Antonia's brother,' said Ellie.

'Pleased to meet you, Contessa.' said Franco with a slight bow.

'Now will you both call me Dee, as I think we will be working together. Tell me, where are the boys?' said Dee, looking around.

'They are out working on the docks,' said Antonia, 'loading or unloading the ships, carrying baskets or luggage for the visitors, running errands for people, whatever they can find. The paltry amount of money they earn, they bring back to me. I take half to help keep them and clothe them, and for any medical help. The other half I make them put away, so they can one day, perhaps, pay for some proper schooling. I try to teach them the essentials here, but it is hard for them after a day's work. I have to say Ellie has been very generous to us, helping us with the rent.'

'Ellie told me about you, and I would like to help too. From now on you will not have to pay rent anymore. It seems your landlord wants to sell; we have made him an offer he has found difficult to refuse. So, this place will belong to the trust that I am setting up, and the deeds will be with the trustees. So, if anyone comes trying to collect rent, you send them off with a flea in their ear.'

Antonia sat motionless, unable to say a word. Franco put his hand to her mouth and whispered.

'Close it, dear, you're gaping.'

And they all laughed.

'I have opened a bank account in the trust's name. The manager knows all about you and will sanction your weekly allowance for the running of the shelter. If you want anything larger, you will have to see the trustees. One is at the bank, and I will get Ellie to take you to sort everything out.'

Antonia was shaking, and Ellie rose to get her a glass of water.

'Are you all right?' asked Ellie.

'Yes, but I can't understand what has happened, or how to thank you for such generosity. I know the boys will be so grateful… But what do you want me to do? What do you want from us?'

Dee put her hand on the young girl's arm.

'I want nothing, only for you to look after your boys, and let me come to see you all from time to time to see how everything is going. I have given Ellie some money to tide you over. It is to get things started and buy bunk beds, so you can sleep more boys. Go to see the hospital and tell them I sent you. Find someone to cook for the boys, so you have time to help them. Now, my dear, if you will excuse me, I must go as I have a lunch appointment. But I will be back.'

Dee rose to shake hands with the young couple, but Antonia went forward and threw her arms around her.

'Thank you,' said Antonia, tears running down her cheeks.

Dee looked momentarily taken aback and then put her arm around Antonia.

'No, my dear. Thank *you*.'

Ellie walked out to follow Dee back to the car.

'You stay with them and help them. Thank you, Ellie, for giving me such a wonderful charity to organise. I will enjoy having parties to help raise money for the boys to go to school. And, Ellie, get in touch with the local hospital. They are getting some new beds; see if you can arrange to take the old ones off their hands,' said Dee, as Aldo came forward to collect her.

Dee hugged Ellie, then stepped into the waiting car.

'Keep in touch,' she said. And with that, Dee was gone.

Ellie walked back to the old shelter to find Antonia still in tears.

'I think I could do with some water please,' said Ellie, taking the envelope out of her bag. 'This is for you from Dee. I know you will spend it wisely.'

It was Franco, who opened the envelope to find a large wad of lira notes.

'There must be a fortune here,' he gasped. 'Dearest Ellie, how can we ever thank you for your help?'

'It wasn't me.'

'But you organised it. We could never have done this on our own. Thank you and God bless you.'

★

It was late afternoon, but still hot and oppressive; the breeze that usually came from the sea was still. So, by the time Ellie reached Via Lamarmora, she was flustered and sweating. She banged on the great wooden door. A short, birdlike woman dressed in black from head to toe answered her knock. Her wrinkled face was kind and the colour of a walnut.

'Good afternoon, *Signora*. May I see Professor Puddu, please?' said Ellie.

The door was opened wider as the woman disappeared behind it. Gino was standing behind her, a broad smile on his face.

'Come in, Ellie. This is my aunt, Zia Paula. Zia, this is Ellie.' The woman peered around the door, allowing Ellie to enter.

'Pleased to meet you,' said Ellie.

'Thank you, Zia,' said Gino, politely dismissing his aunt, and turning to Ellie, took her by the elbow.

'Come with me, please.'

He led her up the grand marble staircase. The light streamed in through the lantern skylights, pouring in shafts down the stairs, so different from the sombre colour of the other day. On they went, up to the room where he had made love to her.

Once inside, he pulled her into his arms and kissed her. Ellie struggled momentarily but gave in to him.

'Coffee?' he asked.

'Please.'

Ellie settled on one of the large sofas and listened as he made the coffee in the kitchen. He returned with two cups of coffee and some *amaretti* on a tray.

'You wanted to see me,' she said, as he handed her a coffee. 'I couldn't come this morning, as I had promised to see someone else.'

'I am sorry about this,' he said, sitting beside her and taking her hand. 'I didn't want to drop you into my world without explaining.'

'Explaining what?' Ellie held her breath. This was it; he was going to tell her he did not want her anymore. A heavy sigh, almost a sob, escaped from her. He would tell her about his cousin. He had taken what he wanted from her, and Ellie was sure he was going to drop her.

'Ellie, my son, Angelo, was ill last night. I could not leave him today. My mother has a dental appointment and my sister, who looks after him all the time, has a hospital appointment. My aunt downstairs is not good with the boy.'

Ellie's heart dropped several beats. A son? She had presumed he was single. Ellie suddenly felt lost. He had said nothing about a son. And a wife, there must be a wife. He was married. Her world seemed to crumble as large tears rolled down her cheeks, then anger took over.

Ellie rose and ran toward the door, but Gino barred her way.

'Let me go – please, Gino, let me go,' cried Ellie, spitting her words out.

'No, Ellie, please listen to me. I'm not explaining this very well.'

He put his hand on her arm to hold her, but she flinched, pulling away.

'Ellie, it's not what you think it is. Please, just listen to me. I haven't had time to explain. I was going to tell you, but I needed to know how you felt about me, and to know my own feelings too.'

'Angelo is your son. No wonder you did not want to stay with Carlo when he asked you about Angelo the other evening. Were you frightened he would tell me about your son, your wife?'

'Ellie, please…'

'Let me go!' she cried, pushing past him, and wrenching open the door.

Ellie fled down the marble staircase. Gino was calling her, but Ellie put her fingers in her ears, humming to drown out his calls. She had to get away. Giovanna had said, 'don't let him break your heart'. How could she, plain Ellie, have ever imagined that someone as wonderful as Gino could be in love with her?

Through her tears, Ellie found her way home and up to her room, locking the door behind her. She sat on the bed as large, uncontrollable tears fell onto her lap. Searching in her pocket for a handkerchief she sobbed as if her heart would break. She felt used, a fool, lonely and angry with herself. Someone had clipped her wings.

There was a gentle tap at the door. Ellie held her breath.

'Who is it?'

'Ellie, it is me, Giovanna.'

Ellie got up and opened the door, letting her in.

'God, you look awful. Whatever is the matter?'

Ellie looked at Giovanna and let out a large sob. 'You said, 'mind, he doesn't break my heart,' she cried. 'How could you when you knew he is married and has a son? You never said a word, nothing to me. Why?'

Giovanna put her arms around Ellie and led her to the bed, pulling her to sit down beside her.

'What has happened?'

'He's married; he has a son and a wife. He said nothing. I can't believe he could be so cruel, and I could be so gullible.'

'Ellie, listen to me – please, listen to me.' Giovanna took Ellie's hand in hers and looked at her. 'Yes, he has a son, young Angelo…'

'Why didn't you tell me? I thought you were my friend.'

'Ellie, please, just let me explain – listen to me. Yes, he *was* married, but he is a widower. His wife, Maria, was my best friend at school; we grew up together. Maria died giving birth to Angelo. The loss was terrible – Maria was so young; we all felt it. Gino closed in on himself. He tried to cope with the new baby, but it proved impossible. He agreed that Clara, his sister who lives in the apartment below his, would look after Angelo while Gino taught part-time to help pay for the boy's care. Clara has no children of her own. That was seven years ago, and Angelo has settled well; in fact, it is all he has ever known. Gino has always been frightened of upsetting anything. Although Angelo knows that Gino is his father, he has accepted Clara as his mother.'

Ellie stared at Giovanna. 'I can understand he would want to protect the boy, but I still can't understand why he couldn't tell me. He told me he loved me, and he knows all about me… And you, Giovanna, I thought you were my friend, but you never said a word.'

'I don't expect you to understand, Ellie, but I felt it was down to him to tell you. Don't be too hard on him. Go and see him. Let him tell you and tell him how you feel.'

Ellie retraced her steps to Gino's place, going over in her mind the things she wanted to say to him. Why hadn't he trusted her enough to tell her? When was he going to tell her? Suddenly, Dee's words made sense, 'a tragic young man'; was it the fact that Gino was a widower to which Dee was referring.

The door to the street was open, so Ellie entered and marched up the stairs to Gino's flat; she banged on the door, and could feel her anger rising, she was ready to tell him all the things she had planned to say.

Gino opened the door and looked at her.

'I love you,' she whispered. 'I love you, Gino.'

Pulling her into his arms, he kissed her. 'I'm so sorry, Ellie.'

He held her in his arms, and this time she did not pull away but held on to him.

'I'm not married. I am a widower.'

'I know, I know. Giovanna explained everything to me.'

'I want you to understand that you are my world, Ellie, but you loving me is something else. Can you take on another woman's child?'

Ellie smiled, feeling the tension ease in her body.

'He's yours, Gino. Is he here? May I meet him?'

'Come with me,' he said, closing the apartment door behind him.

Gino took Ellie by the arm and led her down the narrow corridor. He tapped on the bedroom door.

'I'm awake, Papa.'

They both entered. Angelo was sitting in bed reading a book. He looked a little flushed and looked younger than his seven years, with large black eyes and a mop of dark curly hair, the spitting image of his father.

'Angelo, this is Signorina Ellie, whom I told you about has come to see you.'

'*Buonaserra, signorina,*' Angelo said with a broad grin.

'*Buonaserra*, Angelo. I hope you will be better soon.'

The boy turned to his father and, in the innocent, disarmingly honest way of children, said, 'You are right, Papa, she is pretty.'

Ellie blushed.

'I'm glad you agree,' said Gino. 'Settle down now. You can read if you like, but rest, okay?'

Back in the sitting room, Gino took Ellie in his arms again, kissing her gently on the forehead.

'I hope you understand. I never wanted to put him through

meeting different women, never knowing where he was, so I have always kept him away from my social life. Most people think he is my sister's child; only my close family knows he is mine.'

'I understand, really I do.'

He disappeared into the kitchen and brought back two glasses of wine. He handed one to Ellie and sat beside her on the sofa.

'Tell me, Gino, was it a love match? Did you love her very much?'

'It was an arranged marriage, but for all that, I loved Maria. Not with a passion, though; not with the love that I have come to know with you. I loved her, but I was not *in love* with her.'

Ellie looked at him and smiled. He was not married.

'Listen, Ellie, a crowd of us are going to the beach tomorrow. I want to take Angelo; he should be better by then, and I think a day by the sea will do him a lot more good than just lying in bed. Young Giovanna will be there with a friend and her brother. Come with us. It will give you a chance to get to know Angelo.'

'I didn't know you knew Giovanna; she said nothing.'

'Giovanna is a wonderful girl, but fiercely loyal to her friends. She and Maria were great friends at school.'

'Yes, Giovanna told me.'

'Say you will come. We are all meeting at the caffé at ten o'clock. We can catch the tram to Poetto. All you need to do is bring a towel and your bathers. It will be a glorious day.'

Later that evening, Ellie walked down to the Via Manno to find herself a swimming costume. She was searching through the various styles when a voice behind her said.

'Not that one, this one.'

Ellie turned to see Gino standing there with the young woman he had been with the other evening – his cousin. He was holding up a blue-and-white polka– dot bikini with bright pink straps.

'You have the figure for it,' he said, a wide, mischievous smile across his face.

Ellie blushed; she wished she didn't do that.

67

'This is Giulia, my horrid cousin who thinks she is in love with me.'

Ellie turned to the girl who had put her lower lip out in a pout and was scowling at Ellie.

'Don't take any notice of her; she's a childish brat,' said Gino, patting Giulia on the shoulder.

Giulia stuck her tongue out at Gino, then walked off.

'That one will come to a sticky end, mark my words,' he said. 'Now, let's sort out this bikini.'

That night, Ellie lay awake tossing over the day's events. She thought about Dee, what she had said about her parents. How perceptive she was. Ellie thought about how much she loved Gino and understood now why he had not told her. Angelo was young; he needed his father and could not share him with anyone else. Gino loved her. The thought of that made her feel secure. He was gentle and kind. Sighing, Ellie wondered what her parents would say – then suddenly realised she did not care. Ellie wanted to be part of Gino's family, part of his life; and that was all that mattered. She had found her wings.

CHAPTER SEVEN

Ellie arrived at the Caffé Genovese just before ten o'clock. The crowd of young people inside were chattering and greeting one another. The noise was so deafening they could barely hear each other over the din. Ellie, standing on the edge of the group, looked for Gino, when Giovanna came forward and put her arm around her.

'I'm so glad you came. Are you all right?' she said and taking Ellie's hand, Giovanna led her over to a short boyish looking man with a dark beard and woolly hair.

'Predu, this is my friend Ellie. Ellie, this is my brother, Predu.'

Predu took Ellie's hand and shook it hard. 'Welcome, Ellie. Come and join us.'

'And this is Giuseppe, my friend. He is a baker, and he has brought some fantastic goodies for us all.'

Giuseppe was tall, clean-shaven but with a black mop of unruly hair. They all shook hands as they greeted one another.

Suddenly, Gino was there. Ellie felt him beside her before he said anything.

'Good morning,' he said, gently kissing her on her neck. Ellie was not prepared for her reaction as a thrill shot through her and felt her heart miss a beat.

'Good morning. Are you well? Have you got Angelo with you?' she said, aware that she was blushing.

'I have,' said Gino, smiling at her. He had seen her reaction to his kiss, and it pleased him.

'Papa,' said Angelo as he tugged on his father's shirtsleeve. 'Papa, can I have an ice cream, please?'

Gino looked at his son and frowned. 'Do you want one now? Why not wait until we get to the beach?'

The boy did not argue but looked crestfallen.

Ellie looked at Gino, tilted her head to one side, and raised her eyebrows.

'All right,' said Gino 'You'll spoil him.'

'Come with me,' said Ellie, taking Angelo's hand. 'Let's go and find out what flavours they have. Do you feel better today?'

'Yes, I do, thank you, *signorina*.' Angelo's broad smile lit up the whole of his little face.

'How about you call me Ellie rather than *signorina*? It makes me feel so old.'

'Thank you, Ellie.'

He stood in front of the counter, looking at all the various flavours.

'Well, what would you like?' asked Ellie.

'Strawberry and vanilla, please.'

The girl behind the counter took a cornet and filling it with the two flavours, then wrapping it in a paper napkin handed it to Angelo.

'Thank you,' he said, a big grin again spreading across his mischievous looking face.

Ellie paid for the ice cream and took Angelo's other hand.

When they returned to the table, everyone was having coffee.

'Here,' said Gino. 'Come and sit by me. This is yours,' he said, pushing a coffee towards her.

He moved up to make room for Ellie, and she lifted Angelo onto her lap, where he sat licking his ice cream.

Finally, when everyone had decided where to go and how to get there, they all walked down the Via Regina Margherita to the port, where they caught the tram for Poetto.

Excited by the outing with his father, Angelo chattered away to Ellie, showing her the different landmarks as they passed in the tram. The big white building of the Lido and D'Aquila sprawled in front of the tram route on the seafront. The buildings were from the thirties and had all the characteristics of that wonderful era.

It was a glorious day, with a gentle breeze off the land and a clear blue sky. They all laughed and chattered as they piled out of the tram.

'Look,' said Ellie, pointing to the retreating tram. 'Just look at those young lads hanging on to the back.'

Gino laughed. 'We all used to do that when we were younger. A free ride – such fun.'

'I bet you were always in trouble.'

'Why would you think that? He said looking a little nettled. 'Come on, we've hired a *casotto* so we can all change.'

The soft, silver-sand beach was crowded with *Casotti*, which were beach huts, some small, others large with big glass windows, some with verandas but all painted in individual colours and of different designs. The sand formed mounds and dunes against the huts making it deep in places. On the beach, people lay under multi-coloured umbrellas or played with their children. Everything seemed bright and colourful under the golden sunshine.

After much laughter and searching, they finally found their hut, then took it in turns to change. When Gino emerged from the hut, he took Angelo's hand and led him into the sea, holding Ellie's hand on the other side.

'You look great in that bikini. I could ravish you right here and now,' he whispered.

'Behave,' said Ellie, but was happy to know he approved of the skimpy bikini he had chosen.

They swam and splashed in the water, Angelo enjoying the time spent with his father. On the beach, some of the group had built a sandcastle, while the others chatted and smoked together.

Lunchtime came, and they all took it in turns to change in the beach hut. Gino took Angelo to wash the sand from his feet at the communal tap on the beach. Then they all wandered down to a nearby restaurant for a pizza and some wine. The meal was a typical rowdy affair, with all the friends talking and joking and making hand gestures to emphasise their point of view.

Gino took a glass and half-filled it with wine, then topped it up with water.

'Don't tell Clara,' he said, as he passed the glass to his son.

'Thank you, Papa,' said Angelo as he sipped the wine.

Ellie sat back watching them, envying them their easy, laid back life, so different from her strict upbringing.

'A penny for them?' said Gino, watching her intently.

She laughed. 'I was just thinking how wonderful this all is, how relaxed and enjoyable. I envy you this lifestyle.'

Gino took her hand and squeezed it. 'I knew you would love it.'

Predu was the first to rise. 'I have to go. I promised a friend I would help him with his car.'

They split the bill and all chorused, *'Ciao.'*

Giovanna and her friends went for a rest under the umbrellas, leaving Gino with Ellie and a sleepy Angelo.

Gino picked up his son, gave him a piggyback, then took Ellie's hand and they walked along the beach together at the water's edge, Ellie stopping now and again to pick up a shell or stone that caught her eye.

As they neared one of the other cafes by the area of the Piccolo Marina, they saw a man taking photos of people for souvenirs. Gino sauntered over to him.

'Please, *signore*, would you take a photo of us?'

'But of course, *signore*, such a beautiful family.'

They stood together, Gino holding Angelo with one arm, his other arm around Ellie. Then he put Angelo down between them, his hand resting on the boy's shoulder, his arm still around Ellie as they looked lovingly at one another.

'Your address please, *signore*, and I will send them to you.'

Gino asked for two copies of each, paid the man, and gave him his address.

'It will be a wonderful reminder of today, darling,' he said, as he tenderly pinched Ellie's nose.

It was late afternoon when they all packed up their belongings and returned on the tram to the Via Roma. Gino carried his sleeping son up to Via Lamarmora and gave him to his sister, gently kissing him on the cheek.

'He has had a marvellous day. He should sleep well. Thank you, Clara.'

Gino, turning and taking Ellie's hand, pulled her up the stairs to his apartment, closing the door behind them, and took her in his arms.

'I have been longing to do this all day,' he said, picking her up and carrying her to his bed.

The familiarity of his touch, and his lovemaking, filled Ellie with immense pleasure as the two of them made love.

Later, a breeze stirred the curtains at the French windows as Ellie lay stretched out on the bed and sighed.

'What are you thinking?' he asked.

'How much you have changed my life. I never realised how much I could love someone. If you knew love like this with your wife, you must have been lonely after Maria died.'

'Ellie, after Maria died, I didn't have time to be lonely. I moved from full-time teaching to part-time to help my sister and my mother with Angelo. My mother has a rather nervous nature and finds it difficult to cope. There was always something to do. Now he is older, and he goes to school, it is easier. As for Maria, yes, I missed her, and I loved her, as I told you.' He sighed. 'With you, it's different, though, for I am *in love* with you.'

'Why is it different?'

'Because for the first time in my life, I feel at one with someone. You have become my soul mate.'

He drew her closer to him, kissing her tenderly, sending wonderful shivers through her as he made love to her once more.

Ellie woke with a start and looked at her watch; it was eight-thirty and dark outside. Gino stirred and pulled her toward him again.

'Come here,' he murmured, 'come and make love to me again.'

Ellie put down her watch and turned to her lover. 'You beautiful, beautiful man… but I ought to go; it's late.'

'Darling Ellie, one more kiss.'

The caffé was buzzing with young people as usual when they entered. Ellie had insisted that it was time to go home, but he had persuaded her to join him for a meal first.

'I'm starving after all that wonderful lovemaking; I need to build up my strength,' he said, a broad, mischievous smile on his face.

She blushed and put her finger to her lips.

'Shush everyone will hear you.'

'I don't care if they do.' He said taking her hand and squeezing it.

After the meal, they walked up to the side street near her house. He found the dark doorway and pulled her into his arms.

'I don't want to let you go,' he said, kissing her again and squeezing her arm.

'Goodnight, my love,' she said and walked toward the house. At the door, Ellie turned to wave, but he had already gone.

Ellie was at the caffé early the next morning, waiting for her lesson. Gino arrived with his usual cheery smile.

'Look what I've got.'

He sat down, opened an envelope, and took out the pictures the man had taken at Poetto. Ellie looked at the photos. A man and a woman with a young boy. To the casual observer, they looked like one happy family. On closer inspection, the soul-searching look between the couple as they stared into each other's eyes was evident.

'Two for you and two for me, so we shall never forget the day together. Today is a visit to the public gardens. I thought a gentle stroll through the streets to the gardens would be good. It isn't too hot this morning.'

'Don't you have anything else to do today? What about Angelo?'

'He has had two days off school. Believe me, Clara would

not let him have another. And no, the only lesson I had has been cancelled, so I thought we could spend the day together.'

They sauntered up familiar streets to the Piazza Arsenale, and down Viale Buon Cammino to the Via Giardini Pubblici. The gardens were laid out on either side of a long, gravelled walkway. A row of newly planted trees stood in square beds with shrubs at their feet. The lawn in front of the public gallery was green and dotted with flowering oleanders. Towering over it all were numerous jacaranda trees and an ancient Ficus, which spread its branches out across a wide area, giving shade from the mounting heat.

'It's like an English park.'

They sat on one of the large lower branches of the enormous tree, and he put his arm around her, drawing her to him.

'There is so much I want to show you.'

'There is so much I want to see.'

'Hungry?' Gino asked.

Ellie shook her head.

'No, are you?'

There is a silence that falls over Cagliari from midday onwards when people retreat from the summer heat and return to their homes to have lunch and a siesta; when the shutters are closed against the sweltering sun; when people doze in chairs, sleep on beds or make love.

Making their way back to his apartment, climbing the stairs, they opened the apartment door and fell into each other's arms, Gino closing the door with his foot as he always did. Ellie felt his strong embrace as they waltzed toward the bedroom. His lips on her lips as they pulled at each other's clothes, desperate for skin to touch skin. It was a rough, all-consuming lovemaking that finally left them both breathless.

They lay together, each lost in their thoughts. Ellie was amazed at her passion, at how wonderful it felt being made love to by such a strong and passionate lover. The image of him earlier, silhouetted against the light from the window with his dark curly hair, and the feel of him now made her shiver with delight. He too was at peace, knowing she had given herself to him and he had found someone who loved him. He sighed as he held her.

'Making love in the afternoon; this is something I could get used to,' she murmured.

He drew her closer to him and sighed again.

'Marry me, Ellie. Stay with me, be my wife. I love you so much.'

Ellie caught her breath; her heart was pounding in her chest, making her feel weak.

'Darling Gino, do you know me well enough to ask me that?'

'I know all I want to. Please, Ellie, think about it. You have always been there, I just had to find you, and now I have, I never want to let you go, dearest love of my life, and joy of my soul.'

'I don't have to think about it. I love you deeply. When I am with you, I know I am safe. I have never known love like ours. You are my first love, and there will never be another love like this for me.'

He rose, propping himself up on one elbow, gently running his fingers over her cheek.

'Tears, Ellie, what is it?'

'I am so happy, darling Gino.'

He bent to kiss her.

'I promise I will love you forever, I promise I will cherish you all my life. Are you sure you are happy to take on Angelo?'

She lifted her head to kiss him, and he fell back on the bed, holding her to him.

'He is yours and I will do everything I can to make him happy.'

He smiled at her, kissing her gently.

'Gino, will you come with me on Sunday to see the shack? Perhaps we could take Angelo and have lunch together.'

'What a splendid idea. How is your project going?'

'Well, I don't know. I have been so busy, and I want to catch up with Franco and Antonia again.'

'Darling, before I forget, the university ball is on Friday night. It is a special event in Cagliari, and by invitation only. My father is a member of the faculty and he always gets a pair of tickets. He does not want to go this year, as my mother is not very well, so he asked me if I would like to take you. I cannot think of anything more wonderful than taking you to the ball. Will you come?'

'That would be exciting, thank you.'

'Black tie, evening dress, a chance for me to show you off.'

Snuggling closer to him, she began kissing him again.

CHAPTER EIGHT

Ellie heard the guests arrive as they climbed the elegant staircase to the informal sitting room her parents used every day, and where they held more private parties, rather than the big room downstairs they used for formal gatherings.

Her mother had been cross when Ellie told her she had an invitation for the night.

'Where are you going?' asked Isabel. 'What is so important that you can't meet some of our friends?'

'I've been asked to the university ball,' replied Ellie, watching her mother.

There was a flush on Isabel's cheeks, a flash of anger – or was it jealousy?

'How on earth did you manage that? I've been trying to get tickets, but it's impossible, as the ball is invitation only.'

'Gino, a friend at the university, asked me. His father is a professor at the university; he always gets tickets. His father did not want to go this year, so he gave the tickets to Gino so he could take me. It seems you don't know the right people, Mother, when it comes to local things.'

Isabel snorted, coming closer.

'What does he want from you or us?' Isabel demanded, holding Ellie's arm, and digging in her long nails.

'Not everyone does something expecting something in return, Mother. It's time you learnt that.'

Now standing on the landing at the top of the stairs, Isabel once more questioned Ellie.

'Where did you get that dress? I haven't seen it before.'

'No, I bought it in Milan when I went shopping with Polly.'

'You have more money than sense. And she is a poor influence.'

At that moment, the door in the downstairs hall opened and Gino stepped inside. Giovanna greeted him, pointing the way up the stairs.

Ellie looked at him and smiled. He was wearing a midnight-blue dinner jacket, but instead of the usual black tie, he was sporting one in bright pink with a matching cummerbund. He was smiling as he came towards them with all the confidence in the world.

'Gino,' said Ellie, when he had reached the top of the stairs, 'this is my mother, Isabel. Mother, this is Giovanni Puddu, my date for the evening.'

Ellie's mother looked him up and down, smiling her charming smile as she shook hands with him.

At that moment Ellie's father called to his wife to come and be sociable.

'Excuse me. It seems Ian needs me,' Isabel said, turning to join him.

Gino took Ellie's hand and led her gently down the stairs. At the bottom, he pulled her into his arms and kissed her.

'You look beautiful; that dress is stunning, my darling,' he said, cupping her face in his hands and kissing her again. 'I have something that will go perfectly with your dress.' He said, pulling a box out of his pocket. 'I know it's early for your twenty-first birthday, but I found this, and I wanted you to have it for the ball.'

Ellie opened the box, made of dark-navy leather and gilt-tooled, and gasped.

'It's called *Su Lasu*,' he said. 'All the young girls have one in Sardinia to wear with their costume; they are handed down in the family, but I found this one in an antique shop, and a friend of mine, who is a jeweller, mended it and cleaned it. I hope you like it.'

Ellie looked at the beautiful gift. It was like a bow all worked in exquisite gold filigree with a stone in the centre; from the first bow hung a slightly larger one also worked in gold filigree with a stone in the centre, and small stones of garnet and peridot radiated from the centre like flowers with intricate gold leaves.

'I can't possibly accept this, Gino,' said Ellie, gently running her fingers over the piece.

He took it out of the box. It hung on a dark-navy velvet ribbon with an embroidered loop and button catch.

He turned her to look in the hall mirror as he placed the pendant around her neck and fastened it, all the time watching her reaction in the mirror. Ellie was wearing a long dark-blue silk dress that was caught on one shoulder and fell toga-fashion to the floor. It made her look taller and very elegant. The gold necklace looked stunning against the plainness of the dress, and Ellie caught her breath as she stared at her reflection, with Gino behind her, smiling and gently kissing her neck.

She turned and kissed him.

'I don't know what to say. I have never had anything so beautiful.'

'It comes with all my love, darling Ellie.'

He held her close to him, returning her kiss with ardour. Then, drawing away, he added, 'We'd better be going, or we will be late.'

At that moment, something caught his eye at the top of the stairs, and he looked up to see Ellie's mother watching them. Ellie followed his gaze, but Isabel pulled away and they saw the light from the open door as Isabel returned to her guests.

The ball was a grand affair, with people dressed in all their finery. A photographer was standing at the bottom of the wide staircase and they posed for him to take their picture. Gino stood with his arm around Ellie in a devil–may-care fashion, one foot on the same step as Ellie, the other coming forward as if he were about to imitate Fred Astaire. Ellie looked at him, laughing.

Gino steered her up the stairs toward a group of people and introduced her to his friends.

'This is Ignazio,' said Gino, gesturing to a short man with a neat, trimmed beard that lay close to his face. 'And this is his long-suffering wife, Fede.'

Ellie shook hands with them.

'This is Matteo and his girlfriend, Rita.'

Matteo had dark eyes, but there was a wicked twinkle in them.

'No wonder we haven't seen you in ages, Gino. Looks like you have been keeping Ellie all to yourself, you dark horse.'

They all laughed, and Gino introduced her to the others in the group.

'They are all studying archaeology, working with a man called Liliu, a famous archaeologist in Sardinia,' he said.

A man in uniform summoned them to dinner, and Gino took Ellie's arm to look for their place at the table.

The dining room was grand, with an ornate plasterwork ceiling picked out in gold against a cream background. The tables were laid with silver and crystal, which shone and glinted in the candlelight from the large chandeliers that hung from the ceiling. Candles and flowers were arranged on the tables, their scent rising to greet everyone as they stood by their places.

Grace was said in Sardu by a short, thin man, and after the 'amen' the room filled with the babble of voices.

Gino pulled out Ellie's chair for her, at the same time nodding to the elderly man on her left.

'Your first time, young lady?' asked the man.

'Yes, yes, it is.'

'Welcome. I see that rogue you are with has the loveliest-looking woman in the room on his arm.'

Ellie blushed at the compliment.

'Now I've embarrassed you. I am sorry. I am Professor Pinna. I taught your young man when he first came to the university. His father and I are old friends.'

Ellie smiled at him. 'I expect you have many stories to tell.'

The professor laughed. 'Perhaps,' he said.

The first course came, a delicate selection of meats, olives, and cheeses. Slowly, the chatter died down as people began to eat and drink their way through the meal.

The second course was pasta *Culurgiones*, pockets of dough stuffed with potato, mint and pecorino cheese, served with fresh tomato and basil sauce and topped with grated pecorino. Ellie leant forward to smell the pasta.

'Mmm, what a wonderful aroma.'

'Not as good as my mother makes,' said the professor, 'but good all the same.'

Gino turned to Ellie. 'Are you all right? Here, have some more wine,' he said, as he topped up her glass and then the professors.

The fish course came, a selection of seafood with a delicate olive oil and parsley dressing, accompanied by Sardinian bread to mop up the delicious juice. There was a considerable hush at the tables as people savoured the wine and tasted the amazing food.

When she had finished, Ellie leaned back in her chair and sighed.

'That was exquisite.'

'It's not over yet. We have the best to come, my favourite, roast suckling pig,' said the professor, a wicked grin on his face as he rubbed his stomach. 'If you are going to live in Sardinia, you must learn to eat like a Sard.'

Gino touched her leg under the table, running his hand up her thigh. His touch made it difficult for Ellie to concentrate on what the professor was saying. She turned to Gino, who appeared to be listening.

Smiling, he added, 'It's true.'

The main course came. Ellie took a piece of meat and watched as both men tucked into it with their fingers.

'*Is didus primus,*' she said, and they all laughed.

Lastly came sebadas, but Ellie only managed a bite of the round pastry filled with cheese and honey with a touch of lemon.

Coffee came, hot and dark, rounding off the grand meal. Music began to play in another room. Excusing them from the table, Gino took Ellie by the hand and led her to the dance floor. The music was not too loud, which allowed people to talk and dance.

'Rock-and-roll hasn't caught up with us yet.' he said, laughing.

The band played a medley of the hit songs of the day as he took her in his arms. The feel of him so close to her in public gave Ellie a thrill of excitement. She became aware of the band playing 'I Can't Help Falling in Love with You,' as Gino held her tighter, and then 'Blue Moon' and 'Moon River.' All the popular songs seemed to sum up her feelings. They moved in a slow waltz, and as he held her, Ellie felt his lips brush her forehead.

'I love you, Ellie,' he whispered.

'I love you too,' she said, laying her head on his chest.

He guided her toward the open French window, which led onto the balcony. The night was warm and still. The moon sailed high in the cloudless, star-filled sky. Ellie sighed as he once more pulled her into his arms.

'Come home with me,' he whispered.

They walked beside the port hand in hand, enjoying the magnificent night. The moon laid a long path of light across the water, which was like a sheet of dark glass; the stars reflecting pinpoints of light on the surface of the sea.

They continued in silence, each aware of the other's thoughts, as they walked up to Casteddu and Via Lamarmora. Gino unlocked the door, opened it, and stood back to let her through. He pulled her upstairs and into his apartment, where he took her in his arms, closing the door behind him with his foot in his usual way.

Ellie took off the necklace and laid it on the table. His hands were on her dress, undoing the zip, letting it fall to the floor; his lips were on her lips. Her hands were on his jacket, pulling it off, letting it fall next to her dress. Locked in an embrace they waltzed through the sitting room to his bedroom. At last, they were naked and in bed, skin on skin, wanting each other, holding one another in an all-consuming passion.

The silver moonlight shining through the window fell across the room and over the bed where they lay in each other's arms. Gino raised himself on his elbow and stroked her face.

'You look beautiful in the moonlight,' he sighed.

Ellie pulled him towards her to become lost in his caresses once more.

Later, as they lay in each other's arms, Gino stroked her body with his fingertips.

'I love you, Ellie.'

'Are you sure?' she teased.

'I am very sure,' he said, smiling. 'Marry me, Ellie. Live with me and Angelo here in Sardinia. I promise I will love and cherish you forever. Don't go back to England, please.'

A silence fell between them. Ellie didn't dare move or say anything; frightened it would break the spell of the moment.

'Are you okay?' he asked.

'Yes, but you have already asked me, and as I said before, you don't know me,' she whispered.

'I know you, Ellie. I know that the times I am away from you I cannot stop thinking about you. I know that you light up my day and that you are the ray of sunshine in my life. I know I want to be with you forever, have children with you, grow old with you, share my life with you.'

Ellie felt the tears slip from her eyes and fall down her cheeks. Never in her wildest dreams had she thought she could find such happiness, such peace, or such completeness. He loved her, and that was the most precious thing in all the world.

'You are very quiet. Have I frightened you?' he asked.

'No, but I can't believe that someone as wonderful as you could love someone like me.'

'My darling Ellie, I'm the lucky one. You are unique, kind, generous, and loving – what man wouldn't want to marry you?' He turned her face toward him. 'Darling Ellie, please say you will marry me.'

'Yes, I will, darling, darling Gino.'

He took her in his arms again and gently nibbled her neck.

That night Ellie stayed with Gino. They shared their love, their hopes, and their joy. Ellie lay in his arms, hoping she was not too happy, afraid of tempting fate. Sleep would not come, so she rose to look out of the window. The moon light fell into the street below. A shaft of light making it bright on one side of the street while the other lay in darkness. The moon also cast a beam across the floor and onto the bed. Ellie turned to look at Gino. He looked so beautiful, the arch of his naked back, his neat buttocks, and long legs. She sighed. He turned to lie on his back. His hair was ruffled on the pillow, his eyes closed, his face relaxed in sleep. A sudden shudder ran through her and slipping back into bed beside him, she gently kissed his neck.

Ellie loved everything about him. His gentle touch on her back, or a friendly pinch of her elbow. The quick squeeze of her hand, or a brush of fingers against hers. She had never known such contentment: and felt so alive, and so very much in love. So, this was love, an all-consuming love – not a love based on duty, as her parents, but pure love, the love that comes once in a lifetime. The need to be with each other, to hold one another. To know what he was thinking before he said anything. Could a love like this last forever? Ellie hoped so. There was always that heart-stopping moment each time they met, the breathless lovemaking, but also the heavy empty feeling when apart. Polly was so right: love certainly gave a woman wings.

Gino stirred and touched her and said sleepily, 'What are you thinking?'

'About love. It is such an unfamiliar experience. I never realised how wonderful it could be. I have seen others in love, but never felt it myself, not true love. I never thought I would ever feel like this. You have become my waking thought, my sleeping dream. You are the love of my life, darling Gino.'

'They say love helps the world go around, and with you it has. I love you too, darling Ellie.'

They ate breakfast together the following morning, looking an odd couple as Gino sat in his jeans and faded T-shirt while Ellie was in her evening dress. He rose, walked over to his bookshelf, and took down a package wrapped in brown paper.

'This is for you,' he said, holding out the parcel.

'What is it? Haven't you given me enough already?'

'This is for the soul,' he said, a wide grin on his face.

Ellie opened the gift, taking out a book.

'*Anime Oneste* by Grazia Deledda. Dearest Gino, it's a first edition! Where did you find it?'

'I have been looking for it for some time. I have a friend who owns a beautiful bookshop; he found it for me. The stories are rich in the Sardinian tradition. I think you will like it.'

Ellie opened the book and a card fell out from inside. She bent to pick it up and read the inscription.

'It is in Sardu. It means, *with great kindness you gave me a gift I will never forget.*'

'What gift did I give you?'

'Your love.'

'Thank you, darling Gino. I shall enjoy reading it and treasure it,' she said, kissing him.

'The pleasure is all mine,' he said, returning her kiss. 'Now, I'll call a taxi. You can't walk through Cagliari dressed like that.'

'Why not? I went to the ball last night.'

He laughed and called a taxi.

'I can see your parents at the same time,' he said.

'No, please, Gino. They have a heavy weekend with lunches and meetings; please understand they will not be receptive to anything now. They have a busy week ahead of them. Could you come on Monday week, in the evening? They will be free then and will have time for us both. Besides, I want a week to know that you love me and want me with no one else knowing. Can you understand that?'

'I can. If that is what you want, Monday week it is. But I will be round later to collect you to take you out for lunch.'

The taxi dropped Ellie off at the house. Gino had already paid the driver, so she got straight out and walked up the steps to the front door. Once inside, Ellie headed for the grand staircase up to her room. She was just at her bedroom door when her mother called to her from the sitting room.

'Where do you think you have been all night?'

Ellie's heart sank as she turned to face Isabel, who was standing, her hands on her hips, looking for all the world like a fishmonger's wife calling her wares.

'Where the hell have you been?' Isabel repeated. 'You little tramp.'

'Well, it takes one to know one. You know I was at the university ball, and afterwards, we all went out to breakfast,' Ellie said, moving out of range as Isabel came toward her.

'You don't really think a man like him is interested in a girl like you? Look at yourself, you are no oil painting. He needs a woman. He obviously wants something from you, or us – a favour.'

'Why would he need anything from us? His family has more influence in Cagliari than you could ever dream of.'

'He will take what he wants from you, then leave you. You do not understand what these Italian men are like –'

'He is not Italian, he is a Sard,' Ellie cut in.

Isabel looked at her blankly for a moment, then continued. 'Whatever. He is only after one thing, and when you have given it to him, he will leave you for one of his own kind. You mark my words. A good-looking man like that could have the pick of Cagliari; why would he want a plain Jane like you?'

Ellie let her mother rant on; she knew Gino loved her and that was all that mattered.

'If you have slept with him, you have played your ace card. He won't be back; I can assure you. You brazen little alley cat.'

'And you would know all about that,' said Ellie, opening her bedroom door; walking in and locking it behind her.

Later, she could be heard singing in the shower.

CHAPTER NINE

Where are we going?' Ellie asked Gino as they walked through Casteddu.

He had arrived to collect her just after midday. Angelo was with him, and they walked hand in hand, the boy between them, skipping and jumping to keep up with them.

'I know a place where they make the best pizza in Cagliari, and it is Angelo's favourite place to eat, so I thought we could spend the time together as a treat for him.'

They entered the restaurant through a black-and-orange plastic curtain, to be assailed by the wonderful aromas of fresh-baked pizza and wood smoke. They were greeted by a short dark haired man with a red-spotted handkerchief around his neck and a large apron around him which seemed to envelop him.

'Signor Giovanni, a pleasure to see you, and you too, young man.' He said as he bent to ask Angelo, 'Have you been good?'

Angelo smiled up at him.

'Oh, yes, Zio Andrea, I have been incredibly good. That is why Papa has brought me out today with his new friend.'

'Andrea, this is Signorina Ellie Montford.' Said Gino.

'Charmed, *signorina*,' said Andrea, and he took her hand, brushing it gently with a kiss. Then, turning to smile at Gino, he said, 'Yes, my friend, yes.'

Ellie blushed, and Angelo laughed.

'You have gone the colour of a ripe tomato.'

And they all laughed.

Andrea showed them to a table in the corner, away from prying eyes.

'You will leave everything to me, please, *signore*?' said Andrea.

The meal was a lively affair, as they talked, laughed, and ate their way through the dishes put before them: antipasto with large olives, finely sliced homemade salami and delicate slices of Pecorino Sardo, followed by three large pizzas, each cut into six slices so they could mix and match the flavours.

Ellie, sitting back, watched Gino and Angelo as they laughed and chatted together. This would be her life, living with this beautiful man and his wonderful young son. She sighed; what more could anyone ask for?

Gino looked at Ellie and took her hand. 'We could all go to see Franco and Antonia tomorrow. Are you doing anything, Angelo?'

The boy shook his head, making a face. 'I can't, Papá. I have a birthday party I really want to go to. Can we do it another day?'

'Of course,' said Gino, ruffling his son's hair. 'And you?' he asked, turning to Ellie. 'What are you doing tomorrow?'

'Nothing. It's Sunday, so my parents will be home, having a day of rest.'

'Great, so tomorrow we will go to the shack,' said Gino reaching across the table to hold Ellie's hand.

'Papá, are you going to marry Ellie? If you do, can I come and live with you?'

'Would you like to?' asked Gino, taking his son's hand.

'Yes, please, Papá. Yes, please.'

'Aren't you happy with Clara and Zio Giuseppe?' asked Gino, looking concerned.

'Yes, I'm happy, but it would be better living with you and Ellie.' Gino laughed.

They finished their meal, paid the bill, thanked Andrea for all his trouble, and then walked back to Via Lamarmora.

'I will take him to my sister's and see if I can borrow her Vespa for tomorrow. Then I will walk you home.'

'No, Gino, you stay with Angelo. I will be all right. It's not far, and besides, I need a walk after that meal.'

'If you are sure then I will see you tomorrow outside your house – early, about eight,' he said, smiling.

'Make it eight-thirty and you have a date.'

The following morning, Gino saw his sister Clara and collected her scooter as he had arranged. He pulled it out from under the huge staircase and pushed it into the street. He rode down to Ellie's house.

Ellie was waiting in the hall, ready to greet him.

'What a glorious day.'

'Come on,' he said to her, 'get on the back.'

Ellie climbed on the pillion seat, and they rode up to the Piazza Constituzione, then on down the Via Regina Margherita to the port. She found it an exhilarating ride, holding on with her arms around Gino's waist as he navigated through the traffic towards the old iron bridge across the port to Giorgino. Ellie noticed, again, the round tower and the old boatyard with the ribs of a boat lying on its side and found them fascinating. The smell of the sea was strong here, and she breathed it in with delight.

They came to the part called Bagni Giorgino and Gino stopped. He left the scooter under a shrub, out of the rising heat of the sun, and they walked hand in hand toward the shack. Ellie let out a cry of surprise as it came into view.

'Look, Gino! They have replaced the missing boards and painted it bright blue. And look at the white windows – it all looks so fresh, so clean. They have been working so hard. It is such a shame you didn't see it before they started the work on it.'

Franco and Antonia were outside and came to greet them.

'Come and see what we have done,' Antonia said, taking Ellie's hand and dragging her towards the shack.

'Antonia, please wait, can I introduce you to Gino?'

'I am so sorry, Ellie, forgive me. I am so excited about everything; I have quite forgotten my manners.' And turning to

Gino said. 'I am pleased to meet you Gino, and this is Franco, my brother.'

They all shook hands and then Antonia showed them into the shack. They had painted the inside brilliant white; red-and-white gingham curtains hung on poles at the windows. Chairs were new or had been repaired and painted white or blue, with the same gingham fabric on the seats. Tables, which were scrubbed clean, had a bottle on each containing freshly picked wildflowers. The whole place had an air of homeliness about it.

'We didn't have enough paint to do all the chairs, so the boys painted the others blue.'

'They look wonderful. Everything is so bright. It is a credit to you all.'

'This way,' said Antonia, pulling Ellie into the large room at the back of the shack. It too had been painted white and filled with bunk beds of all different colours.

'We got the beds from the old hospital. Dee told me to see them and mention her name. They were going to throw them out, but the boys collected them, and a local man helped to convert them into bunk beds for us. They gave us a load of blankets they didn't want. We spent a day washing them all and hanging them out. The boys all painted their beds in the colour they wanted.'

Ellie looked at all the brightly coloured beds and smiling turned to Antonia and hugged her.

'I have found someone in the area to cook for them.' Continued Antonia, 'I have also started afternoon classes. The boys take two afternoons off a week, so they can at least learn to read and write and count. So many people have come to help with the painting and repairs they have been so generous with their time. Dee seems pleased. She came yesterday and brought the woman who looks after the trust to explain the things I can do. Dee calls it The Blue Shack Trust. Dear Ellie, what would we have done without you?' said Antonia, stringing her sentences together in her excitement.

'It wasn't me, Antonia. It was Dee,' said Ellie.

'When Dee saw it yesterday, she seemed pleased and is coming back on Tuesday with some friends. You must be here – please, both of you, please come.'

Franco arrived with coffee and invited them all to sit at one of the scrubbed tables. Tommaso approached Ellie.

'Thank you, *signorina Ellie*,' he said and held out a bunch of fresh wildflowers he had been holding behind his back. 'These are for you.'

Ellie took the flowers and bent forward to kiss Tommaso, who immediately put his arms around her neck and hugged her. His reaction overwhelmed Ellie and she pulled him close to her.

'Thank you, Tommaso. I am glad you are here. Signorina Antonia will look after you, I know.'

After coffee, Ellie and Gino said their goodbyes, promising to come on Tuesday with Dee. They found the scooter and made their way back to Gino's house, where he returned the bike to its place under the stairs.

In his apartment, Ellie found a vase for the flowers and put them on the table.

'They are so pretty,' she said, with a smile.

'You know, Ellie, you have done a wonderful thing for those boys,' he said, pulling her into his arms and gently kissing her forehead.

'It wasn't me, it was Dee, who made it all happen.'

'Maybe, but you helped… Lunch?'

'Yes, please.'

They sat in the Caffè Genovese and ordered antipasto followed by a main course of pasta, and a bottle of red wine and some water.

'It's Sunday, a day to take leisurely and enjoy,' Gino said, taking hold of Ellie's arm and squeezing it in his now-familiar way. 'Now, before I forget, I called in at the university last night and these were in my locker.'

He took an envelope from his pocket and handed it to Ellie. 'Another good souvenir,' he said, beaming.

Ellie took the envelope and opened it.

'Our photos from the ball! You look such a loveable rogue in this photo,' she said, laughing.

He smiled and pinched her arm.

'You know,' he said, 'it will be good to see Dee again. I haven't seen her in ages.'

'I didn't know you knew her.'

'My mother knows the family. Dee's parents were killed in the bombing. She came back from school to find the house razed to the ground; all her possessions gone. She was just fifteen. Her grandparents took her in, but her grandfather stood up to the Germans and was arrested. A week later, they found his tortured and naked body in the street near their home. It was then that they all moved to the country. Her brother went into hiding in the mountains to organise raids on the Germans. They lived up in the old bandit caves. It was a dangerous time. The Germans captured him and took him to the Continent. They never saw him again, although they spent a fortune trying to find him.'

'How awful.'

'Aldo's father – you know Aldo, Dee's chauffeur? – he went with them all to help. It was when Dee's grandmother took her to the country that our two families met. My great-grandfather was among the group that organised the Sagra Sant'Efisio on the back of a truck during the war, much to the annoyance of the Germans but to the delight of the Sards. He later had to move to the country to be with his wife.'

'It must have been dreadful during the war. Was your father involved too?'

'My father helped the resistance. After 1943, when we joined forces with the Allies, when Cagliari took a tremendous pounding, British or American men were sometimes shot down or washed up on the beaches. We took them up into the mountains behind Cagliari or hid them in the vast caves under the city until we could get them safe passage to Spain or the Continent, or we gave them work in the fields of sympathisers.

There was resentment when the partisans made raids on the Germans and the reprisals fell on the local villages; when women became widows and children were left fatherless, as the Germans rounded up the men and gunned them down in front of their families. It was a terrible time to be in Sardinia.

'I was only young, and so I remember very little, just always feeling hungry until we moved out into the country, where everyone helped everyone else. When the war ended, there were no communications. Still no food. After they strung Mussolini up and the war was over, it was even worse. No food, no roads. Distrust among lifelong friends and family, as I said it was a bad time in Sardinia and there were over thousand buildings either lost or destroyed in Cagliari.'

Ellie was silently thinking about the country at war. The beautiful Saint Anna church almost destroyed. The scars were still there in Cagliari, but somehow, they had picked themselves up and put their world back together again. The church, now fully restored to its former glory.

'And Dee?' she asked.

'Dee travelled to Italy to try to find her brother. She met Giuseppe, who was also looking for his brother, who had been taken by the Germans. Giuseppe is about ten years older than Dee. He took her under his wing, and when they married, they came back to Sardinia to live in his family house in Cagliari. He travels a lot, and I think Dee is lonely, so a project like this will be good for her.'

CHAPTER TEN

On Tuesday morning, Gino and Ellie arrived early at the shack to see if there was anything, they could do to help Franco and Antonia. They found them busy hanging out the washing on several lines, which leaned at various angles. A wonderful aroma of pasta sauce hung in the air.

Antonia came forward and embraced Ellie. 'I'm so nervous. What will we do if Dee decides she doesn't like what we have done or thinks we have spent the money unwisely?'

Ellie looked at Antonia and took her hand. 'Don't be silly. You said Dee was thrilled at what you had achieved in such a short time. I know Dee loved it, otherwise, she wouldn't be bringing people to see it.'

'I hope you are right,' replied Antonia. 'By the way, young Tommaso is here. He begged me to let him stay, and it is so difficult to refuse him. Just to warn you.'

Ellie smiled, and Antonia went back into the shack to straighten the tables and make sure everything was in order, for the umpteenth time.

Dee arrived at ten o'clock and walked towards the shack with Aldo at her side and a couple of people following in her wake.

Antonia turned to Ellie. 'Who are these people? I didn't realise Dee would bring others with her. We won't have food for everyone.'

'I have no idea, but don't fret. Dee would not do anything to upset you. I'm sure it will be for the best,' said Ellie, placing her hand on Antonia's arm.

Gino greeted Dee, kissing her on both cheeks. Dee smiled up at him and held him by the arm and patted his hand affectionately.

Introductions were made all-round, and finally, Dee turned to the two young men who were standing on the outside of the group.

'This is Carlo,' announced Dee, pulling her young protégé towards her. 'He is from the *l'Unione Sarda*. He will give us a good write-up in the paper, and his colleague, Sandro, who will take pictures.'

At that moment, Tommaso stepped out of the shack. He was holding a bunch of wildflowers in each hand and he had a wide, mischievous grin on his face. He approached Dee and handed her the first bunch.

'These are for you, with all our thanks,' he said with a slight bow.

Dee looked taken aback, then put her arms around the small boy and, taking the flowers, kissed him. Ellie saw a tear fall on Dee's cheek, which she hurriedly brushed away.

'These are for you,' said Tommaso, as he handed the other bunch to Ellie, who became aware the others were all clapping as she took him into her arms and hugged him.

The photographer lost no time in taking pictures of the flowers being presented to both Dee and Ellie.

'Come along, Carlo, follow me,' said Dee, giving Aldo her flowers for safekeeping and pulling Carlo into the shack while Sandro followed behind them.

Dee loved what Franco and Antonia had achieved. Ellie thought Dee looked like a girl showing off her new dolls' house to strangers.

Gino looked at Ellie and smiled.

'She's happy,' he said, watching as Dee enthused about the paintwork, the curtains, and the beds.

Once they were outside again, Dee organised everyone.

'Sandro, I want a photograph with everyone in it. Aldo, flowers, please.'

Dee stood in the middle, pulling Franco and Antonia in on her left. Ellie and Gino were to stand on her right. Dee and Ellie both held their flowers. Tommaso made sure he was in front of Ellie, as she always spoilt him.

After Carlo had taken the photos, Dee gave all the details to the reporter as he scribbled away, trying to keep up with her obvious enthusiasm.

Finally, Dee rounded everyone up and, with handshakes, kisses, and goodbyes, they all left.

Franco and Antonia went into the shack and sank onto chairs at the nearest table.

'Wow,' said Antonia, 'that was like a whirlwind.'

Ellie and Gino joined them.

'Tommaso, be a good boy and make us all a cup of coffee, please,' said Antonia.

Tommaso returned later carrying a tray with four cups of steaming coffee and a few biscuits. He handed them around and stood back, eyeing the biscuits.

'Thank you, Tommaso,' Ellie looked at the boy. 'I don't want one, but perhaps you would like it?' she said, handing a biscuit to him and was immediately rewarded with one of his winning smiles as he nibbled his way round the treat.

'You will spoil him,' said Gino, taking her hand and squeezing it.

★

Over breakfast, the following morning, Ellie's father complained that the daily papers had not been delivered.

'I don't understand. At least the local paper should be here.'

'I'm sorry, *signore*,' said Giovanna, 'but the *l'Unione Sarda* has not come this morning, and *The Times* has not arrived either. But I will check later.'

Upstairs, Ellie was reading *l'Unione Sarda* which carried an account of Contessa DeLogu having founded a charity called The Blue Shack Trust with the help of an Englishwoman, Signorina Eleanor Montford. There was a picture of Dee, Ellie, and Gino, with Franco and Antonia. There was also one of Tommaso handing her a bunch of wildflowers and Ellie was struck by how happy everyone looked.

'Your parents haven't seen it yet, as I took the papers. Tell me, Ellie, are those the ones they gave you?' asked Giovanna, pointing to the vase in which Ellie had placed the flowers.

'Yes. I want to press some for my diary. He gave me another bunch the other day, and they are in Gino's flat. He is such a lovely boy.'

'You have done a wonderful thing, Ellie,' said Giovanna.

'It wasn't me; it was the Contessa who made it all possible. Dee has been the benefactor in all of this.'

'But if you hadn't stood up to the Milanese businessman at that luncheon, it would never have happened.'

'How on earth do you know about that?'

'A friend of mine was working there that day and said you were very brave.'

Ellie smiled at Giovanna. 'It was something I started that I couldn't back down on. Not brave, but, as my father said, foolhardy, and Cagliari certainly is very small.'

'Well, good has come out of it,' Giovanna said, sighing.

'Are you all right, Giovanna? You seem very down, and you look tired and pale. Is anything wrong?'

'No, nothing, really nothing,' she said.

'Now when you say it like that, I know there is something wrong.'

Giovanna sighed again, and Ellie patted a place beside her on the bed.

'Now tell me. You know me well enough to know it will not go any further. Besides, it is good to talk.'

Giovanna sat down and let out another long, heartfelt sigh as Ellie took her hand.

'There is this man. His name is Marco. I have known him since childhood, but he was promised to someone else in an arranged marriage. I have loved him for what seems a lifetime, but I know there is no hope for us. We see each other from time to time, to talk or have a coffee, or exchange books and discuss them. Nothing improper, just a deep, deep friendship.'

'Does he feel the same way about you?'

'Yes. Last week, when we had coffee together, he told me his wife is going away to Milan to see her relations and taking the children with her. He has asked me to stay with him. I don't know what to do. I know he isn't happy, but adultery is another thing altogether.'

Ellie thought for a moment.

'You think I'm awful, don't you?' said Giovanna.

'I have said nothing yet. But listen to me, Giovanna. You know you cannot have each other, but you can have some time alone together, on the understanding that it will go no further when his wife comes home. But I beg of you, not at his home, not in another woman's bed.'

Giovanna looked at Ellie. 'You agree?'

'Since I found love with Gino, I've realised that love is the most important thing in this world. To have the man you love hold you, love you, and make love to you, even for the briefest time, is a precious gift. With that love, you can face whatever the world throws at you. As my friend Polly always says, love gives you wings.

'If he comes to your place, light candles and prepare a favourite meal. Touch each other, love each other. And when it is all over, put it in your heart, for it will remain there long after it is over. Have no regrets but love him in the brief time you have. There is nothing so wonderful in the world as a man you love loving you. But you must promise me, and yourself, that you will finish it when his wife comes back.'

'Ellie, I will, I will try to end it.'

'Giovanna, if you think you can't end it, then better not to start it. Promise me, Giovanna, that you'll think hard before you do this, and if you do, may God give you the strength to end it.'

'Thank you, Ellie, thank you. I will think about it, I promise,' she said, putting her arms around Ellie.

At supper, Ellie's mother demanded an explanation about the piece in the *l'Unione Sarda*.

'What on earth did you think you were doing?' asked her mother.

'The Contessa is the lady who said she would help at the luncheon when Father told me not to make enemies.'

'Contessa DeLogu,' said Isabel. 'You should introduce me to her a Contessa could be extremely useful to your father.'

Ellie looked at her parents and rose from the table.

'I have absolutely no intention of doing so. Father didn't approve, and besides, Dee has become a dear friend and I have no wish to lose her friendship.'

CHAPTER ELEVEN

July slipped into August as their time together seemed to fly by. They spent some weekends at the shack, Ellie helping with the washing and Gino working with Franco on any odd jobs that needed doing.

Gino and Ellie shared any free time they had together or with Angelo; it was a time of happiness and joy.

It was on a Saturday morning in late August when Gino went downstairs to collect the Vespa as arranged with Clara, to find her waiting for him.

'Are you seeing the English woman again today?'

'Yes, we are going to Villasimius for a day or two.'

'Angelo told me you want him to live with you.'

Gino hesitated. 'If we get married, yes, I would like him to be with us. But it is something we can discuss when the time comes…'

'I have looked after him because neither you nor our mother could cope, and he has become mine now.'

'Clara, we will not take him away from you, and you know I am grateful for everything you have done, but he is my son…'

'He is mine too.'

With that Clara walked off to her flat, leaving Gino feeling troubled.

Ellie woke and looked at her watch. It was late; Gino would be waiting for her. She hurriedly showered, dressed, and collecting the overnight bag she had packed the evening before, ran down the stairs, and out into the street.

He was waiting for her under the arch.

'You're late,' he said, kissing her.

'No, you're early.'

'Give me your bag, and then you can get on the scooter.'

'You look worried. What is it?' she asked.

'I'll tell you later.'

It was a perfect day, not too hot, with a gentle breeze coming off the sea. The beautiful the south coast road to Villasimius was winding and narrow, with only painted concrete bollards or stones to stop cars going over the steep drop to the sea below. At one point, they had to stop to allow a herd of goats to go past. They became engulfed in the bleating animals as they stopped to chew some tasty morsel of vegetation or stood looking at the couple on the scooter. The old shepherd waved and smiled a toothless smile as he walked by, giving Gino a greeting in Sard.

They found the hotel down on the beach in the village of Villasimius. A local party was in full swing, and the host invited them to share the roast suckling pig with the other guests, in celebration of his daughter's wedding day.

Finally, Ellie and Gino climbed the stairs to their room. Gino opened the French doors wide, allowing the gentle breeze to fill the room. A crescent moon hung in the velvet-black sky surrounded by a million stars, frogs croaked above the sound of the waves lapping on the beach, and a gentle breeze stole into the room.

Ellie stood beside Gino and he drew her to him.

'It's beautiful,' she sighed.

He carried her to the bed and laid her down, her hair fanning out over the pillow.

'Will you tell me what was worrying you this morning? I have been patient in waiting to know.'

'When I collected the scooter this morning, Clara was waiting for me. It seems Angelo told her he would live with us after we marry.'

'What did you say?'

'I told her I am grateful for everything she has done and that, he is my son, and yes, we would want Angelo to come and live with us.

'It must be a wrench for her,' said Ellie.

'Clara said she was the one who cared for him when I couldn't.'

'Is it going to be a problem?'

'I don't think so, but Clara is possessive about the boy,' said Gino.

'I hope not. I don't want to come between brother and sister, father and son, but Giovanna said Clara is obsessive about Angelo.'

'Come here,' Gino said, taking her into his arms. 'No more talk of Clara.'

They made love to one another and Ellie fell asleep on her side, wrapped in her lover's arms.

In the morning, the sun poured into the room through the open windows, and Ellie woke to the sound of sparrows chirping and still wrapped in Gino's arms. She snuggled into him to listen to his breathing. What had she done in her life to deserve someone as wonderful as him? Her mother had said he would not love her. But Ellie knew he did; he would never have let her into his life with Angelo if he didn't love or care for her. She wondered if it would be a choice between her and Angelo; whether Gino would keep things as they were and leave Angelo with Clara. Where would that leave their life together?

Gino stirred, and Ellie turned to look at him. He looked so handsome, his dark hair tousled on the pillow, his long lashes giving his eyes a deep appearance, a shadow of a beard on his face. He pulled her towards him and kissed her on her neck, sending shivers of delight coursing through her, and she let out a long sigh and snuggled even further into Gino's arms.

'Hold me tight,' she said, and Gino held her against his body and tightened his arms around her.

'Love of My Life,' he whispered.

'Mine too,' she sighed.

They spent the Sunday morning on the beach, swimming and sitting in the sun. At two o'clock they showered and changed. Gino had ordered a picnic lunch, and after paying the bill they headed back through the countryside to Cagliari.

Gino stopped at an old gateway and followed the path up to an abandoned shepherd's hut. He left the scooter near the door, collected the picnic basket, and called to Ellie.

'Where are you going?' she asked.

'Come with me.'

They walked through a gate into a meadow. The grass was still golden, as it was sheltered from the sun by overhanging branches of some wild olive trees.

It was cool in the shade. Gino unpacked the basket, and Ellie helped him lay out the meats, cheese, and salad. A bottle of white wine they had put in a plastic bag with ice was still chilled.

'How do you know about this place?'

'I used to come here with a school friend; his father owns the land. They are a very old Sardinian family.'

'What a feast! I'm starving,' said Ellie, helping herself to the food.

'Tomorrow I must see someone for lunch, so no lesson, but I will be back in time to see you at seven-thirty. Don't worry, darling, I will be there. What do you think your parents will say?' he asked, as he gently kissed her.

'I have no idea; you can never tell. My father is fairly laid back, but you can bet your bottom dollar that Mother will have had you checked out.'

He laughed, kissing her again.

They lay back on the grass in the shade of a giant olive tree. Insects buzzed in the afternoon heat, while the cicadas grated their legs in a frenzy as if frightened, they would not be heard above all the other sounds. Ellie lay listening to them all; nature was never quiet.

Gino enfolded her in his arms. Never had Ellie ever felt so secure and loved as she did in Gino's arms.

'Where has the time gone? Nearly September, glorious months of knowing and loving you,' she said.

'I love you, dearest Ellie. If life passes this quickly after we are married, we shall be old in no time,' he said, kissing her.

It was late evening when they returned to Cagliari. They went to the Caffé Genovese for a drink and nibbles, then took the scooter back to Clara. They walked together down to Ellie's house and stood under the large arch. Gino took her into his arms and kissed her forehead.

'You are my life, Ellie, I will never let you go. You are my ray of sunshine and the love of my life. Take care and know that I will always love you,' he said, and he kissed her in a long, passionate embrace.

'I love you too,' Ellie said. 'There are not enough words for me to tell you how much I adore you, darling Gino. I can't wait to tell my parents.'

Another quick kiss and he was gone, leaving Ellie to climb the steps to the front door.

Her parents were not at home, so Ellie went up to her room. Soon she would become engaged to Gino. Her heart missed a beat.

On Monday morning, Ellie sat at the breakfast table with her parents and announced that Gino was coming to see her this evening and that she wanted them to meet him.

'This is important, Father, please, I would appreciate it if you could find some time for me, for once.'

Her mother looked at her over the top of her coffee cup. 'What can possibly be so important that we have to see him together?'

Ellie braced herself. 'I have asked him to come at seven-thirty for a drink. All I ask is that you are civil to him and hear him out.'

Her father muttered something about valuable time, while her mother tut– tutted into her cup.

Ellie was on tenterhooks all day, with no lessons to go to, as Gino had said he was seeing someone today and would be at the house at seven-thirty on the dot. She became bored with her own company and went to find Giovanna.

By teatime, Ellie was in a state of nervous excitement. The ticking of the French carriage clock on the mantelpiece marked the passing of time, while the hands on the dial dragged around to seven o'clock. Ellie and her parents were in the sitting room. Ian, a large whisky in his hand nursing it close to his chest as he paced the floor, while Isabel, armed with a double gin and weak tonic, sat fiddling with her pearls.

The clock finally struck seven-thirty. Ian looked at it, checking it against his pocket watch.

'It seems it's not that important if he can't even arrive on time. Has he no manners?' said her father replacing his watch in his waistcoat pocket.

'I hope you have not made a fool of yourself, Eleanor,' said her mother.

Isabel rose.

'We can go in for supper now. If I think it is what you are hoping for from that man, you will be disappointed, my girl. I told you not to give him everything beforehand. He will not be coming. He's probably with his mother asking how to get out of it.'

At that moment there was a knock on the door.

'Come,' chorused Isabel and Ian.

Giovanna entered and walked over to Ellie who, looking at Giovanna's face, suddenly felt a terrible cold shiver run through her.

'What is it, Giovanna? Where is Gino? What has happened?'

'You must come with me. There has been an accident. Gino is in hospital; he is asking for you. Please come. Predu is outside; he will take you to the hospital in his car.'

'What is the matter? Who is in the hospital?' asked Isabel.

'Not now, Mother. I will see you later. Don't wait for me for supper.'

As they hurried down the stairs, Ellie asked Giovanna again, 'What has happened?'

'I'm not sure. He fell from the tram.'

They bundled Ellie into Predu's car, and he sped off to the Civil hospital. It was an extensive building with an elegant portico on the front. Predu parked outside the main door and pulled Ellie into the large, domed hall, which had a grand mosaic floor. At the desk, the receptionist told them where they could find Gino.

Predu took Ellie's hand as they hurried down the endless corridors, and she had to run to keep up with him. They passed large floor-to-ceiling windows and statues of past benefactors and surgeons, the lights in the ceiling marking the measured distance down the long passageways to a room at the far end of the hospital.

Once there, they found a Sister who told them where to find Gino.

'You go in. I'll wait here,' said Predu.

Breathing heavily, Ellie pushed open the door and entered. Gino was lying on a narrow cot; propped up with large white pillows and covered with a hospital blanket.

'Hello, darling,' he said. 'I am so sorry. Whatever must your parents think of me; they must think me very rude, not turning up. Are you all right? You sound out of breath.'

'I had to run to keep up with Predu. What happened to you?' said Ellie, sitting beside Gino on the bed.

'I stepped off the tram in the Via Roma. My leg seemed to give way. I felt giddy. I felt as if I had tripped over something or as if I had been pushed. There were a lot of us getting off the tram, and I lost my balance and fell hard on the road. I must have hit my head, but I don't remember that. The doctors say everything is all right, but they want to keep me in overnight for observation.'

'What do you mean you tripped over something?'

'I thought I felt something round my leg, and a pain in my shoulder.'

'Did you tell the doctors? Does your head hurt? Do you have a headache? Have you been sick?'

'No, I feel fine – a bit tired, that's all. I am sore on my right ribs, and my legs ache; I must have just knocked them.'

'Darling, darling Gino, I thought something terrible had happened. Thank heavens you are all right.'

Ellie bent to kiss him, and he held her tightly.

'I love you, Ellie, I love you. Hold me tight, please, darling, hold me.'

She held him, kissing him tenderly.

'Darling, could you bring my jacket over, please?'

Ellie rose, found the jacket in the cupboard, and gave it to him. He searched in the pocket and brought out a blue and gilt box, which he opened, and took out a ring.

'Come and sit here beside me, darling.'

He took her right hand and put the ring on her third finger.

'It has been burning a hole in my pocket all day. I would have given it to you tonight at your parents, so I want you to have it now. It is a Fede Sarde, and it comes with all my love. I will put it on your left hand when we are married. It represents the ears of corn for prosperity and fertility. It is a traditional design, and it comes with all my love.'

'Gino, it's beautiful, thank you,' she said, looking at the ring, then at him.

'What would I have done if I hadn't found you? I love you so much,' she said, kissing him again.

'We found each other, and I love you, Ellie, I love you.'

Ellie smiled.

'Gino, you have brought me an all-consuming love. Body and soul. You are the only man I want to be with, and with whom I want to have children. I love you so much it hurts.'

'Darling Ellie, I love you too and feel the same way about you. I feel I have been looking for you all my life, and now I have found you. You are my world.'

'I was so worried something awful had happened to you. I don't know what I would do without you in my life...'

'Silly girl, nothing is going to happen to me. We have all our life ahead of us.'

At that moment, a nurse entered the room.

'He needs some rest. You can come and collect him in the morning after the doctor has seen him again. But he must rest now.'

Ellie leaned forward and kissed him again. 'I love you, Gino, dearest love of my life.'

He smiled at her.

'Are you sure?' he asked, with his mischievous grin.

Ellie laughed. 'I'm sure.'

'And I love you too.' he said.

Ellie turned and walked to the door and looking back, blew him a kiss which he returned.

Outside, Predu walked her back to the car and drove them both back to her house.

'How is he?' asked Predu.

'He seems fine. They are letting him out tomorrow, which is good.'

Ellie went straight upstairs, not wanting to see her parents. The thought of the third degree they would put her through was more than she could cope with just now. Ellie opened her bedroom door to find Giovanna sitting in a chair, waiting for her.

'Ellie, how is he? Everyone is talking about it,' said Giovanna jumping up.

'He fell from the tram. He said his leg gave way; that he felt faint. He banged his head on the ground. He said he has pain in his ribs, and his legs ache, but the doctors seem happy with him, and he should come home tomorrow. There was one other thing he said: he felt as if someone had pushed him. There were a lot of people getting off the tram so perhaps he felt as if someone had been too close to him'

'Probably, everyone pushes to get off the tram.'

The two girls sat talking for a while, but Ellie was having difficulty keeping her eyes open.

'I must go to bed; I am so tired, and I want to be up early tomorrow to see Gino.'

They hugged each other, and Giovanna left Ellie to go to bed and think about Gino.

Ellie woke with a start in the early hours of the morning. She felt cold and was shivering and pulled the bedcover up over her. Ellie turned the ring on her finger and thought of Gino, felt a pit in her stomach, and tried to settle down to sleep again.

It was a fitful couple of hours. Everything that she and Gino had done together turned around in her mind. She must have finally dozed and was woken by someone knocking on her door.

Her mother stood in the doorway. Ellie rubbed her eyes and sat up and noticed Giovanna standing in the doorway too and registered the shock and desperation in her expression.

'Mother, Giovanna, what is the matter?' said Ellie, getting out of bed.

Her mother came forward. 'Someone has just arrived to say that your friend died in the night.'

Isabel, unsure what was the matter, stood looking at her daughter as Giovanna rushed forward, shouting for someone to get help.

Ellie heard someone call for a doctor as her world tipped away, blackness rushed in as she fell to the floor.

When Ellie came around, she was lying in her bed, she felt sick and was having difficulty focusing.

'You must take it easy; you have had a terrible shock,' said a gentle voice beside her. 'It's all right, I am Doctor Moreddu. We are alone as I've sent your mother away for the moment.'

Ellie looked at the doctor's kindly face and smiled.

'What happened?'

'I am sorry, but young Giovanna told me your friend Gino Puddu died in his sleep last night. He had a fall, as you know, and he had a clot that travelled to his brain. I know it is of minor consolation, but he would not have known anything about it. I am so sorry, my dear.'

A lump came up from the bottom of her stomach. Tears welled in her eyes and Ellie sobbed as if her heart would break, making it hard to catch her breath. A fog seemed to descend into her mind as she struggled to make sense of his words.

'Now, you must not upset yourself too much,' said the doctor, holding her hand.

'With your permission, I would like to give you a quick examination. Have you been feeling sick recently? Are you off your food?'

'No, but I am exhausted at times.'

The doctor examined her and then held her hand. 'I would like to do a small internal examination, if that is all right, as I believe you are pregnant.'

He carefully carried out his examination and turned to Ellie,

'I thought so, I am happy to say my first thoughts were correct. Congratulations.'

Ellie held her breath – a baby, Gino's baby.

'Are you sure?' she breathed.

'Well, with all my years of experience, I think I can safely say that I am sure,' the doctor said as he squeezed Ellie's hand. 'I won't tell your mother. I think you might want to do that – or not. Is the father Gino Puddu?'

'Yes, yes, he is.'

'I am so sorry, my dear. Now, this is my card. Make sure you come and see me soon. You will need a check-up to see that all is well.'

'Thank you, doctor.'

Ellie's mother returned to the room and strode across to the bed.

'Well, doctor, is my daughter all right now?'

'Your daughter is fine, but I'll want to see her in a day or two when she is feeling more herself.'

He turned to Ellie and patted her on her arm.

'Come and see me anytime.'

And with that, he packed his bag and left.

'What is the matter, Ellie? Who has died? Is it Giorgio, or whatever his name was?' demanded Isabel.

'Just go away, Mother, and leave me alone – please.'

Isabel tutted and walked out of the room, slamming the door

behind her. A few moments later, there was a gentle tap on the door.

'Ellie, it's Giovanna. Can I come in?'

'Yes, please.'

She entered the room and sat on Ellie's bed and held her hand.

'Giovanna, what am I going to do? How is Angelo, has anyone told him?

What about Gino's family?'

'Hush, Ellie, they are all together. The priest is with them and the funeral will be tomorrow. Will you be able to come?'

'Yes, please, if that is all right with the family,' Ellie sobbed.

Giovanna put her arms around Ellie.

'He gave me this ring last night for our engagement. Do you think he knew he was going to die?' said Ellie, turning the ring on her right hand.

'It's beautiful, a real traditional Sardinian wedding ring. But no, no, Ellie, I am sure he didn't know. It is terrible, with you two just about to start a life together.'

'Giovanna, listen to me. No one knows, but I am expecting his child. The doctor has just told me. At least, I have something of Gino's.'

'Dearest Ellie, how wonderful! I am so pleased for you. Whatever did your mother say?'

'The doctor was kind enough to tell me after he had sent her out of the room.'

'You will have to tell her, it's not something you can hide.'

'Not until after the funeral. My mother will go into orbit as it is, and I don't want her upsetting all the family, Giovanna,' Ellie sighed, 'I can't believe he has gone, and I can't believe I am having his child.'

'Listen to me, Ellie. They are laying him in the Chiesa della Purissima, just up the road.'

'Yes, I know it. Can I see him? Is it possible?'

'Ellie, are you sure you want to?'

112

'Yes, please, Giovanna. But when the family is not there. I need to see him one more time.'

'I am saying my farewell this evening; do you want to come with me? I will organise it, and then you can come to the funeral tomorrow with us. We cannot bury him until twenty-four hours have passed, but then it must be done as quickly as possible. You can come to the church with me tonight, and then we will collect you in the morning and bring you back after the funeral. Your parents are out tonight, so they won't know where you are.'

'Thank you, Giovanna, thank you. Whatever would I have done without you over the past months?'

That evening, Giovanna came with Predu to take Ellie up to the church. Ellie had dressed in her blue dress with matching cardigan that Gino had loved so much and carried a single rose she had bought earlier.

They walked up the Via Lamarmora and entered the church. A priest came forward to welcome them and to give his benediction.

'Would you like me to accompany you, my child?' asked the priest in a gentle voice.

'No. No, thank you. I would like to be alone with him, please.'

Ellie braced herself as she entered the room. Walking slowly toward the open coffin. A chill ran down her spine and she pulled her cardigan around her, as much for comfort as for warmth.

Gino was resting in the silk-lined coffin. Ellie moved towards him, her eyes fixed on his, closed as if in sleep, half-expecting him to open those beautiful eyes and tell her he loved her.

Ellie became aware of the heady, sickly scent of lilies and noticed that the area was filled with the flowers.

She touched the silken lining and placed the one red rose beside him. Moving closer Ellie touched Gino's forehead and stroked his hair. He was cold and lifeless. A tear fell onto his cheek as she bent to kiss him for the last time and a large lump rose in her throat.

'Darling, my darling Gino, we are to have a baby. I did not

know before, but he is ours. I promise I will love and cherish him forever. I only wish you could have seen him, or her.'

Ellie suddenly felt faint and held on to the side of the coffin.

'Goodbye, my darling, beautiful man. Go to Maria until I join you. I love you.'

A sob came up from the pit of her stomach, and Ellie became aware of the priest coming forward and putting his arm around her for support as he led her away.

She turned to look at Gino one more time. Her lover was gone, lost to her forever.

Giovanna came forward to take Ellie and hugged her to try to console her.

'Are you all right, Ellie? Father, can you hold her while I say my goodbye?'

When Giovanna returned, she put her arm around Ellie again and took her from the priest.

Ellie clung to Giovanna.

'He looks as if he is asleep. I have seen him like that so many times when he was sleeping,' she cried.

At home, Giovanna came and sat with Ellie.

'Come now, you must get some sleep. I will come and see you later. You have not eaten anything. You must try to eat something. And you must let your grief out; you can't sit here and bottle it all up.'

'Giovanna, I feel as if the breath has been sucked out of me.'

'Ellie, I want to remind you what you said to me about Marco. Do you remember what you said? Love him, hold him, make love to him, so he will always be in your heart. Remember that, Ellie. Gino will always be there. You will think of him with sadness, but also joy; knowing that you loved each other.'

Ellie sobbed, and Giovanna once more put her arm around Ellie to comfort her.

'Now, please try to eat at least a few of these. You must eat something, or you will be sick,' Giovanna said, handing a plate of sandwiches to Ellie. 'Are you sure you want to come to the funeral tomorrow?' Giovanna added gently.

'Yes, oh, yes. Please will you take me?' said Ellie with a sob.

The night passed in complete oblivion for Ellie. She stayed in her room, trying to fight the nausea that plagued her.

★

The service passed in a haze. Ellie did not want to believe the coffin lying on the catafalque held her lover. His last words to her had been that he loved her, and she had told him she loved him too. Uncontrollable tears fell down her cheeks at the thought of the love of her life.

In the church, Angelo stood beside Clara, Gino's sister. He was red eyed from crying. He had lost his father and his dearest friend. Ellie looked at all the family, the family that should have been hers.

Predu came forward and put his arm through hers. Looking at her and gently nodding his head, he led her up to the catafalque, crossing himself as he bent forward to kiss the coffin, now closed, and covered with flowers. Ellie watched and went to follow him, but when she tried to go forward to kiss the coffin, she felt faint. Predu held on to her, then led her back to her seat and stayed with her.

Life was so brief, and one could never know what was around the corner. But Gino had shown her how to live, to love, to laugh, and to cry. Now, he had been taken from her. Life would never be the same. But she would have his child.

The wake that followed would have put any Irish funeral to shame. The tables groaned under the weight of all the food while the wine flowed as people rose to tell stories about Gino as the man and the boy. Ellie listened to them all, tucking them away in her mind to recall later.

Angelo came up to her and climbed onto her lap.

'Why has Papa gone to live with Jesus?' he asked, his eyes swollen and red from crying.

115

'Perhaps Jesus wanted him.'

'But I want him. He's my papa. Jesus has his own father, Joseph; why would he want mine?'

Ellie smiled a wan smile.

'You must be brave Angelo. He is at peace, and you can talk to him every night in your prayers, and perhaps you will say one for me too?'

'I will, Ellie, I promise. You will come and see me, won't you?'

'Of course.'

He slipped off her lap and went to play with his cousins.

A tall, nervous-looking woman came up to Ellie and touched her on the arm.

'My dear, I am Gino's mother. I am sorry we are meeting under such sad circumstances. We have both lost him. He told me he had asked you to marry him, and that you had said yes. I cannot tell you how happy you made him. I do not think I have ever seen him so happy. Thank you, my dear, for that.'

'I loved him very much. I don't think I will ever get over losing him.'

'Time is a great healer, and you are young. My dear, do not tie yourself to the dead – life is for the living.'

She opened her handbag and brought out a small silver box and handed it to Ellie.

'This was Gino's rosary; I would like you to have it,' and bending forward, kissed Ellie on the cheek. 'Thank you for making him so happy.'

'Thank you,' said Ellie, but Gino's mother had turned to go back to the family.

Ellie opened the box. Inside was the beautiful coral and silver filigree rosary that had belonged to Gino.

It was late when they dropped Ellie back at the house.

'Are you sure you will be all right?' asked Giovanna.

'Yes. I will see you tomorrow. Thank you for everything. Thank you, Predu, for everything.'

Giovanna kissed Ellie and waved goodbye.

Ellie climbed up the stairs to her room. The landing was dark, but there was a thin strip of light coming from under the door to the sitting room. She was just about to open her bedroom door when the sitting-room door opened. The shaft of light from the room caught her as Ellie tried to make her escape.

'Ah, there you are!' said her mother in an exasperated tone. 'Where the hell have you been all day?'

Ellie entered the sitting room and removed her sunglasses. It was obvious she had been crying and looked distressed, but that was no excuse as far as her parents were concerned.

'You haven't answered my question. Where have you been all day?' repeated Isabel.

'I went to Gino Puddu's funeral.'

'Isn't that the junior professor who died?' said Ian offhandedly, peering over the top of his newspaper.

'Yes.'

'Why would you go to his funeral? You didn't even know him,' said Ian.

'But I did. I told you, he was the man coming to see you both on Monday evening. I have been having Italian lessons with him.'

'But what about the old professor? You should have been with him!' said Ian.

'He was ill so Gino took my lessons.'

'So it's Gino now. He's your professor, don't you have any respect these days? He was your professor, so he is Professor Puddu –'

'No, Father,' Ellie cut in. 'He was Gino. We became close…'

'But he's married,' said Ian, rising from his chair and crumpling his paper.

'A widower…'

'With a child.'

'You have been doing your homework. Yes, a young son called Angelo.'

'You have been with him alone every day?'

117

'Yes, Father, and he asked me to marry him, and I said yes, and that is why he was coming to see you.'

Ellie heard her mother's sharp intake of breath but ignored it.

'Professors and students are not supposed to have relationships,' said Isabel. 'Your father can't have a scandal like that connected to his name. What were you thinking, Eleanor?'

'We loved each other, and we were to be married.'

'Over my dead body!' roared Ian.

'Have you two been sleeping together?' asked Isabel with a look of disdain, as if it was the worst thing that could happen.

'Yes. And I am expecting his child. The doctor told me on Monday when he came.'

Ian fell back into his chair. 'My God, what a scandal! You will have to go back to England Isabel. We will all have to go back. I can't stand the shame of it all.'

'For goodness' sake, Father. People fall in love and they have children. Just because Mother won't give it to you anymore, doesn't mean she doesn't get it elsewhere...'

'Eleanor!' barked Isabel, colour rising on her face.

'Don't push me, Mother. And as for you, Father, your copybook isn't without a blot or two.'

An uncomfortable silence fell in the room, and Ellie, feeling that she had won that round, turned to go to her room.

'Eleanor will have to go home at once. You can follow later. What will people say?' said Isabel, downing her gin and tonic in one.

Ellie closed the door behind her.

Upstairs, she lay on her bed and wept bitterly for Gino and what might have been.

CHAPTER TWELVE

Ellie's parents were true to their word, and Isabel worked on the arrangements for them all to return to England and Ellie's grandparents'.

Ellie spent a morning shopping for presents for Angelo and Tommaso and bought them each a gold filigree cross on a chain for a keepsake. She also purchased a book for Angelo and put his cross in an envelope inside the book and wrapped them up together. Ellie also bought a silver bracelet for Giovanna as a reminder of their time together.

The following morning, Ellie went to see Clara and young Angelo, hoping they would be in and knocked on the apartment door. It was Clara, who opened the door.

'Hello, *Signorina* Montfort. What can I do for you?' asked Clara.

'I have come to say goodbye to Angelo. Is he here?'

'You'd better come in,' said Clara, opening the door to allow Ellie to enter.

'Go through.'

Ellie went in the direction Clara was pointing and came into a large sitting room like Gino's upstairs. Clara stood in front of Ellie, a look of defiance on her face.

'He's not here. My husband has taken him away for a week with his family. We thought it would be an excellent idea; he can play with his cousins to put last week behind him.'

'I'm sorry he's not here. I am going back to England at the end of the week, and I wanted to give this to Angelo. It's a book on archaeology. I thought he might like it, and perhaps it will remind him of me,' said Ellie, handing over the package.

'That is kind of you, thank you. But *signorina*, when you go back to England, it would be better if you did not keep in touch with the boy. He is settled in this family, and I am his legal guardian, as Gino never changed his will.'

'But I don't want him to think I just walked out of his life without a goodbye.'

'I will tell him you called. I will also give him your present. But remember, he is mine now. So, if you will excuse me, I have several things to do.'

With that, Clara walked to the door and held it open until Ellie walked out. Ellie turned to say goodbye, but the door was already closing behind her. Clara had made her intentions clear and that did not include Ellie in Angelo's life.

Ellie returned to the house to find Giovanna in her room.

'Whatever is the matter? You look as if you have seen a ghost,' said Giovanna, coming across to Ellie and putting her arm around her.

'I saw Clara, to say goodbye to her and Angelo, but she has taken charge. Angelo has gone with his uncle to be with his cousins. Clara does not want me to see the boy anymore – I'm to have no contact with him. I know it is for the best, but I feel so lost, so cut off.'

'Clara has always been very possessive of Angelo. I think Clara found it difficult when he went out with you and Gino. She feels he is hers and would have found it almost impossible to cope when you married, as the boy would have lived with you. But, Ellie, you have Gino's child. You can love and look after the baby and it is yours. Think about the positive things, not the negative ones.'

'Thank you, Giovanna. I will miss you. And you, how are you? How is your life panning out?'

Giovanna looked at Ellie and grinned. 'I have this for you. I know it is special in England, so I wanted you to have it,' she said, handing Ellie an envelope. 'Open it carefully.'

Ellie did as Giovanna asked and caught her breath.

'It is a lock of Gino's hair. I cut it when we were in the chapel. I knew he wouldn't miss it.' She said with a smile.

'Giovanna, what am I going to do without you? Thank you. It will be precious to me. And, how are you?'

Giovanna touched Ellie's arm.

'I have decided to let Marco come to stay with me. It will be hard when he goes, but I only have one life. Besides, losing Gino has made me realise that nothing is promised.'

'Dear Giovanna, I am so happy for you,' said Ellie, with a smile. 'I have this for you,' she handed Giovanna the small package she was holding. 'I hope you will wear it and remember me.'

Giovanna opened the present and took out the silver bracelet and put it on her wrist.

'Oh, Ellie, it is beautiful. Thank you, my dear friend,' she said, throwing her arms around Ellie.

The following morning, Ellie went to see Franco and Antonia.

'Come in! Coffee!' they chorused.

Ellie sat at the table while Antonia made the coffee.

'Thank you for coming to the funeral. I saw you there, but I didn't register much, I'm afraid. It has all been very hazy,' said Ellie.

'We heard you are going away. Why are you going back to England?' asked Antonia.

'My parents are ready to retire, and now that Gino has gone, I have no reason to stay here.'

'But you could stay here and help us; we can always find you a job. It wouldn't pay a fortune, but I know that you would be happy here,' said Antonia.

'You might be right, but I have to go home first. You see, I'm expecting Gino's child and my mother is insistent that I go home with her.'

Antonia put her hand on Ellie's arm. 'I am so happy that you have something wonderful of his. Take care of yourself and come back to see us when you are ready and have the time.'

'I have a little something for Tommaso. Please give him this and tell him it comes with all my love.'

'Ellie, thank you. I know he will love it. He will be sorry not to have seen you.'

Ellie hugged Franco and Antonia and fought off the tears that threatened to break her resolve.

'Thank you for everything, Ellie. Please keep in touch.' Said Antonia, with a break in her voice.

With all the goodbyes said, Ellie walked back to the port, found a taxi, and went to see Dee. She was in her sitting room having her usual cup of strong coffee.

'My dear girl, how lovely to see you,' Dee said as Maria let Ellie into the room. Dee rose and came forward to put her arms around Ellie. 'How are you? Such a terrible loss. You must be devastated. But I understand your parents have lost no time in organising their return to England. Do you have to go with them?'

'I do. My mother is insistent, and Father needs some support.'

'I am always here if you need to return, you know that.'

Ellie fought back the tears she had been struggling with all day.

'Tell me, Ellie, what else is the matter, my dear?'

Ellie smiled at Dee.

'You know me too well. I am expecting Gino's baby, and my mother is at her wits' end, and is sure that the scandal will harm Father's chances of a knighthood.'

Dee chuckled.

'The English and their honours and titles. Everyone is a Count here; they are two a penny in Sardinia. All you need is friends in the right places and money. I'm sure it's the same in England.'

'My mother can't or won't see that. Besides, she wants to go home to grow roses in her garden and drink proper cups of tea. Not that I think Isabel will stick it for long.'

'You know, you could always come and live here. The house is large enough, and I would love to have you.'

'Thank you, Dee, but I don't think I can face Sardinia on my own just now, perhaps in a few years, I will bring back the baby to meet the family. Hopefully, Clara will let me see Angelo then.'

'Well, if you change your mind, I am always here. But don't pin your hopes on Clara; she is a hard, possessive woman. Clara was jealous of you and Gino and frightened you would take Angelo away from her when you married.'

It was an emotional farewell between the two friends, with promises to keep in touch.

The day before Ellie left, Giovanna came to see her.

'Can you come down to the kitchen; there's a young lad who insists on seeing you and won't leave without speaking to you.'

Ellie followed Giovanna down to the kitchen to find Tommaso sitting at the table, eating a large bread roll cook had given him.

'Tommaso are you all right?' asked Ellie going towards him.

He rushed from the table and threw his arms around Ellie.

'Thank you for my present. I will always wear it, and when you come back, you will see it again. Do you have to go?' he sobbed.

Ellie pulled him into her arms and hugged him.

'Now you must be a brave boy. Be good, make me proud of you, and do as Antonia and Franco tell you. You will always be in my thoughts.'

'I will, I promise. Thank you, Ellie, thank you. But you will come back won't you.'

CHAPTER THIRTEEN

Isabel accompanied Ellie home. Ian was to follow the following week after he had handed over to someone, as there was talk of opening the embassy again in Cagliari as the console had been in Rome since the war.

Once back in England, Ellie found it difficult to settle. She missed Sardinia, missed Gino. Her mother only spoke to her to urge her to put the baby up for adoption or to push her toward Simon.

'If you married Simon, there would be no need to tell him about the baby; then you could keep the wretched child. Men are so stupid, he would not know. When the baby comes, you just say it is early. Don't be a stupid little bitch and tell him, or he will never marry you and then I will never get you off my hands.'

'I thought you didn't want me to marry him as he had nothing to offer?'

'Well, he does now. And he's daft enough to marry you.'

After that outburst, Ellie kept out of her mother's way and took to walking across the fields and woods, needing to be on her own.

One afternoon, about two weeks after returning home, Ellie was sitting on a large log that had been carved out to form a seat. It was set at the edge of a stream that ran near the wood on the far side of the farm. She was sitting thinking and crying and turning the ring on her finger that Gino had given her.

Ellie was not aware of anyone coming across the field and was surprised when the large Ridgeback snuffled at her. It was Simon's dog. Putting her hand up to shade her eyes, she saw Simon standing silhouetted against the afternoon sun.

'Hello,' said Ellie, smiling.

'Hello, Ellie. I heard you were back, but you haven't been to see me. Are you all right? Our mothers are trying to arrange a party for your return...'

He stopped and looked at his long-time friend and sat down beside her.

'Ellie, what's the matter? You can tell me. Why are you crying? You always used to tell me what was wrong.'

'This is different.'

'Why is it different? We still know each other well, and you know how I feel about you.'

'That is why it's different,' she said with a sob.

'Whatever it is, I am sure it is nothing we can't sort out between us.'

Ellie shook her head.

'Ellie, do I have any hope with you? I know we said we would wait until you were twenty-four, and I know your mother thinks of me as a clod, but do you think you could marry me?'

She smiled.

'You're not a clod, but I can't marry you, Simon. I can't.'

'Come, Ellie, tell me what it is. What's the matter?'

Large tears fell onto her lap. Simon took her hand in his and held it, waiting for her to speak.

Ellie sighed.

'When I was in Sardinia, I met and fell in love with a man. We were planning to marry, but he had an accident and died.'

Simon listened, not daring to move.

'And you love him?'

'Yes. And I am carrying his child. I didn't realise I was pregnant until after he had died. My mother is being unbearable and says that the shame of it all will make her the centre of all the gossip and doesn't want my scandal to sully her good name.'

Simon looked at Ellie.

'I have loved you for as long as I can remember, and now you need someone to help you. Ellie, the baby will need a home, a father, a family. You know I have always loved you. Let me look after you both. I promise I won't make any demands of you. I just want to marry you and do everything I can for you.'

'You are a wonderful man, but I can't do that to you. How can you be expected to love another man's child?'

'It's yours, Ellie, and that's all that matters.'

Ellie sighed. They were the very words she had said to Gino about Angelo.

'You know it's frowned upon to have an illegitimate child, and you know, too, that either your mother will make you give up the child, or you'll struggle on your own with no help from your parents.'

'My mother said I should marry you and not tell you and pass the baby off as yours, but you know I couldn't do that to you, Simon.'

'Listen to me, Ellie. I have an excellent job with the Foreign Office. We can live in London. No one down here will know anything about it, and nor will they in London. Most important of all, you will be away from your mother. Just think about it, Ellie, promise me. Have you any idea what those homes for unwed mothers are like? They will make you work night and day until the baby arrives. When you have the baby, it will be taken away and given to someone else. Is that what you want for this child?'

'No, Simon, no,' she said, falling into his arms.

'Then think about what I have said, please, dearest Ellie. We are friends; surely that counts for something. And it will get your mother off your back.'

The following day, Isabel announced she was going to London and wanted Ellie to go with her.

'I have booked for you to see my gynecologist. If you are determined to have this child, then you must make sure everything is all right. I want you to take this seriously, Eleanor. I do not want you to go to the local doctor, as I know his receptionist cannot keep her mouth shut. Besides, I do not want any half– wit for a grandchild.'

Much against her will, Ellie accompanied her mother to

London. Ian drove them to the station, and they travelled together in relative silence.

Ellie thought about the time that Simon, Polly, and Laurence's Nanny had taken them all to London to see a pantomime before Christmas. It had been a magical day with lunch at Lyons' Corner House, followed by a visit to Hamleys to see all the wonderful toys, then on to the pantomime Aladdin at the Palladium. On the way home, Ellie and Simon had leaned out of the carriage window to see who could get their face the blackest with the smuts from the steam engine. She smiled to herself. Glorious memories.

At Liverpool Street station, Ellie and Isabel took a taxi to Peter Jones to have a light lunch. Later, they walked out into the gathering twilight. Ellie hated the shorter days and missed the sunlight of Sardinia. November in London was miserable and depressing, with a thick fog. The last time she had been here in the winter, they had had to take it in turns to walk in front of the bus in a 'pea– souper' fog, and when the traffic finally came to a standstill, they had to stay in a hotel for the night and Ellie hoped that wouldn't happen today.

Isabel hailed another taxi and gave the address of the doctor's office in Queen Anne Street. Through the window, Ellie watched the pedestrians, like grim shadows walking down the streets. It had started to rain, and people were shrouded in their coats or huddled under their umbrellas. They were always in black macs or grey ones; why not red or yellow? Surely one should have bright colours on the dull days.

The waiting room was large, with a huge mahogany table in the middle covered with magazines for all interests and chairs arranged around the walls. An eerie silence pervaded in the room. Logs smouldered in the old fireplace – the smell of winter.

A nurse entered the room and called Ellie's name, and she rose to follow the nurse. Isabel rose too.

'I don't need you, Mother. I am quite capable of telling him how I am.'

'He asked to see me, Eleanor. He's an old friend.' Said Isabel as she pushed forward, dragging her daughter with her.

The consulting room had once been a very impressive drawing room with a decorated plaster ceiling. There was another fireplace in here where logs glowed in the grate. The walls were lined with books and framed awards.

The old doctor came forward and kissed Isabel on both cheeks.

'Hello, my dear Isabel. How are you?' He took Isabel's hand and gave her another quick kiss.

He was grey-haired and had a slight stoop and wore a pinstriped three-piece suit, with a watch chain across the front of the waistcoat, and a bright multi-coloured bow tie that looked somewhat out of place.

'And this is your daughter, almost as beautiful as her mother,' he said, peering at Ellie over his half-moon glasses.

'Good afternoon, young lady. Please sit down both of you.'

Ellie felt her flesh creep.

He asked her all the usual questions – how long she had been pregnant, the date of her last period. Rising, he asked her to go into the next room so he could examine her.

After a close examination, he patted her on the arm and said, 'Put your clothes on, my dear, then join us when you are ready.'

Ellie dressed and stood at the door for a moment to listen to them talking.

'She's about fourteen weeks. I presume your daughter agrees with the termination, Isabel?'

'Yes… And I need this, Geoffrey. I can't allow anything to stand in the way of Ian's knighthood.'

'I see. Well, if you leave her with me today, we can operate in the morning, and then she can go home in the afternoon, all being well. How is that?'

'Perfect. I have booked a hotel to be with her.'

Ellie felt the blood drain from her face and quickly bent down to put her head between her knees. Steeling herself and gathering all the strength she could muster, for there was no way they could know that she had overheard. Ellie entered the room and stood before them.

'Are you all right? My dear, you look a little pale,' said the doctor, peering over the top of his glasses.

Ellie forced a smile.

'Yes, thank you. I think I got up off the bed too quickly, and I need to powder my nose; would you excuse me, please?'

'Perhaps you would be kind enough to give me a sample at the same time? It's out of the door and down the corridor on the left.' The doctor turned to Isabel. 'Now, my dear, Isabel, how are you?'

Ellie picked up her purse and took the sample bottle the doctor offered her, thanked him, and walked out of the door, closing it behind her. She turned right and let herself out of the front door. Once outside, she fled down the street and turned up another to get as far away as possible.

It was dark and still raining. Ellie looked along the row of houses. One had no basement light on. She slipped down the steps, closing the gate behind her, to hide in the darkness. Tears of anger stung her eyes. How could she have been so stupid as to have trusted her mother? Her tears turned to sobs. She did not hear the basement door open and almost jumped out of her skin when someone touched her arm.

A middle-aged woman was standing in the light of the doorway.

'Now then, dearie, what is the matter? You'd better come inside. No coat in this weather – you will catch your death of cold. And you look as if you could do with a cuppa.'

Ellie followed the woman into a neat living room and looked at her rescuer. Her hair was a salt-and-pepper grey, and she was tall and thin, with a kind face.

'Sit down, dearie. You look all in.'

Ellie sat on the chair beside the fire, tears falling onto her lap, and watched as the woman took the metal poker and prodded the fire into life, and then swung the kettle over it to boil the water for tea.

Ellie felt cold and began to shake.

'Here, have this,' said the woman, taking a shawl off her chair and wrapping it around Ellie's shoulders. Such kindness from a stranger made Ellie cry again.

The woman took the boiling kettle into the kitchen to make the tea and returned with two steaming cups on a tray.

'Now, now, dearie, you drink this. I have put a drop of brandy in it to warm you up,' said the woman, holding out a beautiful Spode teacup.

Ellie took the cup and nursed it in her hands, trying to warm herself. The smell of the brandy rose from the hot drink and relaxed her.

The woman took her cup and sat opposite Ellie on the other side of the fire, sipping her tea.

'My name is Betty Wright, and you can call me Betty. I am the house keeper for the big house upstairs. Only one old bachelor, well set in his ways, but generous to a fault. So, he won't mind you being here. Will you tell me your name?'

'Eleanor, but my friends call me Ellie.'

'So, Ellie it is. What has happened? Is there anything I can do? Will you tell me?'

Ellie took another sip of her tea and took a deep breath.

'I don't know where to start.'

'I find the beginning is usually the best, dearie.'

Ellie told her about Gino, her time in Sardinia. About Simon, about the baby and her mother. Finding Betty easy to talk to and was surprised as the words came tumbling out; never realising how much she needed to talk to someone.

Finally, Ellie told her about the appointment.

Betty gasped.

'What are you going to do? Have you anywhere to go? Do you have any money?'

'Yes, I have a key to Simon's house and enough money for a taxi. I can go there and stay with him.'

'Are you sure you will be all right, dearie?'

Ellie smiled at Betty. 'Yes, thank you. Thank you for listening to me, and for the tea. I was so frightened that my mother would find me. It has been wonderful to have someone to talk to, without being judged. Thank you.'

'I will go up to make sure everything is in order and then hail a taxi, and you'll get straight in. Now, can I get you another cup of tea?'

'No, thank you. That was just what I needed.'

Betty took hold of Ellie's hand and held it tight.

'One more thing, Ellie. I know it's none of my business, dearie, but if your Simon loves you, if he will take on another man's child and if he will stand up for you against your mother… well, being *in love* is all very fine, but *love* is something else. Love comes in many forms: gentle or passionate, obsessive, or free, unrequited, or shared. Some are happy just to love, while others need love and to be needed. Whatever form it comes in, grab it, Ellie, for it can slip away and you will live to regret it, leaving you to become old and bitter. You had a great love with Gino, but who is to say it would have lasted forever? Some loves are like shooting stars lighting up the sky, while others are a constant light, always there. You have Simon, who will, I am sure, love you and the baby forever. He will be your constant light and he will care for you. Being cared for is the most wonderful thing. Think about it; don't throw it away without a thought. After all, you have known Simon for many years now.'

Ellie thought a moment about *love* and *in love*. Gino had said the same thing about Maria. Perhaps there were many kinds of love.

Betty squeezed Ellie's arm.

'The love you had for Gino only comes once in a lifetime. If you are lucky, friendship and companionship are lasting, and I don't think you will regret being with Simon,' said Betty, putting her arm around Ellie. 'Listen to me, telling you what to do. You keep the shawl, dearie; you can always return it another day. You can't go out there without a coat, it is far too wet and cold.'

Ellie smiled at Betty and handed back her teacup. Betty took their cups into the tiny kitchen, collected her cardigan, and let herself out of the door. Ellie followed her up the steps and watched as Betty flagged down a taxi.

It was dark. The street lights shone on the wet road. Ellie pulled the shawl around her shoulders and opened the taxi door. Turning to Betty, kissed her on the cheek.

'Thank you, thank you for everything, and for being so understanding.'

'Off with you, dearie, before you catch your death of cold. Take care and remember what I said.'

Ellie gave the cabbie Simon's address, and, with a quick wave, they set off.

'Cabbie, can you tell me what house number and street that was where the lady lives, please?'

He told her Betty's address, and Ellie sat back in her seat and watched the world go by and wondered if her mother was still looking for her, or if Isabel had gone to the hotel, or back home.

They drove in silence and arrived at Eaton Mews. The cabbie dropped her outside the door, and Ellie thanked him and paid, giving him a small tip.

'I'm afraid that is all I have.' Said Ellie looking distressed.

'Give me a smile and that will be fine.' Said the cabbie laughing.

She smiled and thanked him again as he waved and drove off.

Ellie fumbled in her purse to find the key and let herself in his flat, went upstairs, and turned on the light. She loved Simon's home. There was a large sitting room, simply furnished with two armchairs and a big sofa with velvet cushions; Persian rugs were on the floor and floral Colefax and Fowler curtains hung at the windows. Books were everywhere, on the shelves, on the table and in piles on the floor. Ellie knew how much books meant to Simon, but she was still surprised to see so many. The collection seemed to get larger every time she came here. Ellie realised she did not really know much about his personal side, only that he was her very best friend.

Ellie turned on the electric fire, pulled the curtains, and went into the kitchen to make herself a cup of coffee. She found a spare blanket in the cupboard in his bedroom and was surprised to see a photo of herself and Simon on his bedside table. She picked it up and looked at it and smiled, Lawrence or Polly must have taken it on the farm while haymaking, they were brown from working in the fields and looked happy. She put the photo back on the table and turned out the light, in case her mother came looking for her, then settled on the sofa with her coffee to think over what Betty had said.

Simon arrived home to find Ellie curled up on the sofa, fast asleep. His spirits rose when he saw her. He opened a bottle of wine, found two glasses, and sat down beside her.

Ellie woke with a start, and seeing Simon, threw her arms around him and burst into tears again. In jumbled sentences, she told him what had happened and that her mother was looking for her.

Simon rose and picked up the telephone receiver. He dialled the operator and asked for long-distance to be put through to Ellie's home number. It was her father who answered.

'Sir, this is Simon Smythe here. I have your daughter with me in London. Please tell your wife that Ellie is safe and won't be coming home for a while.'

'Why is Eleanor with you?'

'I think, sir, that's a question for your wife to answer. All you need to know is that Ellie is well and with me. Good evening, sir.'

Simon put the phone down and turned to Ellie.

'I don't know about you, but I need something to eat. Will an omelette be all right? I'm quite a dab hand at making them.'

Ellie smiled and nodded. She was lucky to have such a sympathetic friend. Simon was starting to prepare the meal in the kitchen when the phone rang.

He picked it up.

'Yes, she is with me, and no, you can't see her. Ellie may be underage, but only by a few weeks. I suggest you go home and leave Ellie to me. Good evening.'

And with that, he put the phone down.

They sat over the meal together and Simon took her hand.

'Ellie, I know I will never take Gino's place, and I know too, you will always hold him in your heart, but is there a possibility you could find a place for me too?'

'Simon, I'm very fond of you, you know that. We have always been the closest of friends. I see you even have a photo of us in your bedroom, I could not help seeing it when I looked for a blanket. They were happy days.'

'Yes, it reminds me of happy times and I've always loved that photo of you.'

'You're an old romantic at heart.' She said.

'Not so much of the old, please. But Ellie, listen to me. After today, you must know that your mother will put pressure on you to give the baby away. Isabel will stop at nothing as she cannot accept that I want to marry you because I love you and want to look after you both. She will be relieved it has avoided a scandal that she thinks would reflect badly on her and her husband. Please, Ellie, I beg of you, for all our sakes, think about it. Perhaps we can pick up again from before your time in Sardinia.'

The doorbell rang. They looked at one another.

'Your mother. Go into the bedroom and I will get rid of her. Stay up here. Do you understand?'

Simon ambled down the stairs into the hall and opened the door. Isabel pushed her way in, but Simon stood to bar her way up the stairs.

'Where is my daughter?'

'Ellie is upstairs. No, you cannot see her. You have already done enough damage.'

'Simon you don't know the half of it,' sneered Isabel.

'I know all I need to know.'

'She's pregnant with another man's child,' said Isabel, 'I bet you didn't know that. Eleanor has no idea what it will do to her father and his position in the Foreign Office. He's up for an honour and this will not help.'

'Being in the Foreign Office myself, Isabel, I'm sure one illegitimate child will not make a lot of difference to your husband's position. If it did, I fear there would not be many lords in the House. Ellie has told me everything. I know all I need to know. Now, if you would be kind enough to leave my house… or I will physically remove you.'

'Eleanor's my daughter and is underage. I will call the police and say you are holding her against her will.'

'Then treat her like a daughter. As for holding her against her will, that would be difficult to prove, and I would tell them you were going to have an illegal termination with your friendly gynecologist.'

Isabel opened her mouth and closed it again and, turning on her heel, walked out of the door.

Simon locked it behind her and went upstairs to find Ellie.

That night they lay in his bed and talked, he in his pyjamas and she in one of his large t-shirts. Simon felt he had to be so careful with her, but with luck, Ellie would marry him, and he would be the happiest man alive.

'Do you remember the first time you came to stay with us, Ellie? You were only about six and I was nine. We all had to come home for the terrible January. You and Polly shared a room.'

'Yes, I remember. I think we spent most of the night talking and were always tired in the morning. I remember the first time I tried to milk one of the cows. Polly was in stitches as she watched me trying to get the milk into the bucket.'

Simon sighed as Ellie continued.

'It was so cold, we had to break the ice in the cattle troughs in the fields for the animals to drink. But coming back into the kitchen to the smell of baking bread, sitting at the table for hot chocolate or Ovaltine, then going into the dining room with Nanny to do our schoolwork with the fire roaring in the grate… wonderful memories. I was so happy with your parents; they treated me as if I was one of the family. Happy, carefree days.'

Simon smiled as he too remembered those carefree days.

'Your mother used to bake bread every day. Polly and I used to bake cakes on Tuesdays, Thursdays, and Saturdays, and no sooner had we baked them than you boys would come in and eat half of the cakes. Do you remember how Laurence had his hand slapped by your mother because he always took three pieces of bread or toast?' Ellie said, laughing.

'I remember everything,' said Simon. 'Like the time you were out in the yard and fell in the mud. You were covered from head to toe, but you just got up, wiped yourself down, and got on with whatever it was you were doing. I think that was the time that I realised you were special…'

'And you told me you would marry me one day.'

'And you told me not to be so soppy.'

They laughed at the shared memories.

Ellie dropped off to sleep, snuggled up to Simon for comfort.

The following morning, Simon made coffee and brought it to Ellie, who had slept in his arms. He looked at her, still asleep, and his heart ached for her. Catching his reflection in the mirror he looked rough and unshaven; he had slept little, savouring the closeness of the woman he loved and praying she would be his.

Ellie stirred and sat up. An aching pit was in her stomach – fear, sickness, or loneliness; it was there every morning.

'That coffee smells wonderful. Would you promise to wake me like this every morning?' she said, falling back onto the pillows.

'Yes, if you marry me, and for as long as I can.'

'I can't marry you until I'm twenty-one. I will need my parent's permission.'

'We can marry today. I can get a special licence; I have some very influential friends and connections. You only have to say the word, dearest Ellie.'

They sipped their coffee together.

Ellie looked at him. She had woken in the night and lain thinking about what Betty had said. Her mother's behaviour certainly would not change. Ellie had heard about the homes for unmarried girls and knew she could never give Gino's baby away. Simon had stirred and pulled her into his arms, and she had finally dropped back to sleep.

'I'll marry you tomorrow,' Ellie said, 'but on one condition: I want Betty Wright as my witness.'

Simon took her hands in his and kissed her fingers.

'Darling Ellie, you won't regret this, I promise.'

That day, Ellie's mother made a nuisance of herself by ringing Simon's phone, until he was forced to take it off the hook.

Simon rang into the office to ask for compassionate leave as he was about to be married. On learning of his need for a licence, his friends and colleagues rallied round and promised to organise the documents for the marriage.

Ellie went out early to go shopping and found a smart outfit for the event. Simon took a taxi to find Betty and tell her Ellie's wish. Betty and Simon made some arrangements together, after which he collected the licence from the office. All his colleagues gathered around him and wished him the best of luck.

Simon took another taxi to Regent Street, where he chose a ring, with a guarantee from the jeweller he would change it if it did not fit or if Ellie didn't like it.

He phoned his parents to tell them the news.

'Simon, how wonderful!' said his mother. 'We are so happy for you. Where is the service?'

'At Chelsea Register Office but come to the mews first.'

'We will be there. Do you want us to bring up Ellie's parents, or are they already in London?'

'No, but thanks. Ellie doesn't want them at the wedding.'

There was a silence at the other end of the phone.

'But they are her parents.'

'Forget it, please, Mama. They have been dreadful to her. Trust me here, please. I will explain sometime.'

'Are you all right, Simon?'

'Over the moon, Mama. Over the moon.'

He put a call into Italy to tell Polly the news.

'Oh Simon,' she enthused,' You should have let us know before and we could have come over.'

'I didn't know myself until this morning.' He said laughing.

'Come and spend your honeymoon here. All the best of luck and give Ellie my love. Take care, Simon. Love you both.'

And in typical Polly style, she rang off.

That night Simon asked a friend if he could sleep on his sofa, but Ellie would not hear of it, insisting he stayed with her. As a compromise, he slept on the sofa.

'It's bad luck to see you before the wedding.'

The following morning, with all plans in place. Simon sent a taxi round to collect Betty, who arrived in a smart navy-blue dress over which she wore a very expensive blond mink coat with matching mink berret. Simon's parents arrived at the flat and introductions were made all round.

A–J was wearing his best three-piece suit and looked uncomfortable as he played with the collar and tie. Bea looked amazing with her hair swept up in a french twist with a fashionable little pillbox hat which matched her pale blue tweed suit.

Ellie was wearing a loose-fitting dress made of very pale pink silk, a matching coat edged in darker pink and a neat pillbox hat completed the outfit. Her bouquet, which she had ordered, was of the same pink and cream as her outfit and looked stunning. Simon was wearing his best suit, and the two of them made a handsome pair.

Simon opened a bottle of champagne and shared it round.

'I know it's a bit early for this, but it isn't everyday I marry the woman I love.' Said Simon beaming from ear to ear.

Bea came forward and took Ellie's hand in hers.

'You look wonderful, and I know you will make Simon extremely happy. I know, too, that he will look after you, my dear. I could not be happier for you both. I feel you have been a part of our family for such a long time already. I'm just sorry your parents aren't here.'

A-J came over and took Ellie in his arms, giving her a big bear hug.

'Welcome, dear girl, welcome to our family.'

'Thank you, A-J. I promise I will look after him.'

'I know you will, dear girl.'

They all climbed into a taxi and headed to the registry office for the quick service. After they had been pronounced man and wife, Simon gently took Ellie into his arms.

'Darling Ellie, never doubt my love. I promise to always look after you both,' he said, giving her a quick hug.

Ellie smiled at him, but deep down there was that small pit in the bottom of her stomach, a moment of sadness. Betty came over and put her arm around her and whispered, 'Be happy, Ellie, be happy.'

'I will, Betty. You look amazing, and what a beautiful coat.'

'It was a present from the gentleman I work for. He said it was to keep me warm. I told you love comes in many ways,' said Betty with a wicked twinkle in her eye.

A photographer stepped forward.

'Smile, please. Pictures for the album, with compliments from the boys at the office,' he said. Simon smiled.

'Trust them to organise something.'

They had lunch at the Ritz, where they were given an excellent table that was laid out with flowers, beautiful crystal glasses, and a magnificent cake.

'Who did this?' asked Ellie, looking at the elegant table.

'We did,' said Simon. 'I could not have done it without Betty's help. The man Betty looks after is a great friend of the manager's, and when Betty told him about us, he said he wanted to help.'

It was a beautiful meal, and Simon held Ellie's hand under the table and squeezed it.

Ellie turned to him.

'Thank you for this. How kind people are.'

A-J rose to give the toast.

'We have known you, Ellie, since you were a child, and you

became part of our family over the years when your parents were away. Now, my dear, we welcome you as a true member of our family. I know Simon will love and care for you – if not, he will have us to answer to!'

Ellie looked at Simon and smiled and Betty clapped.

'Darling Ellie,' said Simon, leaning over and giving her a gentle kiss on her cheek.

That evening Simon's parents returned home to the farm. Simon and Ellie put Betty in a taxi, somewhat worse for the champagne she had enjoyed so much, and they returned to the mews to find a large bouquet of flowers on the doorstep.

Ellie picked them up and opened the card that was pinned to the wrapping paper.

Be as happy as we are and you will be all right
Love to you both
Mario and Polly

'Oh, Simon aren't they lovely, trust Polly to organise something.' She said.

Simon was smiling.

'Happy Ellie.'

'Yes, yes, thank you, Simon,' said Ellie.

'No, my darling, *thank you*.'

Ellie's father, Ian, was mystified about the quickness of the wedding and why he and Isabel had not been invited. But he was secretly pleased that his daughter's scandal would not affect his promotion, which he hoped would be in the form of a gong for all his work in the Foreign Office.

Isabel showed complete indifference. Her daughter was now married, avoiding any scandal for her husband. Isabel wanted and expected the Foreign Office to put her husband's name up for a knighthood; the thought of becoming Lady di Montford was all-important to her, what she had worked hard for, and with that, Lady di Montford could rest on her laurels.

Ellie and Simon settled into the mews house. Ellie blossomed away from her family and under Simon's care. He laid down the house rules about her parents coming to see her, but it proved unnecessary, as neither of them bothered to come or even ring to find out how their daughter was getting on.

It was Ellie's first home; one she could look after without her mother's influence. Simon, who felt as if all his Christmases had come at once, came home from work with a bunch of flowers and helped her with the supper. His Ridgeback came to live with them, and they would take him for walks in the evening if it wasn't raining or sit and read together or entertain new found friends.

Life was wonderful for Ellie. She thought of Gino and he lived in her heart. Thanking God that He had given Gino to her and had known a true love that would remain deep inside her. There were mornings when she woke with the pit in her stomach, but Ellie remembered what Gino had said about love and in love. There was no doubt Ellie loved Simon but was not in love with him, but then, he had enough love for the two of them.

Christmas was wonderful, spent at the farm with Bea and A-J. Ellie settled into family life and was lucky enough to feel well in her pregnancy.

Laurence had called to wish everyone a happy Christmas and to give the good news that Fiona was expecting a baby in March, but had a rough time, but was fortunately feeling better now. Much to the delight of Bea and A J.

Sometimes, though, Ellie woke in the night, when the tears came, and Simon would gently hold her and comfort her until she fell asleep again. Some days he came home to find her crying silently to herself, and he would enfold her in his arms and comfort her. He was sure that time would help.

In the spring, Ellie went shopping for oddments for the house, turning it from a house into a home. On one of her trips, she found a beautiful inlaid box in an antique shop and set about putting all the photos and mementoes from her time in Sardinia into the box, including the beautiful *Su Lasu* pendant. On one of her trips, Ellie found a gold locket and put Gino's hair in it with a photo of him. It made her think of Giovanna and she smiled.

Ellie was still wearing Gino's wedding ring on her right hand and knew that when the baby was born, it would be time to pack it away with all her other memories, to live her life with Simon. But until then she was reluctant to remove the ring, the last thing Gino had given her.

PART TWO

CHAPTER FOURTEEN

SARA
England, late May 2006

Sara opened the front door to the mews house, climbed up the stairs, and dropped her coat onto a chair in the sitting room.

The flat had been in her father's family for years and was always passed on to the eldest with the idea that anyone could use it when they wanted to stay over in London for the night. It was where Ellie and Simon, her grandparents, had started their married life, and then it was handed down to Adam, her father, who had given it to Sara on her eighteenth birthday. Although they had removed most of their things when they left, a few old books, ornaments and pictures remained. She loved the idea that the flat contained pieces from her parents and grandparents, it made it feel more homely and comforting.

Sara made herself a coffee, took it into the sitting room, and sank onto the large, sumptuous sofa, putting her feet up on the cushions. She had had a business lunch earlier and was not hungry. The warmth of the flat and the comfortable sofa worked their magic as she dropped into sleep.

Sara woke to the sound of rain from a late-spring storm beating against the window. She stretched out on the sofa and was just enjoying the peace when her phone rang. Her boss, Rob – did he never sleep?

Sara answered it, only to be assailed by him: no hello or greeting, but straight to the point. Typical Rob.

'I want you to go down to Italy. The manager of one of our branches has put his hands in the till to the tune of ten thousand euros, and he and his secretary have run off to some romantic island until the money runs out or he gets fed up with her.'

Sara smiled to herself. It was amazing how many times men ran off with their secretaries, only to get bored with them once the thrill of the illicit affair wore off.

'Sara, are you listening to me?'

'Yes, Rob, I'm all ears.'

'I want you to go down there and sort it out for me, please. You are the only one I can trust, and the only one capable of doing this. I am sorry to ask you, as I know you are on holiday now.'

'It will be fine, Rob, really.'

'I have arranged for everything. A taxi will collect you tomorrow at one o'clock to take you to Stansted Airport to be there at three o'clock. Go to the EasyJet flight desk; they will have all the details. I have arranged for you to stay in a little bed-and-breakfast until you find your feet. I know hotels are not your thing.

'Ring me when you have something to report. I will text you all the details. Okay?'

'Yes, okay, I'll be in touch.'

He rang off in his usual no-nonsense way.

She rose and made another coffee. Turned over the pile of mail to see if there was anything of interest or urgent. There was not.

Sara had planned to go down to Suffolk next week to see her grandmother, who lived in a little converted cottage on her parents' farm and was looking forward to it, as it had been six months since she had visited the family.

She sighed and rang her father to explain why she would not be down at the weekend as planned.

'Please tell Ellie I am sorry I won't see her this weekend, but I will contact her. And, Papa, give her my love.'

'I will. Take care of yourself, darling girl. Come and see us when you get back.'

Sara smiled and put her mobile phone down. Her father was always there for her, always willing to back her, even if he did not agree with her. When Sara was at university, studying modern languages, she had worked at the travel agency for her pocket money. Rob, the owner, had taken her under his wing, giving her more and more responsibility. He had finally offered her a job as a trouble-shooter, with a good starting salary, all the travel she wanted, and the promise of a promotion in the company. When Sara told her parents about leaving the university, her mother had gone silent on her after the initial row, but her father had encouraged her to follow her heart, to do whatever she wanted. Sara sighed; she loved her father. She knew her grandmother would also be disappointed not to see her; Ellie always made Sara feel so special.

The following morning Sara packed, and the taxi arrived to take her to the airport. Sara checked in at the flight desk and was surprised to find the flight was to Cagliari in Sardinia, not the mainland. She had thought it would be Rome or Turin; that was where they usually had the trouble.

The flight down to Cagliari was good. It was after eight when they circled the city on the way to the airport. The lights shone and twinkled below, and it surprised Sara to feel an unexpected rush of excitement.

They landed and the passengers poured out into the airport. After collecting her case, Sara walked out into the arrivals area. A short man with a thick beard was holding a piece of paper with her name, *Signorina Smythe*, on it. Sara moved forward to meet him.

'Please, *signorina*, let me take your case,' said the man. 'Please to follow me,' he said in his broken English.

Sara gave him the case but kept hold of her overnight bag, which contained her passport and various documents and followed him outside to the waiting taxi.

'Do you know where to go?' she asked in her perfect Italian.

'Yes, *signorina*.'

It was dark and the journey was unremarkable until they came to the old part of the city.

'This area is Stampace,' said the taxi driver with an air of pride in his voice. The narrow, one-way streets were so close that in some places another car could not pass.

The driver found The Place, then helped her out with her

bags and handing them over to the porter. Sara thanked the driver and tipped him.

She booked in and was then shown to her room. It was a small suite, with an adjoining bathroom and a comfortable sitting room. Everyone was so welcoming that Sara immediately felt at home. She thanked and tipped the porter.

Left on her own, she crossed the room to look out of the window. The street was so narrow, and it was possible to peer into the rooms of the houses opposite. Sara watched as the silhouette of someone moving in one of the rooms opposite. She turned to the left and saw a little square with a large, floodlit church.

Sara smiled; she was going to like Cagliari.

Closing the shutters, she unpacked her overnight bag and left everything else in the case; she would sort it out later. Sara sat on the bed and rang her father.

Later, after washing and freshening up, Sara went down to find a restaurant.

The man at the desk came to greet her.

'Good evening, *signorina*. I hope you enjoy your stay.'

'I'm sure I will. Can you tell me where I can get something to eat?'

'Turn left out of the door, go down to the bottom of the road to the church, turn left, and walk up to Piazza Yenne. You will find some excellent restaurants there. *Buon appetito.*'

Sara found a restaurant in the square, which was alive with people, eating, chattering, sitting under the large canvas gazebos. Lights twinkled everywhere and the place had the atmosphere of a grand room. The locals were wrapped in coats or fur jackets, but Sara found it warm in the late May evening.

After studying the menu, she chose the house wine and a set menu and enjoyed the most amazing Bavette steak she had ever eaten, with a helping of roasted vegetables. She sipped the glass of red wine and felt herself relax. The Italian chatter around her made her feel at home. She would enjoy her stay here; of that she was sure.

Feeling tired, Sara returned to her room, undressed, fell into the large double bed, and went straight to sleep.

The metal clang of the bells from the nearby church calling the faithful to early Mass woke Sara. She took a moment to recall where she was, then fell back onto her pillow. The sun was pouring through the window and a gentle breeze stole up the narrow street, pausing to enter the windows. She lay in bed and thought over past events.

Her beloved grandfather had died two years ago, leaving her a small inheritance. Sara had told her boss and taken time off to fly home to be with her family for the funeral. It had been a tough time for her darling grandmother. Ellie and Simon had been inseparable, and now Ellie was having to face life without her right-hand man. She had been beside herself with the loss; she and Simon had been so close for all their time together. The farm seemed strange too without Simon. But over the past two years, Ellie had picked up the pieces and put her life back together. She was so resilient; it was a trait that Sara admired so much in her grandmother.

Sara's father, Adam, had been distraught at the loss of his father, with whom he had always been so close, but as he said, at least with a heart attack it was quick.

Adam had grown up on the farm and had been expected to follow the family tradition of joining the Foreign Office. He loved the farm and the outdoor life, but when a well-paid junior post came up in France for a year, he had taken it.

While there, he followed the usual round of social events, parties with the same boring people who either drank too much or hopped into one another's beds. It was at one of these social events that he had met Jayne, a highflyer who had won a scholarship to a minor public school in England and developed a chip on her shoulder with a need to climb the social ladder. Jayne seduced Adam, taking him to her bed to make sure she would keep him.

So it was that after knowing her for only four months, Adam

took Jayne home to meet his parents, and announced he was getting married, and that Jayne was pregnant. It had upset Ellie, as she felt they would never be happy together.

The wedding was a social affair; after all, that was why Jayne had married Adam, to get her name in *Tatler* and *Country Life*. Jayne had taken her parents out to buy them new outfits for the wedding, knowing that they would never have the occasion to wear them again.

Polly and Mario came over from Italy. Polly, her hair seemed to get redder, no doubt with a little bit of help from a bottle, but her eyes remained vivid green, she was her usual stunning self and Mario, tall and as handsome as ever. They had not had any children and worked tirelessly at the vineyard. They spent time flying around the world to meet new customers or renew old friendships; their love for one another as plain today as it was all those years ago when they first met and married.

Sara had been born seven months after Adam and Jayne's wedding. Adam stayed in the Foreign Office, and Jayne insisted on hiring a nurse for Sara so she could join her husband as he performed his duties, and again, see her name in the social columns.

It was ten years after Sara was born that her father arrived home one evening with a bunch of flowers and a bottle of champagne and told Jayne over dinner that he had thrown in his job at the Foreign Office. He was going home to help run the farm, he announced, as Simon was getting older and was not in the best of health. The row that followed could be heard from one end of the mews to the other. The ranting and raving became grunts and then moans, which finally fell into a lengthy silence.

It was two days before Jayne would speak to him. They moved out of the mews house and down to Suffolk. Adam and Jayne moved into the large farmhouse, and Simon and Ellie moved into the barn conversion that Adam had done for them.

Jayne resented the fact that her husband had left his job without asking her, and her resentment spilt over onto Sara. Jayne was convinced that if they had had a son, Adam would not have given everything up. She resented that he wanted more children while hating the thought of a large family; being a farmer's wife did not have the same ring or prestige as a diplomat's wife, however minor the job. Besides the three-bedroomed mews house had been easy to run, the seven-bedroom farmhouse was another thing altogether.

Sara was packed off to boarding school, much against her father's wishes, at an early age, then sent to a finishing school in Switzerland to polish the languages her grandmother had taught her, and then, finally, on to university.

She had also spent long summer holidays in Italy with her great Aunt Polly and her husband Mario. Carefree days working in the vineyards or shopping with Polly.

Sara sighed. She had hoped to spend more time with her grandmother, but when her boss called, she needed to go.

She turned over in bed. When this was over, she would spend some time with her family. Sara looked at her watch: eight o'clock. Was that UK time or European time?

'Hell, it's UK time,' she exclaimed.

Time to get up and explore. She put her watch on one hour and then showered, dressed, and went downstairs. An old woman sat at the reception desk.

'*Buongiorno, signorina.*'

'*Buongiorno, Signora.* Could you please tell me where I can find a café to have breakfast?'

The woman gave her a voucher and directions to a café by the church of Saint Anna.

The cafe was jostling with local people chatting together, drinking their coffee, and eating sticky buns. It was a welcoming atmosphere. Sara ordered a coffee and a doughnut and sat sipping the hot liquid and enjoying the sugary bun. Somehow, she felt at home amongst these people.

Sara spent the morning wandering around the city, finally finding herself up on San Remy, where there was a Sunday market. Stalls sold goods like antiques, clothes, books, and music tapes. People bargained or haggled with one another, each desperate to get the best deal. By one o'clock the market had packed up and all the people had gone to have their lunch. Sara found a bar nearby, and ordered a drink and a snack, and sat eating, looking out over the city. From her elevated position, she could see right down to the harbour. The sun was warm on her face, the gentle breeze coming off the sea, bringing a freshness to the air.

In the afternoon, Sara looked up the address of the office and wandered down to find it so she could go straight there in the morning, not wanting to be late on her first day. She found the office in the Via Manno. It was just off the Piazza Yenne and she realised it would be easy to get to in the morning.

Satisfied she knew how to get to the office, Sara walked on down towards the port to watch the boats coming and going. Expensive yachts bobbed at anchor in what looked like a new marina. The breeze rattled the riggings, flapping the pennants that flew from the different yachts. The sounds of people tinkering with their boats, yachting activities, came across the port.

She turned to walk along the port, then crossed the road to the Via Roma, where there were several bars. Sara sat outside one, ordered a coffee and sat sipping it, and watched the big red sun sink into the sea, and sighed with contentment.

In the evening, Sara found a restaurant on a side street off the Via Roma that specialised in local food. There were several set-price menus, she opted for a mid-priced one, and enjoyed an antipasto, malloreddus – a local pasta, she was informed by the waiter, who was happy to find a foreigner who spoke such good Italian – followed by a grilled pork chop cooked with butter and sage and rounded off by ice cream and coffee.

Sara made her way back to her B&B. It had been a pleasant day. In her room, she threw off her shoes, sat on the bed, and phoned her father. The two of them chattered together for half an hour until they finally had to say goodnight.

152

CHAPTER FIFTEEN

Monday morning, Sara was up early and standing at the office agency door, waiting for the staff to arrive. Sara introduced herself to them all, explained what she was doing, and went through everything with them. The staff comprised two junior girls, Maria and Olivia, and a young man called Fabio, all of whom ran the office well and were shocked that their boss had left with his secretary.

Maria had secretarial experience, so Sara upped her wages and put her in charge. She was more than capable of running the entire operation but was not keen on taking all the responsibility. When Sara suggested she share it with Fabio, Maria agreed.

The other junior girl, Olivia, was a little shy, so Sara put her to work sorting out the brochures, making the coffee and greeting clients, whom Olivia would pass on to either Maria or Fabio. Sara knew that Olivia would soon develop skills and would be as confident as the others within a month or two.

All that week, Sara saw clients and helped in the office. She had inherited her grandmother's charm, and her natural way with people always paid dividends.

At the end of the week, her boss called her.

'You have done a grand job. I'm pleased with everything,' Rob hesitated, 'but Sara, could you stay on for a couple more weeks until I find a replacement for the office?'

Sara laughed. 'You don't want me home then? I'll stay. I love it here. It will be like a holiday.'

On hearing Sara was staying, her work colleagues took her out for a celebratory evening drink at their usual meeting place. The Antico Caffé was buzzing with locals. They found a table outside on the terrace and ordered drinks and nibbles.

'Are you okay where you are staying?' Olivia said. 'Why don't you rent a flat and have a place of your own for the time you are here? My aunt has a flat she rents out to special people up in Casteddu. You would love it there, even for a short time.'

Sara thought for a moment. She would have to move everything up there.

As if reading her mind, Olivia added, 'We can all come to help you move; then we can come to supper with you. We will bring the food. What do you say?' a broad smile on her beautiful face.

'All right. I'll get a chicken for supper,' said Sara.

'Great,' said Olivia, and turned to the others. 'Sara wants to move to Casteddu. You will help me move her, won't you?'

They all agreed, and Olivia took out her phone and rang her aunt. Turning to Sara, she put her thumb up, thanked her aunt, and rang off.

That night Sara thanked the owner of the B & B, paid her bill, and then went up to her room to pack.

The following morning, her three colleagues were there with Fabio's car. They loaded everything in and drove up to Casteddu. Olivia jumped out of the car and banged on a great door; which was immediately opened by a short, round woman wearing a black headscarf.

'Zia, this is my friend Sara, come to stay. We have brought all her things.'

They all trooped up the first, then the second flight of stairs, and entered a spacious room. It had two French windows, both with shutters. Linen curtains framed the windows, which opened out with a view of the street. Two big sofas sat opposite each other in the room, together with odd armchairs. At the far end of the room, there was a dining table and chairs. Off the main room were the kitchen and a bathroom. The bedroom, which was also large, faced the street. It was cool and inviting.

Sara thanked Olivia and her aunt. The rent was agreed upon and paid.

'No men in the room, *signorina*,' said the aunt.

'No, Zia, she is a good girl,' said Olivia, laughing.

Sara thanked everyone, and they all hurried down to the car and off to work.

It was a busy day in the office, but Sara found time to buy a chicken for the evening as they were all coming for supper.

It was a wonderful evening. Everyone contributed something: Fabio brought wine and a very extravagant pudding, Olivia brought a salad with the antipasto, Sara cooked the chicken and Maria arrived with bread and ingredients for pasta. They all chattered as they cooked together. They laid the table, and everyone sat down to eat.

Sara watched them all and sighed. She had never felt so at home in a place in such a short time.

'A toast,' said Maria. 'To Sara, the best boss we have ever had.'

'To Sara,' they chorused.

'Thank you for making me feel so at home,' said Sara, a lump in her throat. She smiled and thanked them all, overwhelmed, and feeling a tiny prick of tears in her eyes.

'You will be happy here,' said Olivia. 'You won't want to go home.'

Two weeks had passed since Sara had moved into the flat. Olivier's aunt had given her a key to the outside door, so Sara would not disturb the family as she came and went. The whole flat had taken on a look of home. The bookcases bulged with books bought from the market, and flowers grew in pots on shelves and large containers by the windows and out on the balcony. At the antique markets, she had bought some Sardinian pottery and pictures, which gave the place a homely touch.

Sara wondered if she did really want to leave here or whether to ask Rob if she could stay for a while. Sara felt at peace here among these people.

Her phone rang. It was Polly.

'My dear Sara, how are you. I spoke to Ellie yesterday and

she said you were in Sardinia and enjoying it. I have one word of warning. The Sardinian men are romantic and beguiling. Be careful.' She said laughing. 'Take care and keep in touch, love you.'

And she rang off. Sara sighed, Polly was like a breath of fresh air touching base with everyone and then gone.

One evening a few days later, her colleagues took her to the Antico Caffé. They had a superb meal and they introduced her to many of their friends. It was a relaxed evening, which turned into a late do, and Sara had thoroughly enjoyed it.

'Don't be late tomorrow,' Fabio said as they parted. 'We have that important client coming early in the morning.'

'I won't be late, don't worry,' she replied.

Sara woke the following morning with a start and looked at her watch.

'Shit! I'm going to be late.'

She showered and dressed, cursing her lateness. No time for coffee; she could have one at the office. Grabbing her phone and her bag, Sara raced down the stairs. The front door was ajar; she raced out into the street – and straight into someone.

'Shit!' Sara exclaimed as the contents of her handbag spilt all over the granite paving, her mobile phone clattering across the cobbles. She bent to pick everything up, still cursing to herself, and stood up, stuffing everything back into her bag. Sara had not seen whom she bumped into but turned to swear at them. He was tall with dark curly hair and even darker eyes and Sara momentarily thought she knew him but dismissed it.

'I'm late,' she stammered.

'Nothing is worth that hurry,' he replied.

Sara turned to go.

'Not even an apology?'

Sara threw him an apologetic look and raced on down the street. She did not want to be late for this meeting.

She arrived at the office just before the client was due.

'Two cups of coffee, please, Olivia.'

'Both for you,' Olivia replied with a broad grin.

Sara chaired the meeting with the representative from a London travel company who was looking to set up a branch in Sardinia. Everything went very well, and they agreed a deal. There were handshakes all round, and then Sara took him out for a meal.

That evening, Sara joined Fabio, Maria, and Olivia for a glass of wine on the way home at their usual meeting place, the Antico caffè. They were celebrating, as Rob had rung to say how pleased he was with the outcome of the deal.

Some of Olivia's friends were sitting at the back corner table on the outside terrace.

They waved to her to join them, and Olivia introduced Sara to them.

They all sat at the table drinking house wine, sharing nibbles, and chatting. Sara had bought a postcard to send to her grandmother; Ellie would love this place. She jotted a few words on the card, sending her love; she would post it on the way home.

Another man joined them, and he was greeted with hugs and kisses by everyone. Olivia introduced Sara to him.

'This is Luca,' they all chorused.

Sara looked at him and blushed.

'We have already met, but briefly,' he said. 'I see you are not in such a hurry now.'

'Where did you meet?' asked one girl.

'We bumped into each other this morning,' said Luca, sitting down beside Sara.

Everyone continued their chatting. As Luca and Sara sat talking to one another, the rest of the world seemed to fade away. One by one the others left for their supper or evening activities.

'Are you coming, Luca?' asked the girl who had asked where they met.

'Not just yet, Monica, see you tomorrow.'

She shrugged and glared at Sara, then left.

Luca turned to Sara and smiled.

'You've upset her,' said Sara.

'I don't think so. Monica is a long-standing family friend.'

'By the look on her face, I would say it is more than that.'

'Maybe, but she's like a sister to me.'

Sara looked at him and smiled.

'So, tell me about yourself,' said Sara.

'What can I tell you? I am a professor at the university. Like my father, who is a professor of archaeology, and my grandfather, who was a professor of languages. I live in Casteddu, further up from where you are.'

He paused, looking at her quizzically.

'Why are you in Sardinia? What do you do here, apart from bumping into men in the street?'

Sara laughed.

'I came to Sardinia by chance. My boss needed someone to sort out our office here, so he sent me. I never thought I would like it here, but in fact, I love Cagliari.'

'You should get out to see the island. I have to travel around; perhaps you could take some time off and come with me. There are some wonderful ancient sites to see. Are you interested in ancient history?'

'Yes, I love old things.'

'You have Stonehenge. Have you seen it?' he asked.

'Yes, I saw it when I was a child, then with some friends who came to stay. It is amazing.'

'I want to see it one day. Why don't you join me for supper here? The food is excellent, and we can talk.'

They enjoyed a meal together, and then had coffee and a liqueur, neither of them wanting the evening to end.

It was late when they walked up to Casteddu together.

'If we go up this way, there is a post box at the top,' he said, pointing to the card Sara had in her hand, a big grin on his face.

They found the post box, and Sara posted the card to her grandmother.

'Ellie loves receiving cards when I am away.'

Finally, they came to Sara's house.

'I would ask you in for a coffee, but my landlady is a bit of a Tartar,' said Sara.

'Yes, I know. I know her well.'

'Oops!' said Sara putting her hand up to her mouth.

They both laughed. He bent and kissed her gently on the cheek.

'Goodnight, Sara. I hope we can do this again?'

She smiled and opened the large front door to the hallway.

'Good evening, *signorina*,' said her landlady.

Sara looked back at Luca and they both laughed.

CHAPTER SIXTEEN

ELLIE
England, June 2006

Ellie pressed the button on the coffee machine, watching the dark liquid stain the milk. The aroma rose to fill her senses – a flicker of a memory. She pushed the other button, wanting a longer coffee this morning. This wonderful, clever little machine was a present from her granddaughter, Sara, and Ellie loved it. She was not a tea drinker, and this was ideal for a quick pick-me-up.

Ellie took the cup and sat at the large kitchen table. It had been a restless night – sleep had been an elusive bed partner – and she felt tired.

Ellie felt lonely. It had been two years now since her darling Simon had died. He had had a stroke while working in his beloved garden. When she found him, he was still clutching the rose he had picked to bring her, as he always did. She had dried the rose, and it sat in a velvet frame beside her bed with a photo of her husband.

The shock put Ellie into a deep depression. Polly had come over from Italy for the funeral and stayed on for a week to help Ellie with some of the things that needed sorting. When Polly went back home it was Ellie's son, Adam, who had rallied round. He had arranged everything, helping her in every way possible. She was lucky to have such a wonderful family.

Ellie sighed. Sara had rung to say she was not coming down, as she had to go to Italy to sort something out in the office. She had been looking forward to seeing her granddaughter.

Ellie flicked through the mail that either her son or daughter-in-law had left on the table. Catalogues or leaflets; why was it that as soon as you turned sixty the post was full of adverts for hearing aids (deaf aids, her husband had always called them), stair-lifts, Saga cruises or retirement homes, not to mention knickers to keep you dry, together with aids for many, so far, unnecessary things.

Ellie sighed again and turned over the last brochure to look at the remaining post. A postcard from her granddaughter. She smiled, and picking it up, she read Sara's distinctive handwriting.

Hi, Ellie.
Weather great. This is our meeting place – you would love it here,
I know. All love, Sara

Ellie read and reread the card before finally turning it over and caught her breath. The caffé Genovese, now called Antico Caffé – nothing had changed, only the name. How long had it been? Forty years or more. She had buried that part of her life, put it in a box to forget it. In her mind's eye, Ellie could see Gino sitting in his usual seat, reading his paper and waiting for her; she felt the faintest touch of his hand on her elbow, the brush of his kiss on her cheek.

An uncontrollable sob came from the pit of her stomach as the memories came flooding back, and a large tear fell down her cheek.

CHAPTER SEVENTEEN

Sardinia, 2006

Two weeks passed before Sara heard from Luca again and she wondered if he had just been polite but not interested in her. So, when he rang on Friday to ask her if she could meet him at the Antico Caffé at about eight o'clock that evening, it was a pleasant surprise.

The café was busy when Sara arrived, and he was waiting by the gate on the terrace. He dropped her a quick kiss on both cheeks, and they made their way in.

'Hi, Luca,' called a man sitting at a table. 'Come and join me.'

'*Ciao*, Salvatore. How are you?' said Luca, taking Sara's hand and going over to the table on the terrace. 'Salvatore, this is Sara, Sara, Salvatore. He is an old family friend,' said Luca.

'Pleased to meet you,' said Salvatore. Rising, he gave Sara a quick peck on each cheek, then pulled a chair out for her. 'Sit down here, please.'

Luca gestured to a passing waiter for drinks all round and another chair. Everything arrived, plus some mixed meats and olives as an appetiser.

'Cheers,' said Salvatore. 'Now tell me, Sara, what are you doing in Cagliari? Are you on holiday or working?'

'I am working at a travel agency in the Via Manno.'

'Didn't they have some trouble with Piero, didn't he run off with his secretary to Corsica?'

'My, Cagliari is a small city for gossip,' said Sara laughing.

'It is, but how did you meet Luca?'

'She threw herself at me in the excitement of seeing me on her way to work,' Luca cut in, laughing.

'Is that your normal way of meeting people in England?' said Salvatore, looking at Sara with a serious expression.

'I was late for work, and he was in my way.'

They all laughed.

'You look well, Luca. Dig going well? Just yes or no will do.'

'Yes.'

'We need concise answers, otherwise, we have a complete rundown of the day's activity,' said Salvatore, a broad grin spreading across his weathered face.

'Tell me, what are you two doing next weekend? Only Giulia and I are having lunch with Carla and Matteo on Saturday; why don't you come too? You know you would be more than welcome.'

'That would be great; it's a date,' said Luca. 'All right with you, Sara?'

'Fine by me.'

'Right,' said Salvatore, 'I must be going. See you next week.'

He hugged Luca and whispered under his breath, 'You lucky devil.'

Luca and Sara finished their drinks, then ordered a meal.

'They are old friends. Our parents have known each other since school, so we go back a long way,' said Luca, taking her hand and squeezing it gently.

They talked about his work and his hopes as they ate together.

'I followed my father into archaeology. He was always very keen on it as a child. His father used to read him stories of the giants who lived in Sardinia, and now I am excavating giants at Monte Prama. He would have been amazed. And your work, you love it?'

'I do. I gave up university to join Rob, my boss. The job was interesting; he offered me a promotion to be a trouble-shooter for his company, and I jumped at it. Although I must admit my mother wasn't happy about me leaving Uni and going to work without a degree.'

The evening slipped by as they got to know one another, feeling at ease in each other's company.

'Coffee?' asked Luca.

'Please. Can we go Dutch on the bill?'

'Dutch, what is Dutch?' he said with feigned innocence.

Sara was about to explain when he leant over to kiss her on the cheek.

'You are my guest in my country.'

After the coffee, they walked back to Via Lamarmora. Luca took her hand and held it, squeezing it from time to time.

Outside the door to her house, he stood looking at her.

'Thank you for a lovely evening,' she said.

'I am sorry I didn't get in touch over the last two weeks, but I have been so busy, and by the time I dropped into bed it was too late to ring anyone.'

'I thought perhaps you weren't interested.'

He laughed.

'Take care. I will come down from Cabras to pick you up next Saturday morning. By the way, I forgot, can I have your phone number? I have mine here on a piece of paper, just in case you need to contact me.'

He pulled out his wallet and handed Sara a piece of paper with various numbers.

'You should be able to get me on my mobile, but if not, on one of the other numbers.'

Sara looked in her bag and found her business card.

'My mobile is on there. I usually have it with me so that Rob can contact me.'

He took the card and smiled as he put it in his wallet.

'Goodnight, Sara. I can't see you this weekend, as I have to go back to Cabras in the morning, but I just wanted to see you,' he said, pulling her into his arms. He kissed her gently, and when she did not pull away, he took her in his arms and kissed her with a passionate intensity.

'Goodnight again, Sara.'

'Goodnight, Luca, and thank you.'

'Saturday week. Bring your bathers,' he called.

'Saturday week,' she replied.

Sara spent the Saturday cleaning the flat, watering the plants, and pottering. She hung her washing on the line outside her window like the locals, chattering across the small ravine to her neighbours opposite.

In the evening, she made herself an omelette and settled down to ring Ellie. Sara had not spoken to her for a while and had missed the intimate conversations. They had a long chat together, Sara telling her everything that was going on and about the people she had met.

'I understand you are in Cagliari. Where are you living?' asked Ellie.

'In the old part of the city In the Via Lamarmora. The locals call it Casteddu e Susu.'

Sara heard a large intake of breath.

'Are you all right, Ellie?'

'Yes. Yes, I am fine. But if you will excuse me, Sara, suddenly I feel tired. I have been gardening. Hot chocolate and bed, I think. Forgive me, and ring again soon.'

'Are you sure you are all right? Do you want me to ring Papa or Mother?'

'No, darling girl. I have been working in the garden and have just come over tired.'

'Well, if you are sure. Take care. Love you.'

'You too.' And with that, her grandmother rang off.

Sara poured herself a glass of wine and tried to settle into the book she was reading.

She thought about Ellie. She had been Sara's guiding light when she was younger. They were so close that Ellie insisted that Sara call her by her name, as she hated the thought of being called Grandma. With her father in the diplomatic corps and Jayne with him, Sara had spent most of her holidays with her grandparents. Sometimes they had visited Polly in Italy, other times they spent glorious days out on the farm. Ellie's parents had been in the diplomatic corps and had missed out on family life too, but Simon's family had always been there for Ellie, and then for Sara: lovely Bea and caring A-J and Aunt Polly, who lived in Italy with her winemaking husband Mario, holidays there were always special. They always made Christmas special for Sara and she loved them all dearly. A-J would read aloud to them at night, as he loved reading and wanted to impart that love to his family. Sara could not remember a time when her grandfather hadn't had several books on the go at the same time. Ellie spoke to her in Italian and French, alternating the languages, so that Sara was fluent in her late teens, getting top grades for both languages at both O level and then A levels in her GCSE, much to Ellie's delight.

Sara sipped her wine, hoping Ellie was all right.

Sara remembered when she was about ten or eleven, the row her parents had when her father had come home and told her mother he had thrown in his job at the Foreign Office, as he wanted to work on the farm with Simon, Sara's grandfather. Jayne had been furious, and her anger had spilt out onto both Sara and Adam; it had drawn her and her father closer together. She sighed and turned in for the night.

The following morning, Sara rang her father to ask if Ellie was all right.

'Fine. Actually, Ellie is here, and is having lunch with us today.'

They chatted for a while and Sara promised to keep in touch.

After a quick shower and washing her hair, Sara went to the market up on San Remy to see if there were any more bargains to be found. It was hot, without a breeze, and it felt as if a storm was brewing.

Sara found a small pizzeria, ordered a Margherita with extra mozzarella, and took it back to the flat. She opened the house door just as the first blobs of rain fell.

In her flat, Sara put her iPod into the speaker, found a bottle of red wine, and poured herself a glass, opened the pizza, and sat listening to classical music as she ate.

Outside, the storm was raging with thunder and lightning. The air had become chilly, so Sara lay on her bed and pulled up the duvet and fell fast asleep.

It was late when her phone woke her.

'Were you asleep? I'm sorry to have woken you.'

Sara smiled and looked at her watch: nine o'clock.

'Luca, how lovely. I have had a wonderfully lazy day. It is pouring here. Is it raining with you?'

'No, but it's very humid. How are you? Do you miss me?'

'Should I?'

There was silence on the other end of the line.

'No, but I hoped you might?'

She laughed.

They talked for half an hour.

'We have found some amazing things on the dig. You won't forget Saturday, will you?' he said, suddenly changing the subject.

'No, I won't. I will ask Fabio to stand in for me so we can have the weekend together,' said Sara smiling.

'That would be wonderful.' he said.

On Monday, Sara asked Fabio if he would mind working on the coming Saturday as she wanted to go away for the weekend. He was pleased, as the overtime would go toward the payment on the apartment he was planning to buy in Cagliari.

On Saturday morning, Luca collected Sara at ten on the dot in his Cinquecento. He opened the car door for her, took her bag and dropped her a kiss on the cheek.

'You have got your swimming things, haven't you?'

'Yes. Is it far to the villa?' she asked, sliding into the little car.

'No, it's in Villasimius. I thought I would show you some of our amazing scenery. How can you sell it to people if you have not even seen it? So, a beautiful drive along the coast with some time on the beach is called for.'

The coastal road was indeed stunning. Cliffs dropped to the crystal-blue sea, interspersed with stunning white beaches and sandy coves. The pine trees grew down to the shore and green shrubs covered the area.

Sara sighed. 'It is beautiful and still wild.'

'That's its charm. It's still very unspoilt.'

They reached Villasimius and turned off the coastal road. The villa was down a long road, just outside the village and surrounded by Oleanders, palms, and fruit trees.

Luca parked in the shade of some pine trees and helped Sara out of the car, giving her a quick kiss. At that moment, the front gate opened, and a woman came out to greet them.

'Darling Luca, how good to see you,' she said, giving him a hug and kisses. 'You must be Sara. Hello, my dear, I am Carla. It is always a pleasure to meet Luca's friends. Come in, come in.'

Carla was short with long raven black hair and clipped up with a pretty slide. Her eyes were black and smiling.

'This is gorgeous,' said Sara, looking around.

The smell of the lemon and orange flowers wafted through the magnificent garden which was enclosed by a large wall that trapped the heady scents. The villa was of a traditional design, with a wide veranda that overlooked the sea through the pines.

They passed through the garden to the elegant villa that was painted white throughout but decorated with soft furnishings in amazingly vibrant colours.

'Go through, Luca. You know where to go.' Then, turning to Sara, Carla said, 'Follow me, my dear. I am so glad you could come. I am sure you would like to change.'

Sara followed Carla through the house and down to a small hut near the pool.

'Take a towel, and you will find all the facilities inside. We'll be over there,' said Carla, pointing to the terrace.

In the changing room, Sara was surprised to see that the colours in the house were repeated out here, giving the whole place a feeling of brightness.

Sara changed into her bikini and tied her coloured *pareo* around herself. Taking her bag, she joined Luca on the terrace.

The men rose to greet her, and Luca put his arm around her as he introduced her.

'This is Matteo, Carla's husband; then Salvatore, whom you met, and his long-suffering girlfriend, Sylvia.'

Sylvia laughed.

'Drinks?' asked Matteo.

'Later. I want to take Sara for a swim first. It's boiling,' said Luca, bending down to collect two towels off the chair.

Luca took Sara's hand and walked her down through the pine trees to the beach.

He dropped the towels on the sand and led her to the water's edge.

'You can swim, can't you?'

'Yes,' she said, smiling.

He released her hand and raced into the sea, splashing, and calling for her to join him.

Sara dropped her *pareo* by the towels and joined him.

The water was cool after the hot journey, and she relaxed in the sea, enjoying its freshness.

Sara felt Luca come close to her and turned toward him as he stood beside her.

'You look wonderful in that bikini,' he said, putting his arms around her. 'I think you're lovely, Sara. I have missed you. You have been on my mind, making it difficult for me to concentrate on my work,' he whispered, as he kissed her neck, her cheek, and finally her mouth.

When he released her, Sara felt dizzy and swayed slightly, so he held on to her.

'You must know how I feel about you, Sara?'

She couldn't say anything but putting her arms around his neck returned his kiss.

At that moment Salvatore and Sylvia came racing down to the beach and dived into the sea, laughing and splashing each other.

Luca held Sara's hand under the water; the look in his eyes

said everything Sara could want. Her heart missed a beat as she looked at Luca and smiled.

Lunch was long and lazy in the shade of the veranda: pasta Genovese, followed by spit-roast lamb and salad, then mixed Sardinian cheeses, all washed down with several bottles of Rocca Rubia.

'Do you live here all year round?' Sara asked Carla.

'Yes. Matteo is a skilled carpenter; he builds and mends boats at the port of Villasimius. I have a small boutique for clothes, shoes, and accessories. It keeps us busy, and being nearby means we can spend time together at home in the evenings and at weekends.'

'What do you do when you are not with Luca?' asked Carla.

'I work as a trouble-shooter for a travel agent. They had a problem down here, but it is all sorted now.'

'So, will you be going home soon?'

'Not yet. They are looking for a new manager. I love it here and will be very reluctant to go back to the UK.'

'You should stay a while and see the island; it has lots to offer people,' said Salvatore.

'Do you live here too?' said Sara. 'I have a business consultancy in Cagliari, which I visit twice a week. The rest of the time I work from home in Villasimius. The wonders of modern communication.'

'You are staying tonight, aren't you, Luca?'

'No, Carla, thanks, but I have to get back tonight.'

'Next weekend, perhaps?' she said.

'I am hoping to take Sara up the coast to see some ancient sites next week end.

Don't worry, we will be in touch.'

'My God, Luca, you are not going to bore her to death with all the old ruins?' said Salvatore, laughing. Turning to Sara, he added, 'Be careful. If he thinks you are even a little bit interested in the history of Sardinia, he will never stop talking about it, or taking you off to remote, unexcavated sites.'

170

They all laughed, but Sara turned to look at Luca, who was watching her intently.

'He won't bore me. I can't wait to see all the things he wants to show me.'

It was early evening when they all said their goodbyes with a promise to come again soon, and Luca took Sara back to Cagliari.

He parked the car in the Piazza Indipendenza. It was reserved for the people living in the area and closed during the night, so it was quiet. They walked hand in hand down Via Lamarmora from the piazza, past the chiesa della Purissima.

'I thought we could have a coffee at my place, as we pass it first,' he said, a wide, mischievous grin on his face.

Sara followed him further down the now-familiar road until they came to a big painted door. Inside, the hall was very grand with a door to the left. A wide marble staircase wound up to the top floor, where a lantern window let in the evening starlight.

They climbed to the second floor and he let her into his spacious flat. Two large French windows were open, with the shutters ajar, to allow in the air.

Sara looked around the room. Bookshelves full of old and new books covered one wall. On another wall, there was a beautiful collection of Sardinian prints of all the village costumes, paintings by local artists, and a collection of numerous antique maps. On the floor was a large handmade rug in muted colours. Multi-coloured cushions sat on sofas that were covered with natural linen, and the curtains also made of linen, but with Sardinian motifs on the bottom. The room reminded her of her grandfather's study and her own house with her father's books on the shelves.

'It's very cosy,' said Sara smiling. 'How long have you lived here?'

'I moved in on my twenty-first birthday, and I love it. It used to belong to my father and my grandfather before him. A lot of the books and prints were my grandfather's and it is that which makes

171

it feel so homely. Anna, a friend, did the furnishings for me. She is a designer.'

'How strange – my flat in London belonged to my grandfather and then my father and it still has some of their things in it. I find it comforting to know they are still there. Is your father still alive?' asked Sara.

'Yes, but when he married my mother, her parents had died in a car crash, and they moved into her house… Coffee?'

'How sad, losing her parents… Yes, please. Can I help?'

'No. Make yourself comfortable.'

'Are most of the houses up here like this, with large rooms? Because this place is almost identical to where I am staying.'

'Yes, most have sizeable rooms for extended families,' he said, 'They were built for the rich Spanish families, but over the years some have remained as houses while others have moved in, turning them into flats.'

He disappeared into the kitchen and Sara wandered around the room. She walked over to the bookshelves and ran her hands over the spines of the books on archaeology, poetry, and Sardinian flora and fauna. She smiled; all his family's interests were on these shelves, everything that made them tick.

Sara became aware of Luca standing behind her as he gently slipped his arms around her. She felt his breath on the back of her neck; felt the shiver of delight that ran down her spine; felt the quiver in her stomach and felt a sudden longing for him.

She turned to Luca as he enfolded her in his arms.

'I've loved you from the moment you threw yourself at me in the street when your things spilt all over the road and you swore at me.'

She smiled at him. 'And I have loved you ever since you told everyone that we had already met.'

Luca bent to kiss her, gently at first, but with mounting passion. Sara pulled at his shirt as he undid her dress and allowed it to fall to the floor. They seemed to waltz together, shedding clothes as they kissed, and held on to each other. Then he picked

172

her up, carried her to his bedroom, and laid her on his double bed, with a great carved crucifix above it. It was cool in the room as a fan turned slowly on the ceiling.

'Hold me tight, please,' she murmured.

He held her to him, and they gently made love, which turned into a sudden passion that took their breath away.

Later, lying in his arms, Sara turned to him.

'The coffee will be stone cold by now.'

He laughed and kissed her on her nose. Propping himself up on his elbow he stroked a strand of hair away from her eyes.

'Thank you.' he said.

Sara lay looking at him. He was beautiful, his dark hair falling in waves. His eyes were dark, deep, and inviting. His body was beautiful too, and she coveted every part of him.

Luca rose and kissed her on the lips. Pulling on his T-shirt, he went to make fresh coffee.

They ate at the Antico Caffé, a light pasta dish followed by steak, and rounded off with coffee.

'I am not willing to face your landlady, but you could stay with me tonight,' he said, a smile spreading across his face and a mischievous twinkle in his eyes.

Sara leaned over and took his hand. 'I would love that.'

They ambled up to the Via Lamarmora, arm in arm.

Sara tried to remember when she had felt so much at one with someone. There had been other men, brief encounters that she had finally found boring. No one had come so close to her in such a brief time. There was a connection, a bond; he was a kindred spirit.

'You're very quiet. Are you all right?' asked Luca, stopping to look at her.

Sara looked up at him and smiled.

'I'm fine, really fine.'

Up in the flat, they undressed each other, taking time to see, to touch, to feel, and to know each other.

Luca lay beside her and slept, but Sara lay in his arms thinking about the days that had passed, and how in such a brief time she felt so at one with this man and knew she was falling in love with him. He had stolen her heart and she was in danger of losing her soul too.

CHAPTER EIGHTEEN

Sara woke with a start. Luca was already up and busy making coffee. He came and sat on the bed beside her, dropping her a kiss.

'Good morning, sleepyhead,' he said, kissing her again, and handing her a cup of coffee.

'Good morning. It's Sunday; is there a rush to get up?' she said, pulling herself up to take the cup he offered her.

'I am sorry, but I need to go to the cemetery this morning. My best friend died in a motorcycle accident last year, and it is his birthday today.'

'Oh. How sad. Do you want to go on your own, or can I come with you?'

'Would you, Sara? That would be great, thank you. I was going to ask you, but I didn't know how you would feel about it.'

'Do you want to talk about it? Can you tell me about him?'

Luca took a sip of his coffee.

'Paolo was very special,' he said. 'He, like me, was an only child and we played together when we were younger; we were at school together. Later he trained to be a sommelier; he had a natural 'taste' and was excellent at his job and travelled all over Sardinia and had been on the Continent and was much respected in his field.

'He had come home for a couple of months to work at a new restaurant in Cagliari. Returning home late one night, he was hit by a drunk driver on the wrong side of the road. They arrested the driver and charged him. He is in prison now, but it won't bring Paolo back. Such a waste.'

Sara put her hand on his arm. 'I'm so sorry, how incredibly sad.'

Luca and Sara stopped off at a florist's and bought a bunch of carnations.

'Carnations last longer in the heat,' said the young florist as she wrapped the flowers in paper.

Luca drove Sara to a village outside Cagliari in silence, each deep in their thoughts.

'Thank you for this, Sara. I would have found it difficult on my own,' said Luca, finally breaking the silence.

Sara put her hand on his and squeezed it.

They parked the car in the shade of an old, large, wild olive tree and walked hand in hand into the cemetery.

The area was filled on one side with old graves, large statues, and marble monuments to lost mothers and fathers, husbands, wives, or children. Photos of the deceased were placed in small oval windows, smiling out at the outside world.

Sara walked on with Luca until he stopped at a row of modern tombs: a large wall with slots in which they put the coffins. Each had a plaque engraved with the name, date of birth, and date of death, together with an oval picture of the deceased.

Luca stepped forward to place his flowers in the vase by his friend's tomb. Sara looked at the photo: a good-looking young man with such a confident smile. As Luca had said, what a waste.

At that moment, a woman approached the tomb with a vase of flowers. Luca turned to look at her and then went forward and took the woman into his arms.

'Dearest Maria, how are you?'

Sara moved away, not wanting to intrude on such an intimate moment between two friends.

Hearing laughter, she turned to watch a group of women dressed in black filling vases with water or removing the dead flowers, chattering, and laughing as they carried out their work. Sara noticed the colour of the flowers, the ruddy faces of the women and the vibrancy of the place.

'Sara,' called Luca. 'Sara.'

She turned to see him beckoning to her and walked over to him.

'This is Maria, Paolo's mother.'

'Hello,' said Sara. 'I am so sorry for your loss.'

'Hello, my dear. Thank you for coming with Luca. I like coming here; it is where I feel close to Paolo. I come to talk to him when I am lonely. Thank you, Luca, great memories.'

With that, Maria walked back to her son's tomb.

Sara took Luca's hand.

'In England, our graveyards are grey and silent; people talk in hushed voices. But here everyone laughs, and they talk to their loved ones; it is more like a social gathering,' she said.

'We honour our dead, we remember them, and yes, we talk to them, so they are always with us.'

Luca put his arm around her.

'Enough sad talk,' he said, as they began walking back to the car. 'Sunday, time for eating and resting.'

They found an agritourism restaurant and joined the many families also enjoying a Sunday outing. They sat at a long table with another family. The waiter came and piled three dishes in front of them.

'The small plate is for antipasto, the bowl for pasta and then the plate is for the main course,' said Luca, expecting her question.

It was a long, leisurely meal as the plates were removed one by one and the next course served. By the time the waiter had removed the last plate, Sara was fit to burst.

'I don't know about you, but I need some exercise, after all that food,' said Sara.

Luca laughed. 'Good. I know just the thing.'

He paid the bill and they drove back to Cagliari. Once in his flat, they fell into each other's arms on his bed.

CHAPTER NINETEEN

A month had passed. Sara was working hard at the agency and loving it. Luca was busy up at Cabras but returned at weekends, so they could spend time together.

He took her to see the ancient sites in Cagliari. They ate out most weekends but sometimes cooked pasta at the flat so they could be alone together. They drove to Poetto, swam in the warm water, ate ice cream, and returned to the flat in the evening to sleep or make love.

Sara's boss phoned her at work on a Monday, after Luca had returned to Cabras for the week.

'How are you, Sara? Are you okay? Can you manage without me?' Rob asked, laughing. 'I need a favour. I know it is quite a way, but could you go up to Oristano? They are trying to sell a travel agency there, and I want you to look at it. Is it possible?'

'I don't see why not, perhaps at the weekend. I will find someone to drive me up there.'

'You are a star, Sara, thank you. Put the petrol and expenses on the company card. If you need a taxi up there, put it on the card. Keep in touch. Keep well,' he said and rang off.

Sara discussed the coming weekend with her colleagues. There was not too much on, so she arranged to take the time off to visit Oristano and spend a few days with Luca. Fabio was only too pleased to, once again, add to his savings with the overtime.

Sara rang Luca and told him what Rob wanted.

'I have ordered a taxi to bring me up, so you don't have to drive down here and then up to Cabras.'

'Cancel the taxi. I will be down Wednesday night so we can be together. I miss you close to me at night,' he said.

'Are you sure?'

'Sure, of what, that you should cancel the taxi or that I miss you?'

'Both.'

'You know, I want to take you somewhere special for a long weekend. We can do it this weekend.'

So, cancelling the taxi and leaving everything in Fabio's capable hands, Sara packed for a break. Luca told her to pack casual wear and not to forget her swim things.

It was late on Wednesday evening when he arrived at the flat. They decided on a meal at the Caffé and walked down the street hand in hand and chatting.

That night, Sara lay in his arms and realised that Luca made her life feel complete.

'What are you thinking, darling?' he whispered.

'How much you mean to me.'

'That's good. Now go to sleep; we have a long day tomorrow.'

It was a lovely morning and they drove in silence out of the city towards Oristano. It was an open area covered with vines, fruit trees, and corn. The lush greenness of the island was giving way to the gold of summer, which would soon turn to brown as the land dried under the relentless sun.

'The Campidano,' said Luca, taking his hand off the wheel and squeezing Sara's knee. 'It is known as the bread and fruit basket of Sardinia. All good produce comes from here.'

They arrived in Oristano, found a parking space, and went in search of a coffee. They found a small café and ordered coffee and water.

'Could you tell me where we will find this agency?' asked Luca, handing the address to the young waiter.

'No problem. If you follow this road down to the end and turn left, you will come to a square. The agency is there. About five minutes on foot.'

Luca and Sara finished their coffee, thanked the waiter and walked down the road, where they found the agency as directed.

'I just want to see how they perform and perhaps talk to the owner.'

They entered the agency. A young girl was sitting at a desk, drinking a cup of coffee. She looked up and smiled.

'Please excuse me. We have had a heavy morning and I have only just had time to have a coffee.'

'Don't worry,' said Sara. 'Is your boss in, by any chance?'

'He is in his office. Who shall I say wants him?'

'My name is Sara Smythe,' said Sara, handing the girl her business card.

The girl disappeared and returned with her boss, a large bear of a man with a full beard and piercing blue eyes.

'Good morning. I am Ricardo Spanu. How can I help you?'

'It's about the agency,' said Sara in a low voice.

The man moved forward and ushered Sara into his office. Luca remained with the girl, chatting to her about holidays.

'Please take a seat, *signorina*. Would you like a coffee or a soft drink?' asked Ricardo, closing the door to his office behind him.

'No, thank you,' said Sara, sitting in the chair he offered her. 'Thank you. I understand that you are thinking of selling this agency. Is that right?'

'My, news travels fast! How do you know?'

'Someone in London told me. Is it true?'

'In London… Yes, I would like to sell it as a going concern and keep on the staff,' he said, looking at her business card.

'How many staff are there?'

'Three: me, Cara, whom you have met, and Giuseppe, who is at lunch. I know your company; it is highly respected in the travel business.'

'Thank you,' said Sara. 'May I ask why you are selling?'

'My mother is getting old and needs looking after. She lives in a small village in the mountains, and I want to be with her.

Besides, there is a young widow in the village I have had my eye on for a few years. So, time to make a move,' he said, a broad grin across his face.

They discussed the asking price, the turnover, and whether he owned the building, which he did.

'If you want to buy the property, that will be fine, but if you want to rent, that will be okay too. I have already had an offer, but they want to run it themselves. They will sack the staff, and that is not what I want.'

'Thanks. I will be in touch in the next couple of days. Thank you for your time. You have my card; please contact my boss, Mr Robert Taylor.'

The man rose and shook her hand.

'It's been a pleasure, *signorina*.'

'Thank you and good luck with the widow.'

The big bear of a man smiled again.

Luca was laughing with the young girl when Sara returned to the reception desk.

'Cara has been to see my dig,' said Luca, with a note of pride in his voice. 'I am off there now to show it to Sara.'

They said their goodbyes and walked back to the car. It was hot, and the car was boiling.

'Did you have any success with the boss?'

'Yes, I think he may well be open to an offer. I'll ring Rob later.'

'I know an excellent restaurant for lunch, and then we can go to the site,' said Luca, reaching over to give her a quick kiss.

Lunch proved delicious: fresh fish followed by strawberries and coffee.

'You will like my dig, although I think it will be rather hot today.'

Before they left, Sara texted Rob about the meeting. His reply was typical:

Splendid work – have a great day.

They drove to the site at Cabras and Sara was surprised to see how much of the area it covered. The heat was overwhelming;

181

even the slightest breeze that came from the sea was hot.

Luca took her hand and introduced her to Francesco, who was one of the team.

'You couldn't have chosen a much hotter day,' said Francesco, laughing, and wiping his brow.

'Come,' said Luca to Sara, 'come and see these.'

Large fragments of broken statues were placed on the ground. Some held shields, some weapons, and they were all tall.

'My grandfather always told my father that there were giants in Sardinia. My father used to read me stories about them. Now here I am, excavating them. My grandfather would have been amazed.'

'How many have they found?' asked Sara, gazing around at the numerous artefacts.

'We don't know yet, as they are all in pieces. It seems someone destroyed them and then buried them.'

'How did you find them?'

Luca laughed.

'They were found back in 1974 by a local farmer called Sissinio Poddi. He ploughed up a stone head and contacted the local archaeological department. They thought it was a fake and that a sculptor had put it there as a hoax – the two circles for the eyes were so weird. They didn't have the money to do a lot of excavating. But having dug more, they found all these extraordinary figures. The Italian Ministry of Cultural Heritage has now found the money to dig, as the giants seem to be of international interest. This is the largest collection of giant statues found in the western part of the Mediterranean. The rest is history, which can only be good. I am immensely proud to be part of it all. Now, it's hot and we should go if we want to get to the hotel before it's dark.'

'Where are we going?'

Luca touched his nose with his finger.

'Wait and see.'

It was a long, hot drive before they finally arrived at the hotel near Oliena. The owner came out to greet Luca. She was of medium height, with long dark hair and dark eyes to match, which were alert to everything.

'This is Sara. Sara, this is Anna. She is the friend who decorated my flat.'

Anna hugged Luca, then kissed Sara on both cheeks.

'Lovely to see you, Luca. How are you? How are your parents? Well, I hope?' She turned to Sara. 'It's nice to meet you, Sara. Come in. The porter will show you up to your room, and I will see you later when you have settled in.'

Sara and Luca climbed up the stairs, which seemed to go on forever until they reached the top floor, where they were shown into their suite. The bedroom was light and airy. It was painted white with wonderful bright colours on the bed and curtains.

It stepped down to a sitting area and bathroom. There was a terrace off the sitting room. Luca tipped the porter and watched Sara as she stepped outside and gasped. There was an outdoor Jacuzzi with a view to die for – olive trees and vineyards, watched over by the huge mountain range.

'Supra Monte,' said Luca as he put his arms around her.

'It's beautiful. How do you know about this place?'

'My parents used to bring me here when I was a child. It has always been rather special. We have known Anna's family for years.'

They unpacked, put on their swimwear and, taking a robe each from the room, walked down to the pool. The swim was refreshing after the heat of the day and Sara lay in the water, loving the feel on her body.

Luca came over and kissed her gently.

'Happy?

'Very.'

Later, they showered together, then dressed to go down for drinks and dinner. They sat out on the terrace, sipping their cocktails.

'How long will you be digging at Monte Prama?' asked Sara.

'It depends on how much more we find. Now, no more talk of business, mine, or yours,' he said, taking her hand in his and squeezing it gently.

'Agreed.' She said.

They walked through the hotel to the dining room. There was a large open fire at the far end of the room with every conceivable kind of meat roasting on spits and a grill. The aroma filled the room and Sara suddenly realised how hungry she felt.

They chose pasta followed by roast suckling pig. Luca ordered a bottle of Nepenthe.

'It's a particularly good local wine and my father's favourite. You will live forever if you drink it. Many Sards live well into their century up here,' he added, laughing.

The food arrived and when the meat came, Sara followed Luca's lead, eating it with her fingers.

'We will make a Sard out of you yet.'he smiled.

They finally rounded the meal off with ricotta ice cream and honey.

Anna met them in the hallway and asked them to join her for coffee and a nightcap. They sat talking together, and Sara listened to the old friends tell stories about their younger days.

'On Sunday there is the Festa del Redentore; you should take Sara to see it,' and turning to Sara said, 'I'm sure you would love it. All the wonderful costumes and dancing, it is very colourful. And then you must see the spring.'

'I forgot that it was the Festa. Yes, that would be great. We could go on Sunday. See the festival then drive home.

'Could you arrange a picnic for our lunch tomorrow, by any chance? I would like to take the tour up to Supra Monte and I thought we could have lunch there. And then another on Sunday. We can go to the Festa and then drive home,' said Luca.

'That's perfect I will arrange that for you. Roberto is here and has asked to take you in the four-by-four at about ten o'clock in the morning, so you can get up in your own time and enjoy a good breakfast. Leave it to me; I will arrange a pleasant trip for you both. Sleep well,' Anna said, rising and putting her hand on Luca's shoulder.

'Roberto is an old friend,' Luca explained to Sara. 'When

I was younger and stayed here, we would go out together and search all the old sites around the area. He was always interested in archaeology, but when his father died, he had to return to look after his mother and the farm. It will be good to see him again.'

Luca took Sara's hand and led her up the stairs to their room. Inside, Sara ran the Jacuzzi, lit some candles, and dropped some lemon oil into the water. Luca came to join her, and they lay in the warm, bubbling water together, talking over the events of the day.

'Tell me what is the Spring?'

'Sorgente su Gologone is the natural spring and a tributary of the river Cedrino. It is quite beautiful and I think you will like it.'

Later, wrapped in large, white towels, they walked out onto the terrace and looked up at the stars. It was a magical scene. A full moon illuminated the mountain towering over the valley. The silver-washed olive groves and pine trees gave the vista an enchanted look.

Luca took Sara in his arms, pulling her towards him.

She sighed.

'I love you so much. We have only known each other for such a short time, yet I feel I have known you forever.'

'Darling Sara, when you find the one you love, the one who touches your soul, it can be in a day or after a lifetime. For some, love comes too soon, and they are not ready, while others find love later in life and have only a brief time to share their happiness. We have been lucky enough to find each other when we can spend a long time together.'

He lifted her up and Sara put her arms around his neck as he carried her to the bed.

The doors to the terrace were open, as were the windows in the bedroom. On the gentle, warm breeze, sounds of the night stole in – the bells of the goats in the pen below, the frogs and cicadas, all mingled with the scent of pine trees.

The soft moonlight fell across the bed as Luca tenderly made love to her.

Sara woke in the morning, still entwined in Luca's arms. He felt so strong, and that made her feel safe. In such a brief time she had come to love him and thanked her lucky stars she had bumped into him that day.

He stirred beside her. His breath tickled her neck and she laughed as he pulled her into him.

They showered together and went downstairs.

Breakfast was a grand feast, with every conceivable food to satisfy guests of all nationalities. Luca had bacon and eggs.

'I need to build up my strength,' he said, taking Sara's hand and squeezing it.

Sara chose yoghurt and fruit, followed by the most delicious freshly baked bread with local butter and homemade marmalade. The aroma of the hot coffee filled her senses. They sat at a table with a view overlooking the pool and then on into the deep valley that stretched out into the distance.

Plants rambled everywhere around the veranda, while the multi-coloured furniture brought a unique style to the place.

At ten o'clock, Luca and Sara went outside to find Roberto and found him waiting by a Land Rover.

The two men embraced.

'Roberto, this is Sara. Darling, this is my old friend Roberto.'

Roberto came forward and kissed Sara on each cheek.

'A pleasure to meet you; but be prepared for us to talk ruins.'

Sara laughed.

'Signora Anna has organised a good trip today, so all you have to do is sit back and enjoy it,' said Roberto, as Luca climbed in beside Sara in the back of the Land Rover.

The scenery was breath-taking as they climbed the twisty road up the mountain. Roberto stopped every so often, to allow them to look at the diminishing village of Oliena and over the new plantation of native trees in the distance.

'We are removing the pine trees and planting native varieties, as it is now a national park.'

Up they climbed, higher and higher, until they reached a wide plateau where a shepherd's hut stood under a huge oak, and they got out to see the view.

'Oliena looks so tiny from here,' said Sara, looking down at the village. She turned to look at the surrounding area.

'All the trees are so big up here; they must be really old.'

'The Piedmontese didn't bother with the ones up the mountains; the pickings were too good in the valleys,' said Roberto with a bitter edge to his voice. 'They stripped the valleys and sent all the timber to the Continent, always taking, never giving.'

Sara looked at Luca, who was nodding in agreement.

Standing there on the plateau, it was eerily quiet, with just the cicadas and birds twittering, not a breath. Then a rustling could be heard in the distant trees as a breeze passed through them, making them sway with its force, on up to where they were standing, brushing their faces and tossing the leaves on the trees. Then on it went, up the mountainside. The silence then returning before the next breeze came chasing up the valley through the trees again.

Luca put his arm around Sara. 'It's magical, isn't it?'

Sara took her camera out of her bag and took pictures of the area and the bird's-eye view of the tiny village of Oliena.

'Come on, you two, stand together,' said Sara to Luca and Roberto.

She took photos of the two friends, and Roberto took one of her and Luca.

'For the album,' he said, handing back her camera.

Sara smiled at Luca as they walked back to the Land Rover for the next leg of the journey.

'Why don't you sit in the front with Roberto, so you can talk together, and I can listen in the back.'

'Are you sure?' asked Luca.

'Of course.'

Once in the Land Rover, they continued to climb up the nerve-racking narrow track to the top of the mountain. The sharp turns dislodging the loose shale, and Sara watched as it tumbled down the mountainside.

At the top, Sara got out to look at the view. Luca came up behind her, putting his arms around her. She felt the warmth of his breath, soft on her neck.

'You can see for miles – odd houses, small patchwork fields, woodland, and scrub, then the mountains in the distance. It is so wildly beautiful,' she sighed.

They all admired the view as Roberto pointed out various landmarks.

After the mountain ride, they returned to Oliena, where Roberto stopped the Land Rover.

'Time for a break,' he said and went inside the small bar to get them coffees.

Outside, Luca and Sara sat watching the world go by.

'I am to take you to another site, where we will have a picnic and see *Sa Sedda'e Sos Carros*,' said Roberto as he put the coffees on the table.

Luca smiled and turned to Sara. 'It is one of the places I was telling you about, where they worshipped the water.'

'A picnic too – how exciting,' she said.

After their coffee and a quick pit stop, they set off once again.

'This is the Lanaittu valley,' said Roberto. 'At the end of the valley is the Monte Tiscali. Inside, they found a Nuragic village that is thought to be their last hideout against the Romans. It is a strange and haunting place, but one to savour another time when you come back.'

'I would love that,' said Sara, turning to Luca and smiling.

'They have been doing a lot of research in the area,' said Roberto. 'When I have time, I go to help with the dig. They did some research on bones found in the Grotta di Corbeddu in 1983 and found they were some of the oldest human bones in Sardinia, dating back to ten thousand BC.'

'Yes, I heard about that. I'm digging at Monte Prama now, and it is amazing what we are finding,' said Luca. 'You should come over and see it sometime.'

The two men chatted about the various digs and their mutual interest in archaeology as Sara sat listening, intrigued by their stories.

They travelled up the mountain pass, Luca pointing out the various sites.

'That's where the caves *Su Bentu* and *Su Oche* are. They named them after the sound of the rushing water and the wind that chases through the caves.'

After a bumpy ride, they arrived at an old shepherd's hut that had a large platform built in front of it. Sara got out of the Land Rover and walked over to the balcony to take in the view. The large mountain range before her, the sweeping valley below where the trees moved in the constant breeze, sighing like the whispering of ancient souls. Sara sighed too. This place certainly had a mystical aura about it.

Roberto and Luca came over, carrying the picnic basket.

Luca looked at her and put his arm around her.

'Are you all right?'

Sara nodded and began laying everything out while the two men drank cold beer from the icebox.

'What a wonderful place for a picnic,' she said, pouring herself a large glass of water.

Time slipped by. They sat back in rickety wicker chairs and ate, talked, or dozed in the shade, brushed by an intermittent breeze.

The sun had travelled from its midday height and seemed to rest on top of the mountain range. Roberto rose, collected everything together, and took the basket back to the Land Rover.

'Are you ready?' Luca asked Sara.

'Yes, why?'

'Not bored?'

'Don't be silly. This is great, and I am learning something.'

'What's that?'

'What it is like to be with people who love archaeology.'

'Hmm,' he said, taking her hand and leading her back to the Land Rover.

They walked up to the ancient Nuragic site. It spread over a wide area – stone walls of long-abandoned houses, stores, and communal buildings. The air was hot as the stones radiated the midday heat.

Luca took her hand again.

'Come and look at this,' he said, a broad smile on his face.

They walked past several round stone buildings to one made from cut basalt stones.

'First, I want you to know that basalt does not come from this area, so it had to be transported here. Second, this is unique in Sardinia,' said Luca, drawing her into the circular room. 'Look at the bowl in the centre for the water, and around in the stonework are rams' heads. They had pipes where the water flowed into the bowl. Whether this place was religious, we are not sure; all I know is that for a barren area of land, it is amazing; and we have no idea why they chose this site.'

Sara looked at the building. It certainly was amazing and she suddenly felt the need to know everything that Luca knew about Sardinia, and that she would be happy to spend her life learning about this wonderful magical land.

'It's amazing. I can see why you spend your time digging and finding out things about the ancient people.'

Luca took her hand and squeezed it. 'Home time. We have had a long day and that pool is calling,' he said.

Back at the hotel, they said goodbye to Roberto and thanked him for his time.

'You must come down and see Monte Prama and I can show you round. I will be in touch soon.' Luca promised as the two friends embraced.

The pool was cool, and Sara relaxed in the water while Luca swam several lengths.

Before supper, they again enjoyed a Jacuzzi out on the terrace.

'Today was wonderful. At last, I feel I know why you became an archaeologist. It is fascinating.'

Luca gave her a sideways glance and grinned at her.

'I'm serious Luca really I am.'

The evening meal was roast meats and delightful desserts. They finally climbed the stairs to their room, where they both fell into bed and asleep.

★

The next day, after breakfast, they walked down the road to see the famous spring at the cave. The morning air was cool, making the walk enjoyable.

They reached the site and walked a very rugged path that led to an old church and Sara ventured in. The side walls were plain, and arched but there was a large painting of Christ with Mary over the altar. It had an air of simplicity that Sara loved.

'Do you think there has always been a site here where they worshipped the water?'

'Probably. Water was very sacred to the ancient people; they understood that water is life-giving and a precious resource. There are lots of ancient wells dedicated to water, the spirit of the water, or whatever they believed in. I want to show you one on the way home, as it is incredibly special to me.'

He held out his hand to her and, taking it, Sara followed him out of the church and down the rocky path where steps led to the source of the river below.

At the entrance to the cave the water was blue, emerald green, then blue again. It was mesmerising, the colours, magical.

'What wonderful colours,' said Sara, 'but I bet it's cold.'

'It comes from the heart of the mountains, so yes, it is very cold.'

They walked beside the stream, watching the water as it passed under the saplings that had grown up along the edge, gurgling and splashing over smooth, shiny rocks and slithering over the smaller stones.

'Ancient man must have worshipped here. I find it fascinating that this hasn't changed in hundreds of years,' said Sara, watching the water chattering between the rocks.

Luca looked at her and slipped his arm around her.

'Thousands of years. You really are interested, aren't you?' he said.

'Yes, I am. Why, did you think I was only saying I was interested?' said Sara, pulling a funny face.

They sauntered, hand in hand, down the stream until it spread out. Reeds grew at the edges and enclosed the area like a huge pond.

'Next time we can go to see the Nuragic village of Tiscali. They say it was the last stronghold of the ancient Nuragic people against all the invaders. When we have more time, I will bring you up here to see it all.'

'I'd love that.'

'Would you? My friends always say I bore them with my sites and digs.'

Sara looked at Luca. He had the look of a proud young boy eager to show off a collection of toys. His enthusiasm was infectious, and Sara wanted to know more, to see all the things he knew about.

'I'm not bored at all, I promise. I find it fascinating and I'm looking forward to learning more.'

'One day, I want to take a year out and travel the island, photographing the sites, and mapping them.'

'That would be very interesting,' said Sara.

It was almost noon when they returned to the hotel, time for lunch, and an afternoon by the pool. They lay on the comfortable loungers under the shade of a colourful parasol, slipping in and out of a dreamy haze.

'Tell me about the Festa,' said Sara, taking Luca's hand and squeezing it gently.

'Well, on the last Sunday in August, which is tomorrow,' he teased, 'the people from Nuoro and around the country celebrate the honour of having the statue of Christ the Redeemer, which sits on the top of Monte Ortobene. They have done since about 1900 when Pope Leo X111 decided he wanted nineteen statues of Christ on nineteen mountains throughout Italy to celebrate the 20th Century.'

'Do the islanders come in their traditional costumes?'

'Yes, from all over Sardinia.'

'Can we see it?'

'Yes, if you would like to. We can have an early breakfast, then go to Nuoro and see the procession. I have asked Anna if we can have a picnic, and then drive back to Cagliari. There is one more place I want to show you and we can do that on the way back.'

'Really, what's that?'

'Wait and see. It's a surprise.'

'Oh, lovely, I like pleasant surprises.' Luca laughed and squeezed her hand.

'I love you, Sara.'

'I love you too, Luca. You have made my life complete.'

He sighed and leant over to kiss her.

As the sun dipped over the mountain, the valley darkened under its shadow, and the breeze that came brought a freshness to the end of the day.

They collected their things and walked up to their room.

Sara turned on the taps of the Jacuzzi and dropped some lemon fragrance into the water.

'Are you coming to join me?' asked Sara, slipping off her *pareo* and stepping into the hot bubbling water.

Luca dropped his towel and joined her.

Later, feeling better and relaxed, Sara climbed out of the Jacuzzi and went for a quick shower to wash her hair.

Sara put on a bathrobe and dried her hair with a towel and wandered up the stairs to the bedroom. Luca was lying stretched out on the bed, his eyes closed, his towel wrapped around him.

She kissed him gently on the lips.

'You're dripping water on me,' said Luca, pulling her down beside him.

'Hold me tight,' she said.

He held her in his arms and Sara sighed a long-contented sigh.

Later they ate in the dining room where Anna came to join them.

'Festa tomorrow?' she asked.

'Yes, we will leave after breakfast and then head home after the parade,' said Luca.

'Fine, I have organised a picnic,' said Anna, 'You will want something to eat, as everything will be shut. I can't have you going hungry.'

'Thank you for everything, Anna; it has been a great stay,' said Luca.

'You have such a beautiful place here,' said Sara, 'It would be wonderful to come back and see more of the area.'

'I will look forward to that,' said Anna, rising, 'Now please excuse me as I have some new arrivals.'

Sara and Luca climbed up to their room.

'Coffee?' she asked.

'Please.'

She made the coffee and they sat together on a wicker sofa out on the little terrace and watched the moon sail high in the dark, inky night sky. The sounds of the Barbargia came in on them, mingling with the clang of sheep and goat bells from the valley.

Luca took her hand and sighed.

'You know, Sara, I feel I have known you all my life, I can't put my finger on it, but I feel a bond and a wonderful connection.'

She smiled and snuggled into him.

'Funny, I feel the same way about you too. Perhaps in another time, we knew each other.'

He smiled and pulled her further into his arms.

By nine o'clock in the sun-filled morning, they stood in the hall to pay the bill.

'Goodbye, Luca, Sara. Please come and see us again,' said Anna, hugging them both. She took a bag off the desk and handed it to Sara.

'This is something for you, for good luck.'

Sara took the package and opened it.

'An owl, in local pottery. How beautiful! Thank you, Anna, thank you,' she said, kissing Anna.

'Your picnic is already in the car. Have a glorious day at the festival.'

With all the goodbyes said and a promise to be back soon, Luca and Sara climbed into the car and set off to Nuoro.

They found a parking place and joined the crowds of people walking up to the main square. The morning sun was already hot as they walked hand in hand up the old streets, formed by blocks of granite in a herringbone pattern, shiny from the thousands of feet over the ages.

The sun's rays caught one side of the street, while the other side remained in shadow, so the breeze that came was cool.

They reached the Piazza Santa Maria della Neve, which was dominated by the beautiful, pink-washed cathedral dedicated to Santa Maria, with wide steps leading up to it.

Luca pulled Sara towards the shade of a tree by the steps to the church. People milled around: the tourists, in summer clothes, looking for a vantage place to take their pictures to show back home. Their pink and red faces unaccustomed to the heat.

People dressed in their varied local costumes. Mothers with babes in their arms, both dressed in the same costume. Fathers and sons in white baggy trousers topped with a black Greek-like tunic. Waistcoats in black velvet or elaborate brocade, and all sporting the *berrita*, which they wore on their heads in individual ways.

The sound of the crowd murmuring, the distant notes of an accordion and singing filled the air with expectancy.

At last, the Carabinieri cleared the Piazza, making sure everyone not involved, was behind the temporary barriers. The sound of jangling bells could be heard as a cart came into view, pulled by two massive oxen.

A roar went up from the crowd as they passed. A man in full costume led the oxen, which were decorated with flowers and embroidered trappings. People threw petals and their scent rose in the late morning heat as they were crushed under the many feet.

Luca looked at Sara and smiled.

'Are you okay?'

'It's wonderful, such an amazing atmosphere.'

He put his arm around her and drew her to him.

They watched as the long procession passed them – groups, from the different towns or villages from all over the island, each wearing their traditional costume.

A group of dancers stopped and danced. The girls in their full pleated skirts matched the men in their costumes; with tiny steps, as they glided in circles and squares and weaved or stomped out the story told in the dance. Gold brooches, necklaces, and heirlooms glinted and flashed in the sun as the girls twirled to the sound of the launaddas.

A roar and whistles came from the crowd. More costumes came from other townships and villages, the colours bright in the sunshine. A new roar going up as people from the village saw their costumes.

Next were the *Tenore* singers; a group of five men stopped and sang. One man sang the tune while the others sang in a polyphonic harmony, giving the song a strong resonance.

Sara felt the hairs rise on the back of her neck as the music filled her senses. Ancient sounds recalled for a modern-day.

She became lost in the sounds, the colours, the vibrancy of these people with their roots going back into the mists of time, with their traditions and folklore, taking part in a Festa that was theirs, although willing to share it with the tourists.

Finally, the procession of the Sardinian women brought up the last of the groups. Each woman was dressed in her costume representing all the groups here today.

Sara watched mesmorised as the last of the women passed by and stood watching them as the crowd enveloped them on there way on through the village.

'Are you ok?' asked Luca, looking concerned.

'Oh yes thank you. It is wonderful, Luca, thank you for bringing me. But where are the people going now?' asked Sara.

'They will climb up to Monte Ortobene and say Mass and give thanks for the statue,' he said, looking at his watch. 'Do you want to go with them? Or are you ready for a steady drive home?'

'I'm ready.' She sighed. The music still going around in her head.

They wandered back down through the narrow streets of the old town to find their car.

It was hot inside the little car and Luca switched on the air conditioning to full.

'I thought we could take the scenic route home so you can see some of our beautiful countryside.'

Sara looked at him and smiled.

'That would be wonderful.'

The drive proved to be twisting with wonderful views over the valleys and up the mountains.

'I Can't believe how green everything is up here. So many trees and the contrast of dried grass and the green trees are beautiful.' She said.

'Various oaks, sweet chestnut, wild cherry all go to make up the forests, which cover over half of the island, so you see why it's so green. The shepherds practice goat farming up here, where the goats roam in the forests, eat the nuts, feed the trees and clear all the ground, keeping it open and a guard against fires.' Said Luca.

A silence fell between them as Sara watched the landscape slip by.

Passing Fonni, Tiana, and Sorgana, Sara watched as tiny mountain villages that seemed to cling to the mountainside gave way to the cultivated lands around and then turned to forest again.

Suddenly, they turned left off the major road down a track through the trees. Luca stopped the car in front of an enormous lake.'

'Largo Gusana,' he said, anticipating Sara's question. 'Time for a picnic under the shade of the trees and near the water.'

They found an area covered with grass tufts and had their picnic in the shade of a clump of olive trees.

Luca unpacked the basket as Sara lay back in the shade, listening to the birds singing and chirruping, while a gentle breeze rippled across the lake and brushed through the trees and grasses, giving a brief respite to the heat of the day.

Luca settled down with his back against one of the old olive trees and Sara leant against him.

Fresh ham, olives, and tomatoes were wrapped in greaseproof paper. Sara made sandwiches with them. Taking a bite before handing Luca his sandwich.

'Mmm, wonderful, I'm starving,' she said.

'So, I see,' said Luca as he took the sandwich Sara offered him. 'Remind me not to take you on my year out. I wouldn't be able to keep you in food,' he added, a broad grin on his face.

They lay back on the grass and watched a hawk as it lazily hovered on a thermal.

'Well, I have one more place to show you and we need to get there before dark,' said Luca as he packed up the picnic things.

They climbed into his car and set off once more. The sun was running just above the mountain tops setting them alight with its last golden beams. The temperature had dropped, and the air was fresher, as a gentle breeze brushed the trees and grasses.

Luca finally pulled off the road into a courtyard area. The gates were closed, and he got out of the car to unlock the gates, drove the car in, then closed them behind him.

'Where are we?'

'Sara, this is one of my favourite places in the whole of Sardinia, and being a professor of archaeology, I have a key to most of the sites.'

Just then an old man came out of a nearby building and shuffled toward them.

'Professor! How good to see you, my dear friend,' he said, coming forward and shaking Luca's hand.

'I'm on my way home. I know you will lock up. Good luck,' he said, smiling a mischievous smile.

Luca opened the car door for Sara and introduced her to the man.

'Efis, this is Sara. Sara, this is Efis. He looks after this site and is an old friend.'

'Hello, nice to meet you,' replied Efis.

'You too,' said Sara.

Efis looked at Luca and nodded his head. He went out through the gates, locked them behind him, and shuffled away into the fading light.

'This place seems to have a dreamlike quality about it,' said Sara, looking at the buildings, which stood out against the hard-baked ground in the late afternoon light.

Luca took her hand and led her along a path, past old stone buildings. They came to an oval outer low wall with another one inside the shape of a keyhole. In the centre was a great triangular hole. They walked through the opening towards the great entrance. There were steps down into a well, steps that looked as if a machine had carved or cut them, they were so precise. The roof also had steps, matching the ones in the ground.

Luca led her down the steps to the edge of the water in the well. He turned and pulled Sara into his arms.

'This is the sacred well of Santa Cristina. I have always loved this place and found it fascinating. It is associated with the moon, and every eighteen and a half years its light falls directly into the well from that hole above,' he said, pointing to the corbelled ceiling. 'I may be a man of science, but the ancient people worshipped the sun, the moon, and water. What would life be without them? I believe this is much older than the Pre-Nuragic people and that it was a calendar for predicting the seasons. If you look, the stones are cut so precisely and with such incredible accuracy, it had to be done by skilled engineers. The stones and buildings around the well are not made with the technology the well– makers had. I believe the well-makers could have been from a previous civilisation, but it is impossible to prove.'

He looked at her.

'Am I boring you?'

'No, it's fascinating.'

A hush fell in the well.

'Sara, darling, I know you love Sardinia,' he said, pulling her into his arms again and kissing her gently. 'Will you marry me? I know we have not known each other very long, but long enough to know I want to spend my life with you. Do you love me enough to give up everything and come and live with me in Sardinia? Would that be too much to ask? Will you at least think about it?'

The world seemed to hold its breath as if it were waiting for her answer.

'Darling Luca, what an amazing place to ask me to marry you, and yes! I don't need to think about it; I love you too.'

He put his hand in his pocket and brought out a small blue box. Opening it, he took out the ring he had chosen for her.

'This comes with all my love, Sara.' He said as he slipped it on her right-hand finger.

'It goes on your left when we marry.'

'Darling, Luca, thank you, and thank you for such a wonderful day,' she sighed as she looked at the intricately fashioned filigree gold ring. 'It's beautiful. I love it.'

He held her to him and kissed her, and as he did a breath of air passed through the well, as if the world could breathe again. Then the night sounds came in on them as they climbed up the ancient steps towards a new life together.

CHAPTER TWENTY

That night Luca asked Sara to move into his flat with him, and she was happy to agree. The following day, Sara gave Olivia's aunt notice, thanked her for all her help and paid her a month's rent in lieu, to give her time to find another tenant.

Luca stayed for the morning to help move some of her things, first down the two flights of stairs, then up the two flights to his flat.

'I can do it over the week.' she said.

'It looks like a greenhouse with all your plants. Are you all right now?' he laughed. 'See you at the weekend,' he said as he kissed her. 'I miss you already.'

After he left for Cabras, Sara did not go straight to work, but spent some time finding places for her books and the ornaments that had been so lovingly collected during her stay in Cagliari. It was a job she would enjoy finishing in the evening; it would help to pass the time while Luca was away. Sara would bring the last of her things over from the old flat during the week, so it was in place by the weekend, and they could spend time together.

They had decided not to tell anyone they were engaged until they had found time to talk to their parents. So, it remained a wonderful secret for the time being. Sara put Luca's ring on a chain around her neck, so she could at least wear it.

When Sara arrived at the office, Olivia was busy going through a pile of old photos.

'A friend of mine, Bruno, is doing a tour of the ancient parts of Casteddu e Susu and he is having an exhibition of all the old photos he has collected,' said Olivia, sorting through the photos her friend had left. 'You will love it. He has asked if we could put some of these up in the window.'

'Where is the exhibition?' asked Sara, coming over to see the photos.

'Two doors down,' replied Olivia. 'Bruno has rented the empty shop for the two weeks of the exhibition. He has contacted *L'Unione Sarda* and they have found some old stories that are unusual.'

'Sounds interesting.'

'It will be. Please say you will come?'

So, that afternoon Sara and Olivia walked down the street to see Bruno and look at the exhibition he was busy setting up.

While Olivia and Bruno chatted together, Sara wandered around looking at the photos and reports from days gone by. Bruno had placed extracts from newspapers beside some of the photos taken at the time. Others were waiting to be finished.

Sara became lost in the stories of the inhabitants of Cagliari, especially the ragged children called *piccus is corbbus*, young, orphaned boys with their large baskets, who worked on the docks for a living in the early twentieth century.

Sara stepped forward to look at a photo of a woman standing with a young couple. Beside them were a youthful woman and a tall, dark-haired man with his arm around her shoulders. The man was the spitting image of Luca. In front of them all was a young, olive-skinned boy.

The hair rose on Sara's back as prickles of excitement travelled through her. She could not stop staring. The woman was her grandmother – but it couldn't be. Ellie had said nothing about being in Sardinia.

Sara looked at the write-up:

LOCAL WOMAN HELPS ORPHANED BOYS

Contessa DeLogu has bought a shack in the Giorgino area to help house the many young orphans often referred to as picciocus de

crobi, boys of the baskets, after the boys who worked on the docks
years ago. It is also linked to the life Of Sister Giuseppina Nicoli,
1863 – 1924, who cared for these children.

The Contessa is the wife of Count DeLogu, who is involved
in the new oil business at Sarroch. The Contessa has set up a trust,
called 'The Blue Shack Trust' after the colour of the shack.

When we spoke to the Contessa, she said she could not have
done it without the help of the young Englishwoman Eleanor
Montfort, pictured beside the Contessa…

Sara stared at the newspaper cutting and the photo. Perhaps it was a coincidence, someone else; but although the picture was not very clear, Sara knew it was Ellie.

Olivia came up beside her. 'Are you okay? You look… you look a bit lost.'

'When was this picture taken and where? Do you know?'

Olivia turned to Bruno.

'Can you tell us anything more about this picture?'

Bruno walked over to a desk, opened a large file, and flipped through it.

'It was taken in August 1961. You are in luck: the couple who ran the shack then, are here,' he said. He took Sara's hand and led her over to a couple in their sixties who were talking with a group of men.

'Franco, Antonia, this young lady is interested in your photo.'

They turned to Sara.

'Hello, I am Antonia, and this is my brother, Franco. What can we do for you?' she asked.

'Hello, I'm Sara Smythe. Could you tell me: the woman with the Contessa, who is she, please?'

'She was one who helped us to get everything off the ground. She came into our lives when we were desperate. Her parents were with the Consulate. She had gone to a luncheon with the business people involved in oil and other businesses in Cagliari. She asked them to help us. We had met her at a previous charity do and said she would try to help. Anyway, at the lunch, she asked them to help us, but they put her down and refused. But the Contessa was there, the wife of one of the Sardinian businessmen, and said she would help. The Contessa gave us money and set up The Blue Shack Trust for the boys. We had painted it blue; you see. She helped us find beds, get a cook, and find a teacher to educate the boys. Her name was Ellie Montford.'

Sara gasped, but before she could say anything, Antonia had grabbed one of the men she had been talking to and pulled him into the circle.

'This is Tommaso. With the help of the trust, we sent him to school, where he won a scholarship to university to study medicine. He is now a doctor with a family of his own. He is the mischievous one in the photo standing in front of Ellie. Dear Ellie, she would have been so proud.'

'Do you remember her, Tommaso?' asked Sara, a catch in her voice.

'I do. Are you all right? You look as if you've seen a ghost.' Said Tommaso.

Sara looked at Tommaso. He still had that same mischievous look about him as in the photo, though his hair was brushed down to keep the rebellious mop from springing out everywhere.

'Yes, I am all right, thank you. Please go on with your story. You said you remembered her.'

'Yes, yes, I do,' said Tommaso. 'Ellie was always extremely kind to me. I saw her the first time she arrived in Cagliari. She was with her mother and an enormous car. I remember she tipped me and got into trouble… You look pale – please sit down. Can we have a drink of water, please?'

Sara sat down and sipped the water that appeared from nowhere and tried to compose herself.

'What is it, Sara?' asked Antonia, looking concerned.

'Ellie Montford is my grandmother. I thought I knew her well, as we are close, but there has never been any mention, of her or her family, being in Sardinia. Ellie speaks Italian and I never thought to ask her where she learnt it. My great-aunt married an Italian and I know my grandparents used to visit her regularly when they were younger. I just assumed that Ellie had learnt Italian with them. I am at a loss to understand why nobody has ever said anything.'

Sara took another sip of her water, suddenly aware that everyone was watching her.

'I am sorry. You must think I'm very stupid.'

'Ellie is your grandmother?' said Tommaso a large smile spreading across his face.

'Yes, but she has never said anything about Sardinia.'

Tommaso took Sara's hand. 'She and Dee are the reason I am a doctor, they both helped me, and I shall be forever grateful to both of them, and Antonia and Franco as well.'

Sara looked at Tommaso and smiled.

'How wonderful.' Said Sara.

Antonia took Sara's other hand and held it.

'Tell me, is the Contessa still alive?' asked Sara. 'And who is the man standing beside Ellie with his arm around her?'

'The Contessa is still alive,' said Antonia, 'and you should meet her. She would love to see you and perhaps throw some light on the story. Ellie was incredibly happy here, but it was tragic… The man beside her was Giovanni Puddu and they were to be married, but he died in an accident.'

Sara caught her breath. 'I never realised my grandmother had such a tragic beginning in her life.'

'Here, take this – it's the Contessa DeLogu's address. Go and see her and tell her I sent you. She is still the main organiser for our charity and will be thrilled to see you.'

'You say they took this picture in 1961. But my grandmother married my grandfather in the same year, and there has been no mention of Sardinia,' said Sara.

'Perhaps Ellie had her reasons. They were different times, different standards,' said Antonia, touching Sara's arm.

'I can't believe you knew her.'

'Ellie was probably the most amazing person I have met,' said Antonia. 'She fell in love with Sardinia and was always ready to help. Her parents were old school – strict disciplinarians and undemonstrative. I always thought that was why Ellie loved everyone and everything with such a passion, to make up for the lack of love at home.'

'She certainly is a very caring person.'

'Her parents were working for the British Consulate before we had an ambassador. At that time, they ran everything from Rome.' continued Antonia.

'Do you know where they lived?'

'In the big house in Via Torino, next to the church. It was the old monastery.'

'How long were they here?' asked Sara.

'I think her parents came here in 1960, but they left in 1961 to retire. Are they still alive?'

'No. My great-grandmother, Isabel, died of pneumonia not long after they returned to England, and my great-grandfather, Ian, died about five years later, so I never knew them.'

'Excuse us, Sara, but we have to get back to oversee everything at the shack,' said Antonia, again putting her hand on Sara's arm. 'We have a few homeless young men needing our attention. But please come and see us when you have a moment and go to see the Contessa; I know she would love it.'

Antonia, Franco, and Tommaso said their goodbyes and left, leaving Sara with a host of questions.

'Are you ready to come back to work?' asked Olivia.

Sara looked at her and smiled.

'Yes, thanks. I'm ready.'

CHAPTER TWENTY-ONE

On Thursday, after a busy few days, Sara took the morning off work to find the address Antonia had given her. The sun shone brightly, accompanied by a gentle breeze from the sea, so she decided to walk to the Contessa. It was an imposing house, standing in a garden full of fruit trees and sweet-smelling shrubs. Sara pushed the buzzer on the gate post.

'Who is it please?'

'My name is Sara Smythe. Antonia from The Blue Shack sent me to see the Contessa. It's about my grandmother, Eleanor di Montford.'

'Wait, please.'

Sara waited and wondered whether this was such a good idea.

'Please come in,' said the voice over the intercom. There was a buzz and Sara pushed the gate open.

The door at the top of the flight of steps opened and a woman in a black dress and white apron stood ready to greet her. Sara climbed the steps and entered the grand hallway. Black-and-white tiles covered by Sardinian rugs gave the place a friendly air.

'This way, please, *signorina*,' said the woman, showing Sara into a large, airy room.

An elegant woman in about her sixties sat in a wing chair beside a low table, on which was a glass of water and a book. The Contessa rose as Sara came toward her.

'My dear girl, I am Grazia DeLogu, but Ellie always called me Dee. Please sit down so I can look at you... Coffee, please, Maria,' she said without drawing breath.

Sara sat down in the chair opposite the Contessa.

'The last time I saw Ellie, she sat in that same chair you are in and told me she was leaving. How time flies. Tell me, is Ellie still alive and well?'

'She is, thank you.'

'So, what can I tell you that you don't already know?'

'Well, everything. I did not even know that Ellie had been to Sardinia, let alone lived here. It has never been mentioned. I always thought I knew her and everything about her, as we are close, but it seems not.'

'Don't be too hard on her,' sighed Dee, putting her hand on Sara's arm.

Maria returned with the coffee and *amaretti*.

'Maria, do you remember young Ellie? The young girl who introduced me to the people at the shack.'

Maria smiled at Sara and nodded and made a hasty retreat.

'Forgive her,' said Dee, 'Maria is shy and traditional. I have tried to get her to give up her uniform and wear casual clothes, but she won't hear of it. Although she has given up the white cap, she always insisted on wearing.'

Sara smiled and tasted the coffee; it was hot and extraordinarily strong but hit the spot.

She took a photo out of her bag and showed it to Dee.

'Antonia gave me this picture. I saw it at the exhibition. It shows Ellie with you and Antonia and Franco, also young Tommaso.'

'Ah yes, young Tommaso, grown up to be a doctor. One of our great successes.'

'But who is the man with his arm around Ellie?'

'If you don't know anything, then I will tell you all I know,' said Dee sitting back in her chair. 'Ellie came here to be with her parents for the summer of '61. They were working with the British Consulate. Your great-grandmother was an extremely ambitious woman. All Isabel wanted was a knighthood for her husband.

'Whenever Ellie joined her parents, she had to learn the language of the country or do good works. So, when she came to Cagliari, her father arranged for her to have Italian lessons with old Professor Serra. But he became ill and retired, and so Ellie had lessons with Giovanni Puddu. They fell in love, and he is the man in the picture.

'Ellie used to attend luncheons with her father, and it was at one of these so-called business meetings that we met. I was there with my husband, as he had gone into partnership with an Italian in the oil industry. Ellie had already met Franco and Antonia and said she would try to help them.'

Dee smiled as she thought back to that day.

'I shall never forget this young slip of a girl asking the Italian oil man to help the poor children of Cagliari. He rejected her out of hand and was rude to her, but she stood her ground. I was interested in what she had to say, and I admired her for her courage in the face of such hostility. I told her I would help, gave her my card. Besides, I did not like the man. It was the start of a great friendship with Ellie.'

Dee sipped her coffee and continued.

'Ellie became engaged to Gino, much to the horror of her parents, who had hoped for an advantageous marriage in England. But he had an accident and died. She came to see me after his death. Her parents were insistent on her going home and confessed she was carrying Gino's child. She hadn't known until after he died.'

Sara stared at Dee and caught her breath.

'I begged her to stay here, to come and live with me but she felt she couldn't, not just then, as everywhere reminded her of Gino and found it hard without him. Ellie went home, and unfortunately I never heard from her again.'

'She came home and married Simon Smythe, my grandfather.'

'Did they have any children?'

'One son, my father,' replied Sara.

'Will you stay for lunch?'

'You are kind, but I have to get back to work. May I come and see you again sometime?'

'I understand, my dear, and yes, I'm always here.'

They stood and faced one another.

'Ellie's story was incredibly sad. Do not judge her too harshly. Times were different then. Not as liberal as they are now.'

Sara smiled and followed Dee to the front door.

'Please come again, anytime. It will be lovely to see you and to catch up.'

Sara walked back to the office, her mind racing with questions. Ellie and Simon had one son, Adam – Sara's father. If he was Gino's son, did Simon know? Did Adam know?

Sara stopped off at the Piazza Yenne for a quick coffee and to go over in her mind the conversation with Dee.

She arrived back at the office to find everyone busy and immediately put to work with an awkward customer unwilling to let Olivia help her.

Sara's phone rang.

'Hello, darling,' Luca's voice was soothing.

'Hello, you.'

'I will be home soon. Will you meet me at the Antico Caffè at seven-thirty? My parents want us to go to supper with them. Mother is dying to meet you and Father is curious too. I have some work to do in Cagliari, so it will be a long weekend.'

'Wonderful.'

Olivia was trying to attract Sara's attention.

'I must go. See you this evening. Love you.'

When Sara arrived at the Caffè, Luca was sitting in their usual place in the corner. He looked up and smiled at her, rising to kiss her.

Sara had taken the ring from around her neck and put it on her right finger, as Luca had done.

'I've missed you, darling,' he said, clasping her in his arms.

'I've missed you too.'

'Hope you don't mind going out to supper?'

'No, it will be lovely. I have a bottle of wine and some flowers,' she said, putting the large brown bag down beside her.

'You are amazing. Thank you.'

He put his hand up to order her a glass of wine from the passing waiter.

'You have no idea how amazing this week has been,' he said, his eyes alive with excitement. 'We have been opening more trenches on the Monte Prama site and we have found more of the giants. They are fascinating – tall warriors, damaged, but we are trying to put them together. It is painstaking work, a jigsaw without the picture to help.'

Sara sat listening to him. He was like a boy explaining a favourite hobby or a new toy.

Suddenly he looked at his watch.

'It's late. Why do you let me ramble on like this?'

'Because I love to listen to you.'

'You are lovely, but we will be late for supper. I have told them there is something I want to tell them.'

Sara looked at Luca and smiled as he tweaked her nose between his forefinger and thumb, a small gesture he always did when he wanted to show her, he was thinking of holding her or kissing her.

They arrived at his parents' home, a neat, three-storey house in the marina area. His mother, who was a tall, elegant-looking woman, opened the door and welcomed them into a wide hallway, then took them upstairs to a large sitting room where Sara handed her the flowers she had brought.

'How beautiful! Thank you, Sara,' said Luca's mother, taking the flowers. 'I am Francesca, and this is my husband, Angelo. Excuse me while I put these beautiful flowers in water.'

Introductions were made all-round, and Luca's father smiled at the bottle of Nepenthe Sara had chosen, his favourite.

The dining room, opposite the sitting room, was spacious and the table was laid with the finest china and glassware.

It proved to be a wonderful evening. Luca's parents made Sara feel very welcome. The food was excellent – homemade pasta and beautifully cooked lamb – and the conversation was stimulating as they discussed the possibility of independence for Sardinia, poetry, languages, and, of course, archaeology. Luca told his father about the amazing finds at Monte Prama, while Sara and Francesca talked about Sara's work and Sardinia.

Luca rose, took the bottle of wine, and filled everyone's glass.

'I have been so busy telling everyone about our find that I almost forgot the actual reason for coming to see you. Mama, Papa, I want you to know that I have asked Sara to marry me, and I am happy to say that she has accepted. I only hope you are as happy as I am, as I love her very much, and, amazingly, Sara loves me too.' Luca said, taking Sara's right hand and kissing the ring he had given her.

Francesca laughed, and rising put her arms around Sara, while Angelo hugged his son and then Sara.

'How wonderful! I am so pleased,' said Francesca. 'Luca has been so happy since he met you, and I know you will look after him; that is all a mother can ask of her future daughter-in-law. I'm sure he will do the same for you.'

Francesca hugged Luca, a tear in her eye. 'Darling boy, I am so happy for you.'

Angelo embraced his son and kissed Sara.

'Welcome to the family, my dear. And I have to say you have excellent taste, not only in the man you have chosen but also the wine.'

Francesca took Sara's hand.

'Come and see me whenever you are in the Marina area. I am home most of the time, and it would be lovely to see you and get to know you.'

Sara promised she would as they said their goodbyes.

Back at the flat, Luca took Sara in his arms.

'I love you, Sara. Thank you for making me so happy and wanting to be part of my life. I promise to love you and care for you forever, even if you get fed up with archaeology.'

They laughed.

That night Sara rang her father to tell him her news and sent him a photo of her and Luca together from her phone. Father and daughter sat and talked until the early hours, Sara telling him all about Luca and how much she loved him and what they had been doing together until she had to end the call as sleep overcame her and went to join Luca in sleep as he enfolded her in his arms.

CHAPTER TWENTY-TWO

It was two weeks later when Sara returned to the marina area. She had been busy at the agency, and Luca was up at Cabras until Saturday, so Sara went to see his mother.

Armed with *Dolci Sardi* that she had bought from a shop on the Piazza Yenne, Sara rang the bell of the tall, elegant house. A middle-aged woman answered the door.

'Good day. Is it possible to see Signora Melis?' said Sara.

'Who is it?' called Luca's mother.

'Someone for you, Francesca.'

'I'm Sara…'

'Come in, come in, Sara,' said Francesca, opening the door wide. 'How lovely to see you. This is my cousin, Valeria; Valeria, this is Luca's Sara,' she said, ushering Sara into the hall.

'How wonderful! Forgive me. I have heard a lot about you. But please, will you excuse me? I have an appointment and I am already late,' said Valeria.

The two cousins embraced, and after many goodbyes and *ciao*'s, Valeria left.

'Come in here, Sara. Would you like coffee, tea, or a soft drink?'

'Coffee would be wonderful if it's not too much trouble. Thank you.'

'No trouble. Just make yourself comfortable in here.'

Francesca led her into a downstairs sitting room. There were large sofas with cushions to sink into, a table with magazines and bookshelves with books and photos of all the family.

'Sit yourself down whilst I make the coffee. We use this room for family visitors, as it is so much cosier than upstairs.'

Sara looked around the dayroom at all the different photos. She could hear Luca's mother in the kitchen, singing to herself while making the coffee. Sara put the *dolci Sardi* on the coffee table and turned to look at the photos on the sideboard and shelves.

There was a photo of Luca's parents on their wedding day, dressed in traditional costumes, beautiful in black and white; sepia photos of their parents and grandparents; a shot of Luca as a little boy, smiling and happy.

Sara moved to look at the others. One caught her eye. She picked it up and stared at it. A man and a woman stood together, he with his arm around the woman. A young boy stood in front of them, and the man was resting his hand on the boy's shoulder. There was a familiarity about the picture. She looked closer. The couple were looking at each other as if only they existed in the world. Sara felt her heart race and felt faint at the moment of realisation: it was the same couple as in the newspaper report – Ellie and Gino. The boy was not Tommaso, though, but he was the spitting image of Gino. Sara smiled but felt the hairs on the back of her neck rise and suddenly became gripped by a stab of fear.

Sara did not hear Luca's mother return.

'I love that photo,' said Francesca, putting down the tray with the coffee. Sara jumped. Her mouth had gone dry, and the world seemed to spin.

'Who are they?' she croaked.

'The boy is Angelo, my husband, and he is with his father, Gino, Luca's grandfather, and an English woman Gino was going to marry. Her name was –'

'Eleanor Montford…'

'How clever of you, but then I suppose Luca has told you, as it is strange that they should both fall in love with an English woman.'

'But I thought his name was Puddu, Giovanni Puddu, and your husband's name is Melis.'

'When Gino died, Angelo was living with Clara, Gino's sister, and her husband, Giuseppe Melis, his aunt, and uncle, as

214

his mother had died in childbirth. After Gino died, they adopted Angelo, and he took the name, Melis.'

The room seemed to close in on Sara. Everything seemed distant and she felt sick. She had to get out.

'Are you all right, my dear?' said a voice that seemed far away.

'I'm sorry, I don't feel very well. I need some air. Please forgive me.'

To the surprise and dismay of Francesca, Sara muttered a goodbye, grabbed her bag, stumbled to the door, and wrenched it open. Sara ran up the street. She had to get to the flat before being sick. Racing up the stairs, to the flat and into the bathroom where she threw up.

Feeling weak, Sara fell to the floor and wept.

Everything was going around in her head. Dee's words: Ellie was pregnant when Gino died. Angelo was Gino's son. Was Sara's father, Adam, Angelo's brother? Did Adam know? Did Simon know that Ellie's child was not his? Sara had to know, but in the meantime, she had to get away.

If she and Luca shared the same grandfather, then marriage would be impossible and against the law. An uncontrollable lump welled up in her throat and she fought to keep it down. She couldn't stay. She rose, washed her face with cold water, and packed a few things.

With shaking hands, Sara rang her boss.

'Rob, I need your help. Something has come up and I need to get away from Sardinia. Please can you help?'

'Are you okay? Are you in any trouble?'

'I'm all right. I just need to leave.'

He hesitated for a moment.

'I have a problem in Paris. Could you help there?'

'Perfect.'

She listened as he outlined the problem.

'I will organise everything this end. Fly to Milan and your ticket to Paris will be there. Is there anything else I can do for you, Sara? Do you have enough money? Have you rung your parents?'

'Yes, I have enough money, and no, I haven't rung my parents. Please, Rob, I do not want anyone to know where I have gone. Not for the moment. I will explain when I get to Paris.'

'Take care, Sara, and keep in touch – promise me. If you need anything, put it on the company card or phone me. Do you understand?'

'Thanks, I will.'

'I will contact the office in Cagliari and say you have been called home for an emergency.'

'Thanks, Rob.'

Sara rang off and set about organising everything and then sat at the table to write to Luca.

My dearest, darling Luca,

First, I want you to know that I love you more than anyone in this world. You have shown me a love that I treasure above everything else.

If you love me, please try to forgive me, and please apologise to your mother for my behaviour.

Please do not look for me. We cannot marry, but I will always love you.

Sara

Large tears fell as she reread the note. Then put it on the table next to the keys of the flat. Sighing, she took the ring from her finger and placed it on the letter.

There had been such excitement in the office when she had worn the ring to work, so much joy. Everyone was so eager to share her happiness, and all Olivia could say was that she had known Sara would want to stay in Sardinia.

After one last look, through tear-blurred eyes, she looked around the flat where she and Luca had shared so much love, picked up her case, and walked down to the Piazza Yenne to take a taxi.

'Elmas, please,' she said, putting her case on the back seat.

'Are you all right, *signorina*?'

Sara nodded. Unable to speak, knowing if she gave way now, all would be lost.

The airport was unusually quiet. Sara used her company card to buy a ticket to Milan.

At the airport in Milan, Sara found the information desk. Rob had booked her on a morning flight to Paris and arranged for her to spend the night in a rather smart hotel near the airport.

The following morning, she flew to Paris. In the arrival's hall, a man was waving a plaque with her name on it.

'*Mademoiselle* Smythe?' he asked.

'*Oui.*'

The driver took her case and walked toward the door. Sara followed behind. He dropped her at an expensive hotel near the travel agency. Sara booked in and rang Rob.

'Do you have any idea how much this hotel is a night?'

'I do. Besides, I do not know any good B&Bs in the area! How are you? Can you tell me what has happened?'

Sara sighed and settled herself in a chair.

'I met this man called Luca in Cagliari. We fell in love and he asked me to marry him.'

'That's good, isn't it?' asked Rob.

'I also learnt that my grandmother had lived in Sardinia when she was younger. I had no idea Ellie lived there. The long and the short of it is, Ellie was engaged to a Sardinian called Gino who died in an accident and she had a child by him. That child is more than likely my father, making Gino my grandfather. And Gino was Luca's grandfather, meaning Luca and I share the same parenthood.'

'Sara, have you asked your grandmother?'

'No, not yet.'

'Why not? You could clear this up with one question.'

'Rob, listen, I don't know if my father knows that he might not be the son of the man he thought was his father. Ellie has said nothing about this, perhaps no one knows.'

'Ah, I see. But you must contact them, Sara – please, promise me. My name will be mud if you don't tell them.'

'I promise, Rob. I will go to the agency this afternoon and ring you this evening.'

Sara arrived at the office and introduced herself to the manager.

'We have no problem here,' he said. 'I am not sure why you have come.'

The staff were unhelpful and arrogant as Sara looked through the books and the daily routine. It was just before closing time that they handed her an email with details of what Rob wanted her to do.

That evening Sara found a B&B and moved into the small but comfortable room and rang Rob.

'They resent any interference, but they need some help with the sales.'

'If you have too much of a problem, ring me. Is the hotel comfortable?'

'I've moved to a B&B around the corner – much more me.'

'I give up. Keep in touch and ring your father.'

★

Sara slowly settled into Parisian life, loving the café culture and was happy during the day in her own company.

It was the nights Sara found so hard, longing for Luca's touch, to feel him close to her, to hear his voice, and the tears would come, however much she fought them.

Sara arrived at the office early every morning and got on with her work. She found and fixed a few accounting errors, but nothing major, and wondered if Rob had just invented the job to give her something to do.

Towards the end of the month, the local team slowly accepted her for her skills with the clients and the hoteliers. Bookings rose, and by the end of the third month, she had made a considerable difference to the balance sheet.

During this time, Sara only contacted her father once to say she was extremely busy, avoiding questions by saying that she was fine but was needed in the office. When he returned the call, she blocked it, feeling she could not talk to him yet.

Sara dined out most evenings in the bustling bistros near her B&B. The nights were interminable and filled with thoughts of Luca. The more she thought about it, the more Sara realised she would have to go home and face up to the problem. She needed to talk to Ellie, to know her side of the story; needed to know if her father knew about Ellie's time in Sardinia. Sara needed to know, but was afraid of the truth.

It was after a particularly lonely weekend that Sara phoned Rob. The weather had become cold, and Christmas loomed on the horizon.

'I need to go home. Can you organise things here?'

'Thank God. I only hope you can sort something out. I have kept my promise not to tell anyone where you are, but for everyone's sake, you should go and see your family. They are desperately anxious about you. And my name is more than mud now. By the way, you have done a wonderful job with the sales. Thank you.'

The following morning, Sara told the office she was leaving and was surprised by their genuine sadness. That evening she packed all her things, paid her bill at the B&B, ready to leave in the morning.

The flight to Stansted was uneventful. Sara found a taxi and finally arrived at her parents' farm in time for tea, paid the driver and tipped him.

'Nice-looking place,' he said.

'Yes, it is, thank you.'

Sara picked up her case and walked round into the yard to the back door, which was always open. Her father's two Ridgebacks came bounding up to her, barking and wagging their tails.

'Come in,' called Adam. 'I'm in the kitchen, whoever you are.'

Sara dropped her case in the back hall and headed for the kitchen. The familiar smell of baking and beeswax polish filled her senses and she found herself unable to hold back the tears.

Her father peered over his glasses and the paper he was reading, and then, realising who it was, jumped up and enfolded his daughter in his arms.

'Darling, darling girl, where have you been? We have all been so worried about you.' Adam held her tight in his arms, unwilling to let her go again. 'Whatever was it that made you feel you couldn't come home? I know it was something to do with Luca. But nothing could be so bad that we can't help you.'

'Papa, is Ellie at home?'

'Yes and has been waiting for you. She has been so worried about you. Go and see her, and I will bring a drink over later.'

'Where's Mother?'

'Jaynes' at a committee meeting. The vicar gave her the job of fundraising for the church roof, and she has done a wonderful job. At last, your mother has thrown herself into local things and the village has accepted her and she has found a genuine interest.'

Sara smiled at her father in the realisation that his life had become easier too.

'It's good to be home.' She sighed.

Adam kissed her and watched as Sara crossed the yard to the flint barn cottage, which he had converted from the granary when he moved into the farmhouse. He slipped into his office and lifted the phone.

Sara knocked on the door of the cottage.

'Come in,' said Ellie in answer to Sara's knock.

Sara opened the door to the hall. It was wide, with the staircase rising in front of the entrance. The room to the left was the dining room, and on the right was the sitting room. Sara entered the sitting room and was greeted by her grandmother's cat winding itself around her legs.

Ellie was sitting in her wing chair reading a book. The pool of light from the lamp beside her fell on her greying hair. Her grandmother looked well. Ellie looked up from her book, her face suddenly alive with surprise.

'Sara! My dear girl, where have you been? We have all been so worried. We couldn't get any information out of your boss, and nobody in Sardinia knew where you were,' she said, rising and putting her arms out to hug her granddaughter.

'I'm sorry, Ellie, but I needed to get away to sort my life out.'

'Sit down, child. I knew what the problem was as soon as your father showed me the photo of you and Luca you sent to his phone. We have a lot to talk about. Luca looks so much like his grandfather; it took my breath away.'

CHAPTER TWENTY-THREE

England, May 1962

Ellie could not have been happier. Spending her days furnishing the mews flat, and in the evening, preparing Simon's meal, when they would sit together, and he would tell her what he had been doing and she would show him her recent purchases. Ellie loved shopping for the new baby – a cot, clothes – and Simon was thrilled to see her so happy.

Ellie went into labour on an early May morning. Simon rang the office to tell them he was about to become a father and needed time off. Early that evening, Ellie gave birth to a beautiful dark-haired and dark-eyed boy, the image of Gino.

'Ellie, he's perfect,' Simon told her. 'You are so clever. My parents are over the moon and can't wait to see him. When will they let you go home? I thought it might be nice for you to be in the country – fresh air and lots of excellent food. Nanny is there to help you, so you can rest.'

'That would be wonderful. Thank you for this, Simon.'

They named him Jon after Gino and Adam after Simon's father, so they welcomed young Jon Adam Smythe into the world.

Simon arranged everything, and after a couple of days, he returned to the hospital to take his new family back to the farm.

Bea and A J were there to greet them, and Bea wasted no time in taking the little bundle from Ellie and holding him until Nanny arrived and took her charge upstairs. The bags were unpacked, and with everyone settled, the family sat down at the table to have a celebratory meal together.

Ellie insisted on breastfeeding the baby and would spend quiet time with him in her arms, looking at her precious child, holding him, enjoying him, and settling into some routine.

But things were about to change.

It was in June that A-J received a telegram from the Foreign Office in Nairobi, saying that there had been trouble in Kenya. Words cost money and the yellow telegrams always sounded stilted as the sender tried to convey what he wanted in as few words as possible, and they were usually unpleasant news.

Sorry inform you. Stop. Laurence and Fiona killed up-country. Stop. No other living relatives. Stop. Have had funeral. Stop. Suggest help.

It was signed by the British ambassador in Nairobi.

The news devastated Bea and A-J.

'What about the baby? Asked Bea.

Simon rang the Foreign Office to find out if there had been any further news.

'They were in their lodge, up-country near the border. The weather is cooler and it is a good time to go. They were raided and killed in their beds. We are still looking for any survivors, as they took several members of staff with them, but we don't hold out much hope. One of the house boys escaped. He was in the latrine when he heard the shots, and he managed to slip away. After he was sure the men had gone, he climbed into the land rover and drove back to raise the alarm.'

'And what about the young baby? What can I do?' asked Simon, trying hard to keep it together and focus on what the official was saying. His beloved brother dead – his nephew missing how was he going to tell Polly?

'Are you still there, sir?' asked the officer.

'Yes, I'm still here. It is all rather a lot to take in.'

'There is no news of a baby, but I will make more enquiries. There are things that need to be sorted out there. Any possibility of one of the family going out?'

Simon put a long-distance call in to Polly to break the news and begged her not to come home from Australia as there was nothing she could do. It was a painful conversation on both sides, but Polly finally agreed with her brother.

Two days later, after tearful goodbyes and a tedious journey,

Simon stepped off the BOAC flight to Nairobi. He was met by a high-ranking official, who took him to the Norfolk Hotel.

'I'm sorry to meet you on such a sad occasion. Both Laurence and Fiona were loved and well thought of out here.'

'Thank you. He was a wonderful brother too.'

'I'm sure you would like to wash and brush up. Take your time. We will meet you downstairs in, say, an hour.'

'Perfect,' said Simon.

Later, Simon presented himself at the reception, having showered and unpacked, and the woman at the desk showed him into a grand room, which proved to be the library. The official rose and offered Simon a drink.

'Please sit down. There seems to have been a development since we contacted your family. Our men went out to your brother's place to make sure everything was all right and that there was nothing else we could do and to look for the young baby. One man found the native Nanny hiding in the cupboard under the sink in her room. God knows how she ever got into such a compact space, together with her charge, the young Smythe baby.'

'Alive?' asked Simon.

'Yes. But the Nanny was traumatised. They had only planned on being up-country for a few days and Fiona had wanted to take him with her.'

'Laurence's baby, well and alive?' asked Simon.

'They found him with the wet nurse. She slept with the baby as all the native women do; it is so much easier to get them to sleep, and when they need feeding, it's no problem. She had been woken in the night by strange noises and, realising they were being raided, hid herself and the child in the cupboard and fed him to keep him quiet. Our men found her in a state of shock and unable to move, still clutching her charge. They coaxed and helped her out of the cupboard and took her to the hospital and informed the authorities.'

'Where are they now?'

'At the hospital. We have arranged for you to see him and for a nurse to travel home with you to look after you both.'

'I need to see the Nanny, to thank her. Can you arrange that too?'

'No problem. We at the consulate organised the burial of Laurence and Fiona. As Fiona had no living relatives, her mother having died of malaria earlier this year and her father of black water fever two years ago, so we decided that the child should be sent home to the UK.'

The official took Simon to see his brother and sister-in-law's graves. It was a hot and airless day, making the sweat run down his back. Simon wiped his face, trying to hide the tears he was so fiercely fighting against. He laid the flowers that the consulate had provided, first on Fiona's grave and then on his beloved brother's. The tears came, and he let them flow.

Later, Simon met the baby's nurse and thanked her, and gave her enough money to last her for a year in Kenya.

He made an appointment to see the lawyers and settle his brother's estate, only to find he was the sole beneficiary and had inherited the farm.

'When did he make the will?'

'When he first came out here. I tried to get him to make a new one when he married Fiona, but he never got round to it.'

'Can you sell the farm for me?' Simon asked the lawyer.

'I can. It will fetch a handsome sum as it is excellent land.'

'Please will you see to it, and when it is all settled, please put the proceeds in a trust for Laurence's son.'

Simon gave the lawyer all the details of the family solicitors in the UK. Then shaking hands, he left to see his nephew.

Simon found the small bundle in a cot in the local hospital. He was the only white face among the other babies. He had his mother's dark hair, but there was a look of Laurence in there. He was smaller than Jon although he was nearly three months older.

A nurse approached.

'His name is Adam John Laurence,' she said, lifting him from his cot and showing him to Simon, who looked at his nephew, trying to fight back the threatening tears, but smiled instead.

The journey home was long and tiring. The nurse who

travelled with them looked after the young Adam John. He seemed a contented child as the nurse fed him, changed him, and generally took care of him.

Simon tried to sleep, but he kept thinking about his brother and his untimely fate. It had only been March when Lawrence had rung to say Adam had been born.

'You are late again Simon, I was first and now I have the first grandchild.' Laurence had chided.

Only a couple of months ago his brother was well and happy, now he was gone.

He sighed. He would have to talk to Polly. Would Ellie be supportive? His mind flittered from one thing to another. He thought back to the days when they were all young together. The farm when they were children. When Polly had married her Italian winemaker. When Laurence had gone to Africa to work and had met and married Fiona. How he had loved Ellie and finally married her. No children, and now two. How quickly ones life could change. He would have to find a Nanny to help Ellie.

Once back at the farm, their old Nanny took young Adam under her wing. That night the baby woke Ellie with his cries, slipping out of bed she went up to the nursery and found Nanny in a state of anxiety.

'I can't seem to settle him, and I'm frightened he will wake young Jon.'

'Here,' said Ellie, 'give him to me.'

She sat in the nursing chair and Nanny handed over the little bundle. He was dark-haired like Fiona, but there was the Smythe determination in his cry.

Ellie gently rocked the fretfulness away, cooing at him so he settled at her breast and sucked contentedly.

'You're a natural,' said Nanny.

Ellie smiled.

'You go to bed, Nanny. I can cope; he'll be all right with me.'

After making sure Ellie had everything, Nanny left for her bed.

Ellie stared at the baby as he snuffled and sucked. She thought of the two young babies and felt a wave of untold joy.

Simon had to return to London, but Ellie wanted to stay on the farm for a while until the babies settled.

'You take care of yourself darling girl. Do not do anything stupid. Remember, you are looking after two precious things.'

She laughed and kissed him.

It was the early hours of the morning when Ellie woke to hear a baby crying again, more a scream, as if he were having some terrifying nightmare. Getting out of bed and putting on her dressing gown, she hurried to see what was wrong. Baby Adam had slept well during the week since he had arrived, and she was concerned.

Ellie opened the nursery door and looked in the cot. Adam was red in the face and convulsing with his cries. She gathered the baby in her arms and rocked him gently, humming to him. She tried to feed him, but he was in such a state it took her a while to get him to finally settle. He snivelled as he drew breath and sucked, and Ellie pulled her dressing gown around them both for comfort.

Finally, having fed, burped and, changed him, she put him in his cot, where he fell fast asleep. She checked on young Jon and kissed him. He looked so much like Gino. Ellie sighed and went to find Nanny.

Ellie knocked on her door, but there was no reply. So, she knocked again – still no reply. Hearing nothing, Ellie gently opened the door, to find Nanny slumped on the floor.

Ellie rushed forward to see if she could help. There was a pulse, but very weak.

Calling again and again for help, but none came. Desperate, Ellie descended the stairs, shouting for help. Her foot caught in her dressing gown, and the next moment she was falling in the darkness; unable to grab the stair rail, but just kept tumbling.

Ellie became aware of lights, people talking, shouting orders, pain, then nothing.

Ellie woke. Unsure where she was and called out. Simon was there at her side; he was holding her hand, his face a picture of anxiety. There were tears in his eyes.

'Where am I? What happened? Is Nanny okay? What about the babies?'

'Shhhh, Ellie,' said Simon. 'You are in hospital. You fell down the stairs. You must have caught your foot in your dressing gown, as it was all tangled around you. Nanny is here too; she had a minor stroke.'

'Am I all right? I can't feel my legs.'

'You had a nasty fall, darling. You have bruised yourself badly, so they have given you some powerful painkillers.'

'Are the boys all right?'

'They are, and don't worry, Mama is coping well.'

Ellie was quiet as a wave of emotion swept over her. Feeling numb, unable to say anything, unable to feel anything, as Simon comforted her.

The doctor was called and gave her a sedative.

'Your wife will need sleep; she has had a shock. It will take a few days for her to recover. We will keep her here but then send her home soon. It will be better for her there.'

Simon finally collected Ellie from the hospital and took her back to his parents' house. Bea fussed over her and Simon took compassionate leave to be with her.

'It seems I will do anything to have you home with me,' said Ellie.

Simon smiled and gently kissed her.

Bea hired another Nanny to help, and the family tried to settle down to some normality.

Ellie fed her two young charges, and they were put outside to catch the summer sun.

They put Ellie outside in the walled garden on the warm summer days, with a rug wrapped around her, to build up her strength. She was not eating and had lost weight, sinking into a deep depression. Her badly bruised leg felt heavy, and any effort seemed to drain everything out of her. Simon became more and more anxious as he watched her slip further away from him.

Two weeks after coming out of the hospital, Ellie was sitting in the garden on a beautiful day, a rug tucked around her, dozing in the sun's heat. A young dove being fed by its mother caught her attention. The two cooed at one another, and Ellie watched the affection between mother and baby.

Suddenly, a hawk came out of the sky and tried to snatch the baby dove, while the mother fought against all odds with the hawk. Ellie leapt from her chair, shouting, and screaming at the hawk, but all to no avail, as it flew off with its prize. Ellie looked at the mother dove and burst into tears.

Simon, having heard the commotion, came running out to find Ellie kneeling on the ground, sobbing her heart out.

'He's killed it, he's killed it,' she wailed.

He lifted her into his arms and held her tight.

'Who has killed what?' he asked, desperately searching around him for some clue to the trauma.

'The hawk killed the baby dove and its mother tried to save it. Simon, please help me.'

And with that came a huge sob, pouring out all the pent-up tears she could not shed since Gino's death. Simon held her tight, rocking her and comforting her. At last, releasing the pain she had been holding in.

Ellie drew back from him.

'Take me home, Simon, please take me home, and we can take the boys with us. They will need someone to love and care for them. We can do that, can't we?'

Simon held Ellie close to him and fought back the tears that stung his eyes.

'Of course, we can, darling, darling Ellie. I love you.'

Before returning to London, Bea arranged to have the boys christened in the local church. Their proud parents, Ellie and Simon, watched over by Bea and A-J, held Adam John Laurence

Smythe and Jon Adam Smythe. Afterwards, they all returned to the farm where Simon opened a large bottle of champagne to wet the babies' heads. Bea had asked Ellie's parents, but they had declined, saying they would be out of the Country. Simon rang Polly, but she was still in Australia but wished them both all the best.

And so, Ellie and Simon returned to their mews house in London to start a wonderful life together.

Life was hectic back in London with two young babies to look after. Simon insisted on having a Nanny to help with the boys so that Ellie could have some time to herself. Ellie would go shopping at Hamleys for toys and the White House for matching clothes for the boys. They looked so alike and were often taken for twins. Simon would return from work and play with the boys before they went to bed, and even at that young age, he would read them a story.

Ellie was so tired when she dropped into bed at night that she found the periods of sadness became fewer and fewer. The house became full of laughter and delighted squeals when Simon came home, and he noticed the change in Ellie. The tears had gone, she looked happy and accepted his gentle kisses without pulling away. Simon could not have been happier.

But fate had not finished with them yet.

CHAPTER TWENTY-FOUR

England, 2006

Sara stared at her grandmother.

'So, which one is my father? Does he know who his father is?'

'Yes, we told him when he was old enough to understand, but he was completely nonplussed. He was never worried about it and has always regarded Simon and me as his parents; and has known nothing else, and we doted on him.'

'But you had two sons, one named Jon Adam and the other Adam John.

Which one is my father, Gino's son, or Laurence's?'

'Jon was Gino's son and Adam John was Laurence's son. We had already named Jon, and they were so alike that we treated them as twins, as there were only a few months between them,' said Ellie.

She hesitated, thinking back to that time and then, sighing, continued.

'It was two years after returning to London that young Jon, Gino's son, became unwell. He was fretful, sick, and drowsy. We called the doctor in and he said he thought it was measles. He told us to keep him warm and give him plenty of liquids. But that night Jon became worse, so we called the doctor again. This time a locum came out. He took Jon's temperature and put a glass over the rash that had developed. He said it was bacterial meningitis, that he was one extremely sick little boy and should be in a hospital.' Ellie said with a break in her voice.

'He called the ambulance, and we all went to the hospital. We instructed Nanny to take Adam John to Bea in Suffolk and to make sure they watched him twenty-four hours a day and to call a doctor if there were any signs of fever.

'At the hospital, they put us in a private room so we could be with Jon. That night Simon and I watched over him as he struggled with his breathing and had seizures. It was a harrowing and anxious time. In the early hours of the morning, Jon found peace as he died in my arms. Gino's son was gone.

'Simon held me and baby Jon, and we wept together. He said to me: 'He is with Gino, Ellie, but he won't forget us, you know that don't you?'

'But I promised Gino I would look after his child. I have broken my promise.'

'Ellie, darling you have done everything you could. You cannot blame yourself.' said Simon.

'Although he tried to reassure me, we had done everything we could. I felt so guilty.'

Ellie paused, thinking back to that terrible night when a part of her had been lost forever and sighed. She had carried the guilt of Jon's death for a long time, but time had been a great healer.

'We took him home, had a small service at the church, and buried him in the churchyard where the boys were christened.'

Sara put her arms around Ellie.

'I never realised you had such a tragic beginning to your life. Thank you for telling me. I didn't know if Simon knew, or if Father knew, as nobody has ever talked about it.'

'That was my doing. When I lost Jon, I felt it was time to close that chapter of my life. I had made a new life with Simon. It wasn't necessary to say anything – until I saw the photo of Luca, and you sent Adam the postcard of the Antico Caffè. It all came back to me then, and I knew you would find out about it. But it has been wonderful to talk about Gino and his son after such a long time,' Ellie said, large tears falling on her cheeks. 'And your father has been so worried about you, and Jayne has done everything to console him.' She sobbed.

Sara took her grandmother's hand in hers.

'I am so sorry to bring all this up. It has obviously been painful for you.'

'It is but it has given me the chance to think back and remember the things I have buried for such a long time. But there is one thing you must remember, Sara. When you are young, you think your love will last forever. You are invincible. You do not think of getting old. Hold each caress, each kiss, each part of your love in your heart and mind, for one day you will wake up to find that those tender kisses and gestures have become a touch or a hug. In old age, love becomes different. Time passes so quickly, until the young lover who took you in his arms every night when you whispered all those wonderful words to each other, probably cannot even hear you anymore. Companionship replaces passion; the comfort of one another, like a well-worn pair of shoes, replaces that once– exuberant love. Shared memories are the glue that binds you together. Cherish it now while you can, mourn it a little later when it has faded, but rejoice in having the friend and companion who is lying beside you.'

The knock at the door startled them both, and they wiped the tears from their eyes.

'Can I come in? Coffee, you two?' said Adam as he entered the room carrying a tray with three cups and biscuits. He turned to Sara and Ellie.

'Are you two all right?'

'Yes,' they chorused.

'You must ring Luca, Sara. He has been worried sick.'

'Luca has been in touch with you?'

'What did you expect? He contacted me the first day he returned to Cagliari. His mother had been trying to contact him but could not reach him until he came home. He called your office and begged them to give him your home number, which they did, and he rang me, thinking you had come home. When he discovered you were not here, he tried everything to find you. You should have let us know, Sara.'

'But I did not know who knew what, or if you even knew anything. Ellie had said nothing about Sardinia, and the last thing I wanted to do was upset anyone in the family.'

Ellie took Sara's hand.

'When I married Simon, I put everything of Gino's away, and when I lost his baby, I wanted to give everything to Simon and Adam. I loved Simon. He was my rock; he always stood up for me against my mother. He was my hero, from my childhood. He was willing to take on another man's child – and as it turned out, two men's children. He loved me and never judged me, and I came to love and respect him. It was not the passionate love that I had for Gino – and who knows if that would have lasted? Gino was a bright shining star in my life, but our love could have burnt out just as easily as it came. But you know, Sara, when Simon died, I lost a friend, a brother, a father and a lover.'

Sara put her arms around her grandmother and kissed her and then took her father's hand.

'I love you both. Thank you for telling me. It seems such a coincidence that I should meet and fall in love with Luca.'

Sara's mother returned from her committee meeting and greeted Sara.

'The least you could have done is let us know you were all right. Your father has been out of his mind with worry. Have you rung Luca? Where were you?'

'I was in Paris. I did not mean to stay so long, but somehow it got more difficult to leave with each week that passed. I have rung Luca, but his phone is off, and I can't get his parents either.'

'That boss of yours wants stringing up,' said Jayne. 'He wouldn't tell us where you were, only that you were all right.'

'I asked him not to. I just needed time, Mother.'

'Well, I'm going to do supper. Adam, can you feed the dogs for me, please?

Ellie, you will join us for supper, won't you?'

They all settled into their jobs. Sara took her case upstairs to her room, washed, and returned to the kitchen to help lay the table.

After supper, Sara said good night to Ellie and her parents and went to bed. She tried Luca's number again, but there was still no reply.

The following evening, they were all sitting having a glass of wine before having supper in the kitchen, when the dogs started barking.

'Sara, would you answer the door, please. It's probably the vicar collecting the papers from last night's meeting, and he is afraid of the dogs,' said Jayne.

Sara rose and went to the back door and opened it.

'Where have you been, my darling girl?' asked Luca, dropping his overnight bag and taking her in his arms.

'Luca! How did you know I was here?'

'Your father rang me yesterday afternoon as soon as you arrived home. I saw the staff at your office, and they organised all the tickets for me, made all the arrangements – they were wonderful. I have to say they are extremely efficient.'

'I'm glad to hear it. Dear Luca, I'm so sorry.'

'I knew it was something serious and that you would have gone home. When I rang here and found you had not come home, I saw my mother and she told me about the photo and how you had reacted on seeing it.'

'I thought my father was Gino's son and so we couldn't marry. I panicked. I love you…'

'Sara don't keep the vicar on the doorstep. Please bring him in,' called Jayne.

Luca bent to kiss Sara and then followed her into the kitchen.

Adam stood to shake Luca's hand.

'We meet at last. I was worried we would not find her,' said Luca.

'It was only a matter of time before Sara came home,' said Adam, sounding a lot more confident than before.

Introductions were made all-round, and finally, Ellie came forward and put her hand out to Luca, but he stepped forward and embraced her.

'You look so much like your grandfather, it's unreal,' said Ellie, a catch in her voice.

'I would have recognised you from the photo. You have hardly changed in all those years.'

'Italian flattery…'

'Sardinian,' chorused Sara and Luca, and they all laughed.

'Take Luca upstairs, so he can wash and brush up,' said Jayne. 'I will serve supper in ten minutes.'

Luca collected his hand luggage and followed Sara up the wide staircase to her bedroom. Once inside, he dropped his case and pulled her into his arms.

'I thought I had lost you. When I saw Mama, she was distraught, thinking she had upset you. It was the photo of my grandfather, Ellie, and my father, wasn't it?'

'It was when your mother told me that your aunt had adopted your father, Angelo and that his name was Puddu and not Melis. I had seen Dee and she told me something about Ellie's story, and I thought we shared the same grandfather. Ellie has told me the complete story now and I realise that it was not true. I have been trying to ring you and your parents ever since I have been home, but there was no answer.'

'No, I asked them not to talk to you until I found you. I have been in touch with your father from the time I knew you were missing. He told me about Ellie and Gino. It is a sad story, but one that frees us to be together.'

'Darling Luca.'

He pulled her closer to him. 'My darling. No more secrets, just openness, agreed?'

'Agreed.'

Downstairs, everyone was seated at the table when Sara and Luca entered the kitchen. A leg of lamb was set in front of Adam, and he was carving it into large slices.

'Sit down, you two,' he said, waving the carving knife toward two places near him.

The meat was put in front of them, and the vegetables served, and the conversation was lively as memories and stories were shared, Ellie and Sara, translating for Jayne and Adam.

Luca looked around the table, and then, turning to Sara, whispered, 'Do you not put bread on the table for supper?'

Sara laughed and went to the pantry to collect a large loaf and placed it in front of Luca.

'I forgot,' said Ellie. 'The Sards eat bread with everything.'

After supper, Luca followed Adam into his study to share a bottle of *Fil'e Ferru* that Luca had brought for him.

'Ellie, could you come with us for a moment?' said Adam. 'Could you translate for us? Will you join us in a drink?'

'It will be a pleasure,' said Ellie, sitting down in an armchair.

'Well,' said Adam, leaning back in his chair and savouring the strong liqueur. 'A job well done. Thank you for all your help, Luca. I can't thank you enough.'

'But I did nothing.'

'You were a great support, and I now know how much you love and care for Sara, and that is the most important thing in the world.'

'I know I have already asked Sara, but perhaps this is the time to ask you. I would like your permission to marry Sara. I love her. I loved her before, but when she went away, I realised how much a part of my life she had become. We share the same interests, and I am fortunate that Sara loves Sardinia.'

'You certainly have my permission and blessing. I know you will make her happy, and I know that she will care for you too.'

Ellie smiled as she translated their conversation.

Jayne knocked on the door and entered. 'Come on, you lot. The plates are cleared away and coffee is on the table.'

The smell of the coffee filled the kitchen as they sat at the table once more and told stories of times gone by.

'I must go to bed,' said Jayne eventually. 'I have an early start in the morning.'

With goodnights said, and kisses and hugs all round, Adam and Jayne went upstairs, while Sara and Luca walked Ellie over to the granary.

'I am so happy for you both,' said Ellie, hugging her granddaughter. 'Goodnight.'

'Goodnight,' Sara and Luca chorused.

Luca caught Sara by the hand.

'Can we walk outside before going to bed?'

'Yes, of course. I must let the dogs out. Come with me.'

Sara opened the back door and called the dogs, who bounded out to see what there was to chase in the garden.

The air was cool and still, but with the mild weather, the scent of late roses hung in the air. A crescent moon sailed high in the clear, star-sprinkled sky.

Luca took Sara in his arms and kissed her. 'I asked you once before to marry me, and you said yes. If I ask you again, Sara, will you marry me? I know now you are my world, and I can't and don't want to live without you.'

'I will, I will, darling Luca.'

He took the ring he had given her at the well of Santa Cristina and placed it on her right hand and kissed her.

'I love you, Sara.'

'I love you too.'

The following morning, the house buzzed with activity. Adam was up early organising the day's work on the farm. Jayne had gone to her meeting. Ellie was up and cooking breakfast for anyone who wanted it.

By the time Sara and Luca arrived in the kitchen, there were wonderful smells of toast, bacon, and coffee filling the room.

'Sit down, you two, and I will bring it to the table. Will you both come over to the cottage after breakfast? There are some things I want to show you.'

Luca tucked into bacon, eggs, tomatoes, and toast washed down with cups of coffee.

'My,' said Ellie, 'I would rather feed you for a day than a week.'

Luca laughed. 'I don't find the woman I love every day.'

After breakfast, Sara and Luca walked over to the cottage. They settled themselves on the large sofa while Ellie made more coffee.

On the low table in front of the sofa sat a beautiful antique box.

'I remember seeing that box when I was a child,' said Sara. 'I found it in a cupboard when I was staying with Ellie. I was about eleven or twelve, and I remember how angry Ellie was when she found me with the contents all over the floor. It was the first and only time I had ever seen Ellie really cross.'

Ellie returned with the coffee, and Luca stood to take the tray from her and placed it on the table beside the box.

'I was just telling Luca how cross you were when I found the box and emptied the contents onto the floor.'

'Memories,' said Ellie, sighing and opening the box and taking out a photo. 'I think this is the photo that your mother has Luca?'

Luca took the photo and looked at his grandfather, Ellie, and his father, Angelo.

'It is,' he said, and passed it to Sara.

'It's funny,' said Sara, 'but when I first saw you –'

'You mean when you first hurled yourself at me in the street.'

They laughed.

'Whatever. I was sure I knew you, and perhaps it was from this photo. It must have made an impression on me, as Ellie was so cross.'

'It was a long time ago now,' said Ellie.

'You all look so happy and so young,' said Luca.

'We were. It has been such a long time since I last opened this box. A lifetime. I put everything away when I married Simon, except this ring,' Ellie said, picking up the ring from the box and turning it in her hand. 'I found it difficult to finally end everything, but when I lost young Jon, I knew it was time to live another life; the life I would have lived if I hadn't met Gino. I can honestly say I never regretted marrying Simon. As I said before, he was my friend, my rock and finally my lover. We never had children of our own, but Adam more than made up for that.

'Sometimes I thought of Gino and what might have been, but it was such a passionate love, it could just as easily have burnt out, like some shooting star, and then left us both bereft. I have wonderful memories, which have come alive again after such a long time.'

Luca touched Ellie's hand.

'I didn't know my grandfather, but Angelo has been an amazing father to me. I grew up with lots of cousins, aunts, and uncles, which was great.'

'I don't suppose he remembers me; he was so very young,' said Ellie as she investigated the contents of the box again. 'We had this photo taken on the night Gino took me to the university ball.'

Luca took the photo and showed it to Sara.

'They are on the stairs to the university's main rooms,' said Luca.

Sara looked at the pair. Gino was in evening dress, standing tall and at a rakish angle, with one arm around Ellie and the other hand resting on his hip, one foot on the bottom step, and the other bent behind him. He was smiling and had a devil-may-care look about him. Ellie, who was wearing a blue toga– like dress, was looking at him adoringly.

'Gosh, he was good looking and very dashing. No wonder you fell for him,' said Sara.

'Yes, very much like Luca,' said Ellie, smiling.

Once more Ellie looked in the box and took out a blue and gilt box and handed it to Sara, who opened it and gasped.

'Ellie! This is exquisite.'

Ellie smiled.

'Gino gave it to me as an early twenty-first birthday present so I could wear it to the ball. I was going to wear it on our wedding day.'

'Su Lasu,' said Luca. 'All the young girls have one when they get married in costume.'

Sara looked at the beautiful pendant and stroked the filigree work gently with her finger.

'I want you to have it,' said Ellie.

'Ellie, it's beautiful, but I can't possibly take it.'

'It is time it was worn again, and it couldn't be more appropriate for the wife of Gino's grandson to wear it on her wedding day.'

Ellie again looked in the box and drew out a newspaper cutting. Sara recognised it as the one that had been in the exhibition with the photo of Ellie and Gino.

'I saw this at an exhibition of old photos. That is where I met Franco and Antonia, who run The Blue Shack charity.'

Ellie caught her breath.

'Are they still running the shack?'

'Yes, and they told me to see Dee DeLogu.'

'Is Dee still alive too?'

'Yes, she is. She is a widow but living in the same house in Cagliari. Dee spoke warmly about you. You will have to see her, and we will invite her to the wedding.'

'I should like that. She must have wondered why I never contacted her, but events overtook me here, and then it all seemed to vanish like a dream.'

'So, you still have friends who want to catch up with your life.'

Ellie sighed.

'It's all so long ago, I'm surprised they still remember me.'

'You should know that if you make a friend of a Sard, you have that friendship for life,' said Luca.

'When are you leaving, Luca?' asked Ellie, a tear in her eye.

'I have a ticket to go back tomorrow, as I have some urgent work to sort out. We have a particularly important dig at Cabras and I'm eager to be there.'

'And you, Sara?'

'I am staying for a couple more days. Mother wants to talk about the wedding arrangements, and I want to discuss a few things with Papa. I will go back after the weekend.'

Ellie smiled and looked at Luca.

'I remember Angelo was always interested in archaeology, and Gino used to read him stories about the giants that once lived in Sardinia.'

Luca laughed.

'And now I am excavating them. My father loves archaeology; he is a professor at the university. It was he who inspired and encouraged me to follow him. My grandfather would have been amazed at some discoveries we have made.'

'It will be good to see Angelo again,' said Ellie, a note of sadness in her voice.

At dinner that evening, when all the family was seated around the table, Luca rose and cleared his throat.

'Sara, will you translate for me, please,' he said. 'Adam, Jayne, Ellie, last night I asked Sara to marry me again, and I am so happy to say she said yes.'

A roar of approval went up from all at the table.

'I would like to thank all of you for your help and support. I know we will be incredibly happy.'

'A wedding, how wonderful!' said Jayne. 'We can have it here at the farm.'

'We thought late May next year if that is all right with you and Papa?' said Sara. 'But please, we want to get married in Sardinia. Would you be upset?'

'Not at all, my dear,' said Jayne. 'But in Italy, you must have a civil wedding first, so we can arrange that here and have a party, and then we can come down to Sardinia for the wedding. It will be good for Ellie to catch up with old friends too, and something to look forward to.'

Sara rose and put her arm around her mother.

'Thank you, that would be lovely.'

Then, turning to her father, she kissed and hugged him.

'Is that all right with you, Papa?'

'Perfect, my dear. That way everyone is happy.'

CHAPTER TWENTY-FIVE

Sara drove Luca to Stansted the following morning. They stood outside the airport and Luca kissed her and squeezed her arm in his familiar way.

'Don't be away too long. I need you in my life, Sara.'

'See you on Monday.'

One quick kiss and Luca walked away. He turned and waved to her, and Sara felt a flood of emotion wash over her.

'Take care,' she called.

At the farm, Jayne was already making lists of guests and looking up different companies for quotes on marquees, flowers, and catering. Her mother was in her element organising the wedding.

'You need to book everything so early, otherwise, you can't get the people you want,' said Jayne.

'She's happy,' said Adam.

'And you, Papa, are you happy?' Sara asked.

'I am. Your mother has at last forgiven me, after all these years, for giving up the Foreign Office, and has taken on the role of *noblesse oblige* in the local area. They asked her to raise money for the church and other charities, and she is always busy. We have both mellowed into contentment. But you, Sara, have found genuine love, and I'm so incredibly happy for you.'

'Thank you, and yes, I love Luca,' she said.

'My mother, at last, has some closure,' said Adam, 'which can only be good. I am only sorry that Simon didn't live to see it, but then Ellie might not have opened up to us if he had been alive, frightened of opening old wounds. I know they were very much in love, but it was a different love, with a powerful bond of friendship, which is sometimes better than just love.'

'Will you and Mother come to Sardinia? Will you come and give me away?'

'Try to stop me! Besides, I want to see what is so endearing about your island.'

They laughed.

'I love you, Papa, and I'm sorry for any worries I put you through, but I didn't know who knew what.'

'Don't you worry about that. You are home now and that is all that matters. But, Sara, you must remember there is nothing so bad that you cannot come and talk to me and your mother, or Ellie. Promise.'

'I promise and thank you.'

After a wonderful weekend spent together as a family, Adam drove his daughter to the airport.

'Keep in touch. I know your mother will want to talk to you about the arrangements.'

'Don't be silly, Papa, Mama will organise everything perfectly, and leave you with an enormous bill to pay. Let me know if I can help with anything.'

'I only have one daughter, and all I want is to see you happy, as well as your mother. I know she will organise a grand party.'

'As it will be a register office wedding here, I have decided not to have a wedding dress, but something I can wear for the dance in the evening. I will have the whole hog in Sardinia. I hope that is okay with you Papa?'

'Whatever, my darling girl.'

At the airport, they said their goodbyes.

'For God's sake, and mine, keep in touch,' called her father as Sara made for Departures.

The day after arriving back in Sardinia, Sara visited Luca's mother while Luca was up at Cabras.

Francesca welcomed her in, and Sara gave her the flowers she had collected from the florist's that morning.

'Come in, my dear. How lovely, thank you. Coffee?'

'Yes, please.'

'I won't be a minute. Sit down in the sitting room while I make the coffee and put these beautiful flowers in water.'

Luca's mother returned with the coffee and *dolci Sardi*.

'I am sorry about our last meeting,' said Sara, settling herself on the sofa in the day room. 'You must have thought me both rude and mad.'

'I knew something was very wrong. Now please, will you call me Francesca, as I hope we are to be friends.'

Sara smiled. 'Thank you, Francesca.'

'When Luca came back, he showed me your letter and I told him what had happened. He got your home number from the office, after a lot of persuasion, and rang your father. Adam told Luca about Ellie and Gino. No wonder you were upset. It is an incredibly sad story, but all is well now, and I am so happy for you both. I do not know how Luca would cope now without you at his side. He loves you so much, Sara.'

Sara smiled again and took Francesca's hand.

'And I love him too, so very much.'

'I know. Now come with me. I have something I want to show you.'

Sara followed Francesca up the broad marble staircase to the dining room where they had a meal the first time she met Luca's parents. Francesca opened the door and let Sara enter first.

'I have taken it out of its box, and it looks as good as it did all those years ago,' Francesca enthused.

On the table lay a full local Sardinian costume.

'This was my mother's when she married, and I married Angelo in it. They always get handed down. Sometimes the moths get to them, but all is well. I have hung it outside to take away the smell of lavender and cedar. I wondered, as I have no daughter, if you might like to wear it when you marry Luca?'

Sara looked at the costume. It was magnificent. A red pleated skirt which, when opened, showed blue stripes. A beautiful silk pinafore worn at the front and a waistcoat of brocade with gold, red and blue. A hand-embroidered white shirt with lace at the throat and cuffs. Shoes made of the same brocade as the waistcoat, and a lace headdress.

'It's perfect! Francesca, are you sure? That would be amazing, thank you,' cried Sara.

'We may have to make a few adjustments, and the shoes may not fit, but we have time to sort it all out.'

'Thank you. What a wonderful thought. Will Luca be in costume?'

'He will. He has Angelo's and it should fit him well. When are you thinking of getting married?'

'As you know, Luca is terribly busy up at Cabras, so we plan to have the civil marriage in late May, which will be lovely in England, and then come down to Sardinia for the church wedding.'

'Perfect. That gives us time to organise things here.'

CHAPTER TWENTY-SIX

January 2007

Christmas passed; Luca and Sara spent the time with their parents, as next year they hoped to spend it together.

In January, Sara returned to Sardinia and spent a long weekend with Luca in Cagliari.

She called in to see her colleagues at the Agency, only to be greeted by Maria, Fabio and Olivia, who over-joyed at seeing her.

Sara had arranged that Luca would take her with him when he went up to Cabras and drop her at Oristano, so she could start at the agency that Rob had finally bought.

On a Monday morning, Sara presented herself at the new agency, and greeted Cara, and was introduced to Giuseppe, the young man who had been out to lunch when Sara had come up last year. It was his neat appearance that struck Sara.

'Hello, Giuseppe. We have not met. I am Signorina Sara Smythe. I know we will get on well.'

Ricardo Spanu, the now ex-owner, came out of the office and welcomed Sara like a long-lost friend.

'Come in, come in,' he beckoned. 'Two coffees, please, Cara.'

Sara followed him into the office, and they spent the morning going through the books, orders, and bookings.

'No wonder Rob sends you everywhere,' said Ricardo, 'you know the business inside out. I do not think there is a lot I can help you with. Giuseppe is more than capable of running this office when you are not here, and Cara is magic at the desk.'

'Will it be too much for them?'

'If the sales increase, which I expect they will, then they may need help. But I will leave that to you.' Said Ricardo.

'They can interview someone when the time comes. After all, they will have to work with whoever they choose.'

'Splendid idea. So, I need not come in anymore. You have my numbers, just in case you need anything else.'

'Thank you. So, it is back to your village, and your mother. How is the widow?'

'I am happy to say she is tired of being alone.'

Sara smiled at the big bear of a man, and his blue eyes twinkled.

'Lunch?' he said.

'That would be lovely, but there is work to do.'

He looked at his watch. 'It's one o'clock. Let's shut up and all have lunch on me, and I can introduce you to the best restaurant in town, so you can take clients there and get to know some locals. Always good for a local to introduce a stranger,' he said with a broad, captivating smile.

He rounded up Cara and Giuseppe and they all headed down to the restaurant.

It was late afternoon when they all said goodbye and Sara, Cara and Giuseppe got back to work.

'Is there anything we can do for you?' asked Cara.

'No thank you, but these are my contact numbers. My work number is in Cagliari. Fabio, Maria, and Olivia are at the office there, and will tell you anything you need to know or contact me. We all work together. This is my home number, and my mobile number for out of hours, and my email address.'

Cara took the card and gave Sara one with her mobile number and another with Giuseppe's.

'We will look forward to working with you, *signorina*.'

'Thank you, Cara, and my name is Sara.'

Luca came to collect her and took her back to his bed-and-breakfast.

'Good day?' he asked as Sara slid into his car.

'Yes, and with a large lunch thrown in.'

248

Once there, Luca introduced Sara to his landlady, before going upstairs to have a well-earned shower.

'Do you want to go out for supper tonight?' he asked. 'Have you any plans?'

'No, I'm not hungry, but you must be.'

'Sara, would you mind if we just went to bed? I'm exhausted.'

Sara looked at him and smiled. They fell into bed and he held her to him.

'Tell me about your day,' she said, but he had already gone to sleep.

January slipped by and the warmth of February took over. The island was in full bloom with wildflowers running rampant across the fields. A gentle breeze caressed the heavy blossom on the trees. Sara was enchanted by the beautiful landscape. The greenness of the land, the rushing streams, full, from the melting snows of the distant mountain range the abundant wildlife all filled her soul with happiness and it pleased Luca.

Some weekends they headed off to see various ancient sites or tombs that Sara had read about in her books and marked up to visit, much to Luca's delight. Other times they relaxed in each other's company, not wanting to do anything.

Some days they would head to Cagliari to see Luca's parents, and Sara went to see Fabio and the girls.

'When are you coming back?' asked Olivia on one visit. 'We miss you.'

'I will be back in a couple of weeks to catch up, but you can always contact me on my phone.'

'But sometimes I just want to chat,' said Olivia.

'Well, just ring and say what you want. If I am busy, I'll ring you back, okay?'

Luca and Sara spent the next weekend quietly at the flat. They went down to the Antico Caffè on Saturday evening to catch up with friends and have a meal. On Sunday, Ellie rang, she was so excited about the wedding.

They chatted for a long time until Sara said goodbye as she and Luca were lunching at his parents'.

'Have a wonderful time. Love you.' And with that, Ellie rang off.

Lunch with Luca's parents was always a treat. Francesca was a marvellous cook and Angelo entertained them with his stories.

'How are the wedding arrangements going in England, Sara?' asked Francesca.

'My mother is busy arranging everything and is in her element. I have left it to her, as we discussed most things over Christmas. She is sending out all the invitations for us, so I don't have a lot to do.'

'I have been sorting things out here. I know you said you wanted something intimate here. Well, I thought this might be an idea,' said Francesca, passing Sara the brochure for a venue.

'This looks lovely, where is it?'

'It's the little Church of Sant'Efisio. The owners, who are long-standing friends of ours, have restored the church and done all the buildings up to make a wedding venue and restaurant.'

Sara looked at Luca and smiled.

'I have spoken to my friend,' Francesca added, 'and she is happy to offer you the venue for Friday and the weekend, which means everything can be in one place.'

'How perfectly wonderful, thank you,' said Sara.

It was late when Sara and Luca climbed up the Via Lamarmora to their flat.

'What a lovely weekend. Dearest Luca, I can't wait for the wedding. Tell me, does your mother want some money towards the arrangements? It is a lot to do on her own.'

'What was the word? Dutch, going Dutch.'

'I'm serious, Luca. It is not the grooms place to pay for the wedding.'

'So am I. We can sort it out later. Come here.'

A month later, on the Friday before the wedding party, Sara and Luca flew to England. Adam collected them from Stansted in his Range Rover.

'Your mother has arranged everything, just as you said. The marquee is in the garden waiting to be decorated with greenery, and the florist is coming in tomorrow to start the flower decorations. The vicar has agreed to perform a blessing service and have you sign the register.'

'However, did she manage that?' asked Sara with surprise.

'He owes your mother too many favours. Besides, you do not want to be driving around town and it is easier to do everything at home. Jayne also promised him a meal and drinks, so knew he wouldn't refuse.'

That evening, they all had supper in the kitchen. Ellie was thrilled to see Luca and Sara again, and Jayne had pulled out all the stops for a wonderful weekend. It was an intimate supper, allowing the family to get to know Luca better, and for him to talk to Ellie about the people they knew. Ellie and Sara did the translating once more.

'I have arranged an early breakfast for tomorrow morning,' Jayne said. 'Mrs Lane is coming in to help so I can put the finishing touches to everything. The local hairdresser is coming in to do my hair, and will do yours too, if you wish, Sara.'

'Thank you. Is there anything I can do to help?'

'It all kicks off at three-thirty. I think everything is ready,' said Jayne, again checking her list. 'The caterers have been in today to lay all the tables. The disco is ready for the evening dancing. They will complete the flowers in the morning. Your dress arrived and is hanging in your bedroom. Luca is in the spare room at Ellie's, as it is bad luck for him to see you until you are at the blessing service. I think I have thought of everything.'

'Thank you, Mother, for all you have done.'

'It's been a pleasure and I've enjoyed it,' said Jayne, sounding genuinely pleased. 'But I am off to bed as I have an early start tomorrow.'

They cleared the table and put everything in the dishwasher.

'Mrs Lane is coming in early tomorrow and will sort the rest of this out.'

Luca kissed Sara goodnight. 'Until tomorrow.'

He followed Ellie to the cottage.

'We can have a nightcap and talk about your father and Gino,' Ellie said with an engaging smile.

The following morning the house buzzed with activity. Throughout the morning, friends who were staying arrived, and, after showing them to their rooms, Adam took them and Luca down to the local pub for lunch, leaving the household to get ready.

'Not too much to drink, Adam, please, do you understand? I don't want the marquee stinking of booze before the wedding,' said Jayne.

'Don't worry, I won't do that,' he replied with a wicked grin across his face.

'Adam, please,' said Jayne.

'I won't, I won't, I promise. I want to enjoy this day too.'

Sara refused lunch; she was far too excited, but her mother insisted on her having, at least, a sandwich.

Sara showered and washed her hair, and the young hairdresser put her hair up with flowers to match her bouquet. Then Sara slipped into her dress. It was cream with a midi-length skirt and matching jacket. Her bouquet consisted of pale-cream bud roses and pink Alstroemeria. The men had matching cream roses for their buttonholes.

Jayne stood beside Sara in front of the mirror.

'You look beautiful, Sara. Thank you for letting me have the wedding party here.'

Sara turned to her mother.

'No, thank you for everything. For always being there for me. I know I haven't always been the perfect daughter, but I do love you and Papa very much.'

Her mother put her arm around her daughter.

'Perhaps I have not been the best of mothers, especially when you were younger. You know I resented being taken from London and put in the country, but I wouldn't have it any other way now.'

'I'm glad you are happy.'

At that moment Ellie came into the room.

'The boys are back, and people are arriving, and the vicar is here…' She stopped and looked at her granddaughter.

'Sara, my darling girl, you look so beautiful,' she said, coming up to her granddaughter and kissing her gently. 'Be happy, just be happy.'

Friends and family had gathered in the marquee and were chatting as they waited for the bride. Adam walked Sara down through the guests toward Luca, who stood tall in his dinner jacket. Sara caught her breath, looking at the handsome man she loved and thought she had lost. Luca turned and smiled at her as Adam released Sara to him.

The address was short, the words brief. Luca put the ring on her right hand; it would go on her left hand in the church service in Sardinia. They signed the register, and the vicar gave them both a blessing.

Luca turned to Sara, pulled her into his arms, and whispered, '*Ciao*, my darling wife. You look more radiant today than ever. Thank you for this. I love you.'

'Darling Luca,' she sighed. 'and I love you too.'

People clapped, and then drinks were served. The vicar moved forward to wish them well and then hurried off to find a glass of champagne.

Jayne sidled up to a man dispensing the drinks. 'Make sure the vicar doesn't have too much to drink, or he will measure his length on the floor.'

People came and chatted with Sara and Luca, and they introduced Luca to all the family and friends, Sara translating for him.

Luca's family had declined the invitation, saying that not understanding English, they would feel lost. Sara and Luca had tried to persuade them. They had said they did not want Sara to spend her day translating for them, but that they were looking forward to the wedding in Sardinia.

Food was served, speeches were made and then there was dancing. The time flew, and before they knew it Sara and Luca were dancing the last waltz together, making a very handsome couple.

Gradually, after bacon and egg sandwiches at midnight, people left. Finally, the family and friends who were staying sat around the kitchen table, drinking coffee and recalling stories from the evening.

'I think that was a marvellous success,' said Jayne.

'You did a wonderful job,' said Adam, taking his wife's hand. 'Wonderful, thank you.'

'We have put the presents in the dining room,' Jayne said to Sara and Luca. 'Next week I will sort them out and give you a list of what they are and who gave them. When guests asked what you wanted, I said that money would be best. I'm pleased to say most have done that, so you have something to start with.'

'Didn't people mind?' asked Sara.

'No, not at all. Most people were relieved not to have to choose something. What is the use of them giving you a cut-glass cheese dish or a pair of silver sugar tongs? I told them that a gift of twenty pounds would be more than acceptable, knowing that most people would be much more generous!'

'Your mother knows how to get people to give their money,' said Adam, laughing.

Luca and Sara finally said goodnight and climbed the stairs to Sara's room. He pulled her into his arms and sighed. 'My darling love, Signora Melis.'

CHAPTER TWENTY-SEVEN

Luca and Sara returned to Cagliari to help Francesca, who had been busy organising everything for the wedding ceremony. Wanting an intimate service, Luca and Sara had decided to get married in the enchanting church of Sant'Efisio at Giorgino and had booked the venue for the long weekend.

On Friday night, they held a meal for close friends and family at the hotel at Sant'Efisio. Ellie was nervous at the thought of meeting old friends and fussed about it.

'Ellie, they are friends, maybe you haven't seen them in forty-odd years, but they are friends,' said Sara.

'But I never contacted them, never kept in touch.'

'You had your reasons, and I am sure they will understand. After all, they wanted to come and are thrilled at the idea of seeing you again.'

They all met in the hotel bar beforehand, and Sara and Luca were there to introduce everyone. Drinks were served, and people mingled.

'Ellie, this is Francesca, Luca's mother, and is married to Angelo,' said Sara.

Ellie moved forward to shake Francesca's hand but was immediately kissed on her cheeks.

'I have heard so much about you, I feel I know you,' said Francesca turning to her husband. 'And this is Angelo,' she said, stepping aside to let him come forward.

'Hello, Ellie. I still remember the day we all went to the beach and you bought me ice cream and we had our photo taken with Papa. Do you remember that day?'

'I do, and I still have the photos Gino gave me.'

At that moment, a very distinguished woman stepped forward.

'Excuse me, but I have to see Ellie.'

'Dee!' Ellie exclaimed.

'Oh, Dee, I am so sorry I didn't keep in touch but…'

'No need to explain; Luca has put us all in the picture. It is just so wonderful to see you again. The shack is still going well, and we have raised so much money, you wouldn't believe it.'

Dee stood back and pulled on the sleeve of the man standing beside her.

'You know who this is, don't you, Ellie?'

Ellie looked at the handsome man. His hair neatly combed back, but still sprang up in a rebellious way.

'Tommaso! Is it really you? My, you are a grown man. What do you do now?'

'I am a doctor at the Cagliari hospital. I am married and have four sons, who are my pride and joy. And this, Ellie, is my wife, Rosanna.'

'I am so pleased to meet you,' said Ellie, greeting the woman with thick black hair and hauntingly blue eyes.

'I am happy to meet you too; it is good to meet the woman who Tommaso is always talking about.'

Ellie turned to Tommaso, who was fumbling with his collar and pulled out a small filigree cross. 'I still wear it.'

Ellie found it difficult to hold back the tears and searched for a hanky, feeling completely overwhelmed.

'Here,' said Luca, handing her his handkerchief.

The table was set so that those who spoke English were put near those who spoke both Italian and English so that everyone could share in the conversation.

The evening passed with everyone sharing their stories and memories until, after midnight, Francesca rose.

'I am sorry to break up the party, but there is another day tomorrow.'

Looking at her watch, she added, 'I mean today.'

The following morning, as the guests arrived in the dining room for breakfast, chatting together, Francesca came to Sara's room to help her into her costume. First, Sara put on the handmade shirt, with lace at the throat and cuffs. Next came the skirt. It was pleated and made of red and blue striped material. Each red stripe had been stitched to the next one, so it looked like a red skirt until you moved, and then the blue stripes showed through.

'Gosh, it's heavy,' said Sara as Francesca pulled the skirt around her waist.

'There is a lot of material in it. I think it is like your kilt, only our pleats are smaller.'

The bodice, or waistcoat, was next, and made from a silk brocade with flowers in red, green, and blue on a cream background, and decorated with red and gold ribbons. It was stiffened, making Sara pull in her stomach and stand straight.

'Now I know why all the Sardinian women walk so straight and erect. This bodice makes sure of that.'

Francesca put the apron of blue silk around Sara's waist and stepped back to look at her handiwork and smiled.

'Shoes next. I had a new pair made for you, as mine were too small.'

'They are beautiful. Thank you, Francesca,' said Sara, taking the shoes, which were covered in the same material as the bodice and decorated with red and gold bands.

Finally, Francesca opened a box and took out a delicate lace mantilla and pinned it in place on Sara's head.

'You only need to wear it for the service, then you can take it off. It has been in the family for years and I have no idea how many brides have worn it,' Francesca said, steering Sara toward the long mirror so she could see herself.

There was a gentle tap at the bedroom door and Ellie entered.

'Come in, Ellie, come in and see how beautiful your granddaughter looks,' said Francesca.

Ellie stood and looked at Sara and caught her breath and

watched as her granddaughter gave her a twirl, revealing the blue in the skirt.

'I have this. I said I wanted you to have it,' Ellie said, opening the blue leather gilt box. She took out the *Su Lasu* and placed it around Sara's neck. The dark-blue velvet ribbon and the magnificent pendant stood out against the white blouse.

'My goodness,' said Francesca. 'How beautiful! Where did you get it?'

'Gino bought it for me all those years ago. I only wore it once, to a ball at the university. I was supposed to wear it at our wedding. I put it away after he died; the memories were too painful. But now it is where it belongs, around the neck of his grandson's wife. I'm sure he would be happy with that.'

There was another knock at the door, and Jayne and Adam entered the room. Jayne looked at Sara and smiled as she held Adam's hand. Adam drew in a long breath and tried to stifle a sob.

'My darling girl, you look wonderful! No wonder you wanted to get married down here,' said Adam turning to Francesca. 'Thank you for everything,' he said, taking her hand and kissing it.

The guests were all waiting in the enclosed courtyard in front of the small church, which was only big enough for the priest. They had placed two kneeling chairs in front of the doorway.

Sara took in the scene as her father walked her toward the little church. It was a warm day, but a gentle breeze brushed the trees and skipped amongst the flowers, making it feel fresh.

Luca was standing to one side with his father, whom he had chosen as his best man. Luca was in his traditional costume. He wore a velvet waistcoat buttoned with gold filigree buttons, over a handmade white shirt with another set of gold buttons at the throat and cuffs. The shirt was tucked into a short, black, kilt-like skirt over long, baggy white britches, which were tucked into soft black leather boots. On his head, he wore the traditional berrita.

Sara smiled a broad smile as she walked towards Luca. He looked so handsome, so different, so romantic in his traditional costume and felt as if she was falling in love with him all over again.

Luca turned to look at her. He was taken aback by how beautiful Sara looked, and then he smiled at her.

With Sara on his arm, Adam could not have looked happier if he tried. Jayne shed a tear, and Ellie was tearful too, as her memories came rushing back to her.

A quick kiss from Adam as he handed his daughter to Luca.

Sara and Luca knelt on the two chairs that had been placed in the doorway. Flowers filled the little church and their scent hung in the warm air.

The priest took the ring from Angelo and placed it on the open Bible he was holding. He gave them a short blessing and held the Bible out to Luca, who took the ring and placed it on Sara's left hand.

Finally, the priest said, 'Those whom God has joined, let no man put asunder.'

Luca rose and helped Sara up and took her into his arms.

'My darling, darling wife.'

A cheer erupted from everyone as Luca kissed Sara.

They all moved into the large dining room. The tables were laid out with white cloths, long sprigs of bougainvillea, and bread sculpted into flowers and animals. Each place setting had a material bag, pulled together with a ribbon, containing a single pearl for the women and a pair of gold button cufflinks for the men.

On the large table where Sara and Luca sat with their families, there was a ring of bread decorated with birds, flowers, and strange Sardinian symbols. It had a ribbon to hang it up.

'We take that home and it dries out over the years and will be a reminder of today,' said Luca.

Everything looked so inviting. People found their seats and began chatting to their table companions.

The meal was a traditional Sardinian wedding feast: a delicate fish course with white wine; *malloreddus* and then roast suckling pig with Cannanau wine; *Sebadas* for dessert with Vernaccia; rounded off with *Dolci Sardi* with coffee and *Fil'e Ferru*.

When the talking turned to a murmur and Adam was sure that there was no more food to come, he rose and tapped his glass.

'*Signore,*' he began in his very broken Italian.

'I beg you to please forgive my Italian. Ellie always tried to teach me your language when I was a child; now I understand why.'

There was a ripple of laughter among the guests, and he continued again in Italian.

'I have spent days trying to learn this speech, but it seems it is difficult to teach an old dog new tricks. First, I want to thank Angelo and Francesca, and Luca and Sara, for arranging such a wonderful venue.'

Cheers from his audience.

'Also, with the help of friends and family, it has been our honour to get to know you all.' Turning to Luca's parents, he raised his glass. 'To Signore Angelo, Signora Francesca, Luca and Sara. I thank you sincerely. May God bless you all.'

'*Saludi,*' chorused the guests.

Luca rose and thanked everyone and then took Sara to cut the cake. People moved to other tables to talk to friends or meet new ones. Ellie and Dee sat huddled together and chatted about old times. Dancing began, and the tables cleared to allow guests to sit and chat and drink together.

Olivia came over to see Sara and Luca.

'I'm so pleased everything worked out so well. I was really worried about Luca when he found you had gone.'

'How is everything at the agency?' asked Sara

'Missing you but doing well.'

Rob and his wife had flown in to be at the wedding and Jayne wasted no time in rebuking him.

'Why didn't you tell us she was in Paris? So inconsiderate.'

'Sara works with me and is as loyal as the day is long and asked me not to say anything to anyone. Nothing would let me break that confidence.' said Rob.

'Well, it's all over now,' said Jayne, losing that round.

Dee came up to Sara and Luca.

'Well, my dears, it is good to see you so happy,' she said, holding Luca's arm. 'A little bird told me you are working on a site near Monte Prama; it all sounds extremely exciting. Call in and see me when you have time. Ellie is coming to stay with me next week so we can have a good natter about the old times.'

Franco and Antonia came up to join Luca and Sara, with Tommaso and his wife, Rosanna.

'You must come and visit us,' said Franco. 'We are very smart now, and although we don't have so many young boys, we have some sad cases with young men. Tommaso here helps us out and gives a lot of time to the shack.'

'I have heard so much about you all and I want to catch up,' said Sara. 'In a few weeks, when everything has settled, I will come and visit you. Is that all right?'

'Wonderful we will look forward to seeing you.'

At the far side of the room, Ellie was chatting with a couple.

'My dear Giovanna, how are you? You look great and so happy.'

'Ellie, this is Marco. You remember Marco?'

Ellie looked at the man and then at Giovanna. 'Your Marco?'

'Yes. His wife left him and moved to the Continent not long after you went back to England. She refused to divorce him but left the children with him. I moved in – much to everyone's surprise and my parents' anger, but he needed someone to look after the children. We have four now, two of his and two of our own, and the girl, we called Ellie. And we have two grandchildren. The boy is Marco Junior, and he is on the Continent training to be a chef, and the girl, Rita, is at university here in Cagliari studying hotel management.'

'Dearest Giovanna, I am so happy for you. But how time flies – both of us grandparents. Where did the time go?'

'We were married last year. Marco's wife died and freed us to marry, so here we are.'

Ellie put her arms around Giovanna.

'So many years, so many stories. I am staying with Dee after the wedding, and I will come and see you to catch up with everything.'

'That will be great,' said Giovanna.

CHAPTER TWENTY-EIGHT

By Monday, everyone had left. Adam and Jayne had gone with Anna, the owner of the hotel in Oliena, for a week's holiday. Anna had arranged a tour for them to see some of the sights on the island. They planned to travel around and then return to Cagliari before going home, while Ellie went to stay with Dee for a few days before returning to England.

'I hope you don't mind, Dee, but I want to see Sara and Luca and walk around Cagliari, just to catch up in my mind.'

'You use the house like a hotel,' Dee told her. 'I have some meetings today. Just let me know if you want feeding.'

Luca and Sara were staying in Cagliari for a few days before joining Sara's parents up in Oliena, so they could see all their friends and take their honeymoon later.

'Ellie, if it's not too painful, we would love you to come to supper at the flat,' said Sara. 'I have learnt to cook quite a mean pasta and we could talk over old times.'

Ellie hesitated for a moment.

'Please don't feel you have to. We just thought it might be nice.'

'It would be lovely. Thank you.' said Ellie.

'Tonight, about seven, but come earlier if you wish.'

Ellie rang Dee to tell her about the evening's arrangements and then spent the day walking around Cagliari. The greyness of the sixties had gone. There were cafes everywhere, beautiful boutiques and smart shops. Down at the port, all the cranes had gone, and fishermen no longer sat on the Quayside mending their nets; all were replaced by expensive yachts in a new marina. There was a walkway all along the front and seating, and neat parking for the cars. It had changed, but it was still magical, with the same dreamlike quality.

Ellie sauntered on through Cagliari, looking for something to take with her this evening. She walked up to the Piazza Constituzione to the Antico Caffe. Was Gino sitting there reading his paper, or was it a trick of the light? She wandered over to the terrace and ordered a coffee. The memories came flooding back; snipits of conversation, feeling his hand touch hers, the pinch of an elbow. Wonderful, loving memories.

After the fortifying coffee, she went across the square where she saw a wine shop and found the wine she was looking for. She walked on up to the lion gate, past new little workshops and up to the arch with the Madonna, resting for a moment and thought about her time here – Gino with his friends and his cousin and young Angelo, when she had thought there was another woman in his life. Ellie caught her breath. The day it had rained, and Gino had taken her to his flat and made love to her for the first time. Ellie smiled to herself and sighed. So many years ago. So many poignant memories.

Ellie suddenly realised that one different thing was the noise. The wonderful chirruping of all the finches as they fluttered in the little cages outside the flats was missing, replaced by modern music. No children playing in the streets, laughing and shouting as they played football or sat in groups competing at 'stones.' The washing still hung from the balconies, but not strung across the ravine, so no water dripped over the street.

Ellie looked up the road, towards the church near the top of the Via Lamarmora where they had laid Gino the night before his funeral, where she had said her final goodbye. Where Giovanna had cut a lock of his hair. It was like another life, another time, which it was, but at this moment it seemed like yesterday. Such wonderful memories – sad, but wonderful.

She arrived at the flat just before seven. The big outer door was open, and she went in. More memories came flooding in on her. The staircase, the lantern skylight. She walked up to the

263

second floor and stood outside the door to the apartment, her heart thumping in her chest and heard herself whisper, 'I love you, Gino.'

Ellie knocked on the door, and Sara opened it and welcomed her in.

'Come in, Ellie, come in. Are you all right?'

'Yes, I'm fine, just forgotten how many steps there were up to the flat.'

Ellie walked in. The big room was still lined with books, but more than she remembered. There were the long French windows, the sofas – all there, but different.

'Has it changed much?' asked Sara.

'A little, not a lot, but full of ghosts.'

Luca came to greet her, and Ellie handed him the bag of goodies she had brought with her. Luca looked inside and laughed.

'You didn't forget. Nepenthe from Oliena. Wonderful,' he said, taking the bottle and handing Sara the bag. 'Your favourite too.'

'Limoncello. Thank you, Ellie,' said Sara.

Ellie looked around the room.

'Please have a wander round. Luca will get the drinks and I am in the kitchen,' said Sara.

Ellie took in the scene. The dining table was still there, and in her mind's eye, she saw Gino sitting there in his shirt and jeans, his long legs crossed at the ankles, while she was in her evening dress after the ball. When he had asked her to marry him again. Looking around the room, she saw herself in her mind's eye, waltzing with Gino toward the bedroom, and followed them. Clothes dropped on the floor. The same two beds were pushed together, with the crucifix above. She saw Gino lay her down. Watched the lovers and felt the tears come. Felt the touch of him, felt his breath on her neck. All those years ago, but the memories were so vivid, so alive. Ellie realised she still missed him and wiping her tears, made her way back to the sitting room to join the others.

'Are you all right, Ellie?' asked Sara, handing her a glass of wine and putting her arm around her grandmother.

'I'm fine. Just remembering,' Ellie smiled, still fighting the tears. 'A toast to you both. To a long life, great love, and eternal happiness.'

The following day, Ellie walked down to see Angelo and Francesca, as they had asked her over for lunch to talk about old times. Ellie arrived armed with a bottle of Nepente and *Dolci Sardi*.

'My dear Ellie, come in. Angelo is upstairs in the sitting room.'

Ellie followed Francesca up the wide marble stairs and into the sitting room.

'What a beautiful room,' said Ellie, looking around at the tasteful decor.

'Aperitif?' asked Francesca.

'Please, that would be lovely.'

'Ellie, dearest Ellie, thank you for coming. Sit down, please sit down,' said Angelo, rising and coming to sit beside her.

Francesca returned with the drinks and they toasted each other.

'*Saludi.*'

Angelo turned to Ellie. 'It's been such a long time, Ellie. I often wondered why you never came back to see me. Clara always said you had gone away because my father had died and you did not want to know me anymore, but I knew in my heart that it wasn't true. Did you forget us?'

'No, but when I went home, I was pregnant. Having a child without a father in those days was almost impossible. I had a very dear friend whom I knew long before I met Gino. He asked me to marry him, so we could bring up the baby together. Tragically, the little boy died of meningitis when he was two, and I felt I could not come back again, as everything would have been too painful. But I never forgot you.'

'I am sorry,' said Angelo, taking Ellie's hand.

'You are right, though.' Said Ellie, 'When I visited Clara for the last time, she made it perfectly clear she did not want me to see you again, or to contact you. You were hers and did not want you upset. I understood she wanted to settle you down, but I felt incredibly sad about it. Is Clara still alive?'

'No, Clara died about thirty years ago. I was sixteen. She had been ill for as long as I could remember. My uncle looked after me, and sometimes we would go to stay with my grandmother, Gino's mother, but she became ill after Gino's death, so it was difficult for Clara.'

'Ellie, when Gino died, things changed for Angelo too,' said Francesca. 'I knew him back then; we had been at school together, and he often came around to our house before going home. We have talked it over together and we think there is something you should know.'

★

Young Angelo cried when his father died, and he cried because Ellie never came to see him anymore. Clara changed after the death of her brother. Her mother died from a broken heart from the loss of Gino, her only son. After that, her father became a complete recluse. Clara turned to religion, going to church every day, and paying extra attention to all the saints' days.

Clara's husband, Giuseppe, stayed later at work and hardly spoke when he was at home. At weekends, he would take young Angelo to see his sister and play with her children.

At home, Angelo tiptoed around Clara, frightened he would rouse her to anger.

In the years to come, Clara became ill with her constant praying and fasting and asking every known saint to intercede for her. Finally, after much argument, Giuseppe insisted on taking her to see his father, who was the local doctor.

'She is having a nervous breakdown,' said his father. 'Giuseppe, we should admit her to a special home until she gets better, but the prognosis isn't good.'

The week before she was due to go into the home, Clara became extremely ill, and it was obvious she was dying. Giuseppe called his father, who called the local priest.

Angelo unexpectedly returned home early and tiptoed up to Clara's room to see his aunt. His grandfather was there, his stethoscope to Clara's chest. The priest was beside the bed and Angelo could see his aunt, propped up on pillows, looking pale and gasping for every breath. He moved to be closer to his Zio Giuseppe.

'Father, are you there? Forgive me, Father, for I have sinned,' Clara gasped.

'Confess all to me now, Clara my child, before you go to meet your Maker,' said the priest, going closer as the doctor moved away from the bed.

'I killed him, Father, I killed him,' she croaked.

Angelo moved forward to catch her words.

The priest made the sign of the cross and bent closer to her.

'Clara, who did you kill?'

Clara breathed heavily, every breath laboured, and her words seemed to catch in her throat. Angelo moved forward again and stood next to his Zio Giuseppe and the doctor.

'I killed him,' she rasped. 'He told me he was going to ask the Englishwoman to marry him.' She paused again, trying to catch her breath. 'I wanted the boy,' she paused, struggling to say the words… 'Gino would have taken him away with that woman. The boy would have been his family, not mine. I followed Gino that day. I beg you, give me absolution,' she gasped.

'Clara, do you know what you are saying?' asked the priest.

She Put her bony hand up to her confessor.

'I was on the tram near him. I was veiled. When the doors opened there were lots of people waiting to get off. I pushed him, put my stick between his legs, and pushed him. I saw him fall and I walked away.'

'But he was your brother,' said the priest, aghast.

'Father, please forgive me.' came her whispered plea.

'Are you truly sorry for what you have done?'

'Please, Father,' she rasped with a rattle.

'In the name of the Father…'

But it was too late: Clara had breathed her last and, silenced forever, gone unshriven to meet her Maker.

Giuseppe turned to Angelo and put his arm around him.

'Clara didn't know what she was saying. Please, Angelo, don't take any notice of what she said.'

Angelo put his arms around his Zio and wept.

Giuseppe's father bent forward to feel for a pulse, then closed his daughter-in-law's eyes.

After Clara died, Angelo cleared the house of all her possessions. It was while he was clearing her room that he found a parcel addressed to him in a box under her bed. He looked at it and recognised Ellie's writing.

He opened it. A book on archaeology. He turned to the opening page and an envelope fell to the floor. Angelo picked it up and opened it. A gold filigree cross and chain. He held it in his hand and wept.

He then read the inscription in the book:

To my dearest Angelo,
Grow up to be like your father and you will never go wrong. All my love, Ellie. 1961.

Angelo looked at the inscription and felt tears fall again. Ellie had not just left; she had come to see him.

But Clara must have sent her away, just as he had thought.

He put the cross around his neck. He missed his father and Ellie. It was at that moment he decided to get a job.

He spoke to Giuseppe when he came home that night.

'I want to get a job so I can go to university. Do you mind, Zio?'

'I have been expecting this,' Giuseppe said, as they sat down to eat the pasta Angelo had prepared for them. 'You don't have to work. Enroll at the university; your grades are good enough.'

'But I can't pay for it.'

'Gino left you money in a trust for your education. Clara didn't want you to go, because she knew that when you started university, her allowance would stop.'

'I didn't know Papa had left me anything.'

'There are a lot of things you don't know and it's better that way. I have loved you as a son, but I knew you would never be mine. Clara was different; she could not bear the fact that you would never be hers.

'Your aunt Clara was mentally ill for a long time. She hid it well, I didn't want to see it, but when Gino died and their mother followed soon after with a broken heart, Clara became evil and turned to religion obsessively.'

'I have always loved you, Zio, as a father, although I knew you weren't.'

'I know, I know. But, Angelo, pick up your inheritance and go to university. You have a wonderful girl in Francesca. Marry her; make a life for yourself.'

'And you, Zio?'

'I am free. I have an enjoyable life now. And there is always the widow down the street.'

'Zio, you dark horse!' laughed Angelo.

★

There was silence in the room. Ellie straightened herself and looked at Angelo. She tried to speak, her mouth had gone dry and the words would not come. Getting up from her chair, she went to look out of the window as a thousand thoughts rushed through her mind. Gino had been killed. Clara had taken him away from her and Angelo. A sister jealous of her brother, how obsessively selfish, how cruel.

Ellie turned to Angelo and said in a trembling voice.

'What a terrible thing for you to hear and experience. I am so sorry. But do you think it was true?'

'Zio asked to see the post-mortem report on Gino, and they found a mark, a round bruise, on his right-hand side, which they could not account for. It looked like the tip of a walking stick. He also had some bruising on his legs, which they put down to the accident. Clara was on the tram and pushed him onto the road and didn't even stop to see if anything could be done for him.'

Ellie caught a sob in the back of her throat.

'Angelo and I became very close at university,' said Francesca, 'and then I lost my parents in a car accident. We clung to each other, in need of comfort. After we got married, we moved here, to my parents' house. Then we had Luca and made sure he had all the love that we had lost. We talked of Clara, but never in front of Luca.'

'And you have borne this all this time, Angelo?'

'I told Francesca before we got married.'

Francesca turned to Ellie.

'I said you had the right to know, and that Angelo should tell you, but he didn't want to drag everything up again.'

'I can understand, and thank you for telling me,' said Ellie, taking Angelo's hand. 'We both lost him, but you have found love and companionship with Francesca, and I found it with Simon, and I know we both gained so much from having Gino's love.'

'Angelo still wears your cross, Ellie; he has worn it ever since he found it.'

Ellie squeezed Angelo's hand and smiled.

'Does Luca know about this?'

'No,' said Angelo, 'and we don't want him to, please.'

Ellie nodded in agreement.

'I knew I would see you, as Sara said she had asked you to the wedding and that you had said you would be coming. So, I brought you these few things,' she said.

Ellie opened her bag and brought out a velvet pouch, and a silver box.

'This is Gino's rosary. This one is a locket with a lock of your father's hair. I thought perhaps you might like some things of his.'

Angelo opened the velvet pouch and took out the gold locket. With shaking hands, he opened it and looked at Ellie.

'Giovanna cut the curl from his head when he was in the chapel of rest. I put it in the locket, together with his photo, and it has been with me ever since, but now I want you to have it.'

Angelo stroked the locket in his hands. He opened the silver box and removed the rosary, pulling it gently through his fingers.

'Gino's mother, your grandmother, gave it to me at his funeral.

She wanted me to have it to remind me of Gino. I put it away with all his other things after I lost Gino's son. But I think now is the time they should be with his son.'

'Thank you, Ellie, I will treasure these, and I will leave them to Luca.'

'You will keep in touch now, won't you?' asked Francesca.

'Yes. I am staying in Cagliari with Dee for a few more days, then I will be back to stay for some time. It would be so good to spend the winter here, as England can be so cold.'

'That will be wonderful,' said Angelo, 'and we can spend time together.'

'Right, lunch. I don't know about you, but I am starving,' said Francesca, changing the mood.

It was a long and delicious lunch. They talked about Angelo's time with Francesca and Luca, and Ellie told them about Simon and losing Gino's child and how Adam had come into their lives.

Finally, Francesca made coffee.

'Thank you for telling me everything and for a lovely meal. We will have to do this again but on me,' said Ellie.

Angelo saw Ellie to the door.

'I can't tell you how wonderful it is to see you again,' he said. 'I feel I have found part of my life again. Thank you. Ellie, thank you.'

Later, over coffee, Ellie told Dee what Angelo had said.

'There was a lot of gossip after you left,' Dee told Ellie, 'but it was all hushed up. Gino's family is well connected in Cagliari, so it never came out. But Gino's mother was a nervous woman. Her husband became wrapped up in his work and found his wife's ill health difficult to cope with. After Gino died and the rumours started circulating that their daughter had killed their son, Gino's mother found it intolerable. They say she died of a broken heart. We learnt later that Clara had had many affairs to have a child, but when the realisation dawned that she was the barren one, it hit her hard.'

271

Dee took Ellie's hand.

'I didn't think it would serve any purpose to tell you; Gino was dead and nothing in the world would bring him back. But I wrote to you, care of your parents at the Foreign Office. I had no reply.'

'My parents said nothing, but then they wouldn't have wanted any scandal associated with their names. I am sorry I never came back to Sardinia. It was part of my life here, but after losing Gino and then his son, I could not face up to it all. I settled with Simon and he was my rock.'

'I know how you feel; I missed Giuseppe when he died. But thanks to you, I had the charity, which has occupied my time. The children come and see me, and I have watched them grow into men with families of their own, which has been so rewarding. Tell me, Ellie, did your father get the knighthood your mother so desperately wanted?'

'Yes, but Isabel only lived two years to enjoy it.'

'Funny how people can be obsessed with something, only to find it isn't worth it when they finally get it, or they don't have time to enjoy it. Incredibly sad,' said Dee.

EPILOGUE

Christmas 2017

Ellie opened the dining-room door and looked at the beautifully laid table with a lace cloth, silver cutlery and crystal glass. She wandered around, reading the name cards for all the family and friends.

There were Adam and Jayne, who had flown down for Christmas, eager to see their latest grandchild, Rosa, who had been born a month earlier. Then there were Luca's parents, Angelo and Francesca, who always helped with the grandchildren whenever they could.

Sara and Luca had wasted no time in having children. There was the eldest, Gino Adam, aged eight; Angelo Simon, aged six; Ellie Francesca, aged four – who was beside herself at having everyone together for Christmas; and now little Rosa.

Polly and Mario had decided not to take their usual trip to Australia this year, but to spend it in the company of the family and their latest godchild.

Ellie looked at the other place settings. There were Antonia and Franco, who visited regularly. Tommaso and Rosanna were coming with their sons, Efisio and Jisepu, who were both studying medicine in Cagliari. The other two were on the Continent working in a hospital in Milan. Not forgetting Dee's companion Maria, who always came to help, and had found people to look after the children when Sara and Luca were at work. They had asked Giovanna, but she was taking her family to her mother for Christmas.

Ellie stopped at the bottom of the table where a place was laid, and a candle stood waiting to be lit. Dee, everyone still missed her.

Ellie had been staying with her in the winter of 2013 when

Dee had been taken ill with a slight cold. She had told Ellie not to fuss and insisted on their going out together for lunch. They had returned to the house in the evening and chatted about old times. The following morning Maria found her dead, gone peacefully in her sleep, leaving Ellie bereft.

The solicitors organised the funeral, following the wishes of Signora Assunta, Duminga, Fidula, Rosa, DeLogu – all good Sardinian names, Sara had remarked to Luca, and it was little wonder she liked to be known as Dee. They held the service in the local church the following day. People packed every corner of the church from all walks of life, from dignitaries and councillors to the boys from the shack. It was a celebration of the life of a much-loved woman, friend, and benefactor.

Luca, Franco, and Tommaso together with some of the boys from the shack, were the pallbearers, and Ellie, Antonia, and Sara followed them, each carrying a posy of fresh flowers.

They shared tears and laughter that day at the wake, sitting for a meal and listening to stories of the kindness and generosity Dee had shown to so many. Ellie and Sara wept for losing such a wonderful friend, while Franco and Antonia were beside themselves with grief.

In her will, Dee had left money for the continuation of The Blue Shack Trust and the dig, with a note: 'Long may it continue'. To Sara and Luca, Dee left her house: 'Fill it with children and laughter, as it should be.'

The old house now rang with laughter from the two boys and two girls, the youngest called Rosa after Dee.

In the first year of marriage, Luca had taken time off, and he and Sara had travelled the island, photographing, and mapping various sites. It had been an amazing year of camping in the wilds of Sardinia, living close to nature, a dream fulfilled for Luca, and at the end of the year, Sara found out she was pregnant, the start of a dream for her.

Ellie looked around the table again. Her love for Gino had

come down from another time through the generations to the present day with their grandchildren, and Ellie thought of all the people who had touched her wonderful life and smiled.

THE END

DEAR READER

Thank you for taking the time to read *Love in Another Time* and I hope you enjoyed the stories of Gino and Ellie also Sara and Luca.

If you have any comment, good or bad, I am happy to hear from you, as I love having contact with my readers, some who have become great friends.

Getting feedback is always rewarding, and a review can sometimes persuade other readers to choose one of my books for the first time.

For news, please go to my website:
www.lexadudleywriter.co.uk

If you wish to leave a review, please go to:
https://www.troubador.co.uk/bookshop/romance/
love-in-another-time/

Or me at:
lexa.dudleywriter@yahoo.com
Which would be lovely.

Thank you again.
Lexa Dudley

HISTORICAL NOTE

The Antico Caffé began in 1838 when Lazzaro Canepa arrived from Genova and opened a small meeting place in his name.

In 1855 it was given a makeover and called Caffe Genovese. A meeting place for artists and writers as well as the cities elite.

Here Sibillia waited for Franco, her young lover. Grazia Deledda, the Nobel prize winner of 1926. Emilio Luxu (Lussu) writer and antifascist. D H Lawrence, Sea and Sardinian. Gabriele D'Annunzio a writer who visited Sardinia once, and fell in love with the island and wrote a poem called '*Sale*' He also visited the falls at Villacidro *Sa Spendula* that prompted him to write a sonnet which was carved on to the rocky wall on which abundant water falls in the rainy months. Salvatore Quasimodo, Nobel prize for literature 1959 used to sip cappuccino and discuss his work with other famous writers at the Caffe.

It underwent restoration in 1998 by the Ruggieri family and became Antico Caffe and managed by Richard and Giulia Mura, an amazing team.

It is now under the protection of the Ministry of Cultural Heritage, being an important part of the history of Cagliari.

OTHER BOOKS BY THE SAME AUTHOR

The Whispering Wind

Elise sighed again: she was truly at peace at last. Her world, she thought, could never bring such divine tranquillity. This man had a tender quality; he was gentle, caring, thoughtful and romantic, and what was more, he was hers in this brief moment of time.

The Whispering Wind is a moving story of two lovers, set on the beautiful island of Sardinia, where Elise goes on holiday to escape a loveless and violent marriage.

Whilst there, she meets and falls in love with Beppe, a local Sard. Despite religious and cultural complications, they embark on a romantic and passionate affair.

Beppe shows Elise his island and introduces her to the welcoming culture of the Sardinians and Elise soon falls under the spell of both the island and its people.

But after weeks of blissful happiness, Elise has to return unexpectedly to England to face all the problems she had been so desperate to leave behind…Two lovers, one heartbreaking story.

This is a wonderful book which hooked me almost immediately with its beautiful descriptive writing and well-developed characters. It is at once a passionate love story and a tribute to the beautiful island of Sardinia, so will have broad appeal among lovers of both romance novels and travel writing. It is clear that the author has a deep love of Sardinia and has researched the book well. The island is now well and truly on my list of places to visit. A more detailed review will be published at http://www.amandaswanderlust.com

Children of the Mists

Children of the Mists is a story of enduring love. Set in the 1800s, life on Sardinia had barely changed since the time of the Caesars. Two families, the Sannas and the Canus, are united by friendship and honour; love and laughter, joy and promises; omens and superstitions; youth and experience transcend generations.

However, for Raffaella and Antonio, their passionate love becomes entangled with revenge, death changes devotion. Promises are forgotten. Vendettas cannot be ignored. Ambition clouds judgements. Antonio and Raffaella were promised to each other, nothing would keep them apart, not even family. Committed to each other, they fight for their love against all odds…

Antonio took Raffaella's hand and led her to the shade of a nearby cork tree. It was cool in the shelter of its grey-green leaves. Through which a small breeze rustled above them. He sat on the dry stones that the old tree had grown out of, the roots making the stone split open. He pulled her down to sit next to him.

'Raffaella, my love, I know I can't ask you yet, and that I should ask your father first, but

I must know if you feel enough affection for me to hope that you will marry me one,'

Praise for *Children of the Mists*
A love story that will win the hearts of readers with its many dimensions. An enduring love story that will captivate the reader with its romance, passion, revenge and honour…'

 Matador